# FATAL HARBOR

# FATAL HARBOR

BRENDAN DUBOIS

PEGASUS BOOKS
NEW YORK LONDON

FATAL HARBOR

Pegasus Books LLC
80 Broad Street, 5th Floor
New York, NY 10004



First Pegasus Books cloth edition May 2014

Interior design by Maria Fernandez



Library of Congress Cataloging-in-Publication Data is available.

ISBN: 978-1-60598-562-6

10 9 8 7 6 5 4 3 2 1

Printed in the United States of America
Distributed by W. W. Norton & Company

*As with my first novel, this one is for my parents,*
*Arthur and Mary DuBois.*
*Thanks for believing in me from the very start.*

# FATAL HARBOR

# CHAPTER ONE

In my home state of New Hampshire, death certificates are a formal-looking document, with a light watermark in the center outlining the shape of our fair state. There are seals in each corner, an elaborate light-blue border with lots of swirls and curls, and the official state seal in the center. The paper is thick and has a light pink background, to prevent counterfeiting, I'm sure.

Just below the words CERTIFICATE OF DEATH, in all capital letters, there are sections to be filled out.

FULL NAME OF DECEASED

Next to those four official words, a three-word name had been typed in:

Diane Elizabeth Woods

Below the name, there are other sections of the death certificate to be filled out.

DATE OF DEATH

DATE OF BIRTH

And the usual and customary information of one's life, all filled out in clean, bureaucratic prose, from PLACE OF DEATH to RESIDENCE to PLACE OF DISPOSITION.

About halfway down the list is the phrase that sticks out: MANNER OF DEATH.

I looked at it again.

MANNER OF DEATH.

And typewritten simply is one word:

Homicide.

I woke up with a start, an elbow in my side. A familiar male voice to my left: "Lewis, if you were working for my crew back in the day, you'd hope that falling asleep on the job would be a firing offense. And nothing else."

I yawned. "Felix, in your day, I wasn't within five hundred miles of this place."

Felix Tinios laughed. "Then you missed a lot of action."

I wiped at my eyes, yawned again. We were in Felix's black Cadillac Escalade SUV, parked on a residential street in Brookline, Massachusetts, just outside Boston. It was late October and two in the morning, according to the Cadillac's dashboard clock. I stretched, felt something pop in my back and legs.

"How much longer?" I asked.

"Up to you. This is your little op, now, isn't it? I'm just here for . . . assistance and technical advice."

Along this fine street were houses whose monthly mortgages could support a family of four for about a year or so in some areas of the United States. Most of the homes were dark, save for a few that had that ghastly light-blue glow in the windows from televisions that were left on.

"So, what's your advice?"

The wind came up, stirring leaves along the pavement. Our target house was just up the street, on the left, near a fire hydrant. It was dark. It had been dark since we had gotten here, nearly four hours ago.

Felix stretched as well. "Stakeouts sure do suck," he said.

"That's a statement, not advice."

"Best I can do right now."

I stared at the house, willing a light to go on, a car to pull into its short driveway, anything to indicate that its occupant had finally come home.

But the Colonial-style home with its attached two-car garage and black shutters remained lifeless.

"Didn't think college professors had such exciting lives," Felix said.

"Always a first time."

"What does this clown teach again?"

"The clown's name is Heywood Knowlton, he's in the history department at Boston University, and he teaches a course called 'Marxism and the American Consumer.'"

"What else does he teach?"

"That's it."

Felix grunted. "Nice gig if you can get it. It's going to be a joy to talk to him, when he shows up."

"If he shows up."

"I'm supposed to be the pessimist in this crew, Lewis. Remember your place."

Felix turned in his seat and reached back among our gear, came back with a Thermos container. "Coffee?"

"Not right now, thanks."

Felix poured himself a small cup, took his time sipping it. At first the coffee smell had been a pleasant one; but, having been cooped up in the Cadillac for so long, it was now turning my stomach.

I rubbed at my eyes, nervous and jumpy. It had been a long four hours and I felt guilty for dozing off. I felt like I hadn't taken a bath or shaved in a week, and in the dim light from the nearby street lamp, Felix looked like he had just stepped out of the pages of *GQ* magazine, wearing charcoal-gray slacks and a black turtleneck. For the past couple of days, we had been tracking Professor Knowlton, not because we wanted to audit his class, but because we wanted to talk to him about someone he knew, this particular someone who had put my best friend into a hospital ICU with little chance of recovery.

Our work had begun at Boston University earlier in the day, where we had followed Professor Knowlton from his office, through the pleasant campus of BU, and into another campus building. Through a pretext call, Felix had found out that after a faculty meeting, the professor was going to a function on Newbury Street celebrating another history professor's book publication. Felix and I had set up surveillance on either end of the street, keeping the restaurant entrance in view, cell phones in our coat pockets, as people walked about us on the cool October evening.

But he never showed up. After a while, after seeing other BU faculty members dribbling out, each carrying their co-worker's book—and I had to smile when one woman with a pinched face and oversized glasses walked by, volume in hand, and said to her younger male companion "There is no God if a dolt like him can get anything more complicated than a cookbook published"—Felix slid into the restaurant and came out, shaking his head.

We had missed him.

Now Felix said: "What news from the hospital?"

"Still in a coma, still in ICU."

"Nothing more than that?"

"It's enough."

Felix drummed his fingers on the steering wheel. "We've been at this two days now. You still on board for what you've got planned?"

"I am. Why do you ask?"

"Because time's gone on, that's why. I've found that over time, well, things cool down. Perspectives change. What was once clear is now a bit foggy."

Up ahead on the road, something scurried across from one row of shrubbery to another. Too small for a dog, too big for a cat. A fox, maybe? Here, in the dense suburbia of Brookline?

"Nothing's changed, Felix. Not a damn thing."

"He might not have anything for us."

"He just might, and that'll be worth it."

Between us on the seat was a small handheld radio. Every now and then there was a small burst of static. Felix swiveled in his seat, put the Thermos away. Back in the rear were two black duffel bags with our respective gear, and underneath our seats were our respective weapons. I had a 9mm Beretta, and Felix had a 9mm Glock. Two different styles of pistols, but the same caliber, helpful if we were to get into a firefight and needed to share ammunition.

Not that either of us was planning to be on the receiving end of a firefight. It was just good to be prepared.

Felix said, "Another half hour."

"Why not."

And among our other preparations back there were plastic Flex-Cufs, a black cloth hood, some short lengths of rubber hose, some half-gallon containers of water, and other assorted pieces of gear to commence mayhem.

Then the radio crackled.

"Dispatch, B-four."

B-four was a patrol unit for the Brookline Police Department.

"B-four, go."

"B-four, respond to Wellington Street. Caller reports suspicious vehicle parked for an extended period of time, apparently two men inside. Vehicle large black SUV."

"Dispatch, B-four, responding."

Felix quickly turned the key to the Cadillac. "Lewis, I do believe it's time to depart these fair shores."

"No argument here."

With lights off, Felix drove us down the street, slowed without halting at the stop sign, and made a turn. I admired his tradecraft. If we were still being watched by a curious neighbor or two, they wouldn't see taillights flickering as we braked, so whether we went left or right wouldn't be known.

Once the turn was made, Felix switched on the headlights, and we sped up through the quiet suburban streets of Brookline. Felix made a series of turns, going one way and then another, until I was severely, completely, and utterly lost. There was an impressive navigation system in his rented Cadillac, but he refused to use it. Earlier, he had said: "It takes a lot of work to stay disconnected in this wired world of ours, but you've got to do it. Otherwise, one of these days you'll be sitting in court, watching some sharp prosecutor explain in full detail your driving record on the night in question."

On this night, we soon left the confines of Brookline and entered Boston. Once we were out of the city where the police were on the prowl, I sensed Felix relaxing, and I did too, though right after that I was quite tired.

Felix said: "Always nice to set your own schedule for meeting public servants. The ones you meet at this hour of the night tend to be grumpy and suspicious."

"Even when they're working for the public good?"

"Especially when they're working for the public good."

"If you say so," I said, and maybe I was being paranoid, for I swung my head around one last time to check on our progress.

Nothing.

Good. Meant the Brookline patrol cruiser was still back there in Brookline, doing its job. The fair people of Brookline were getting their tax money's worth this early morning, for the police were indeed preventing a number of crimes including kidnapping, assault, and possible torture.

A series of crimes I was fully prepared to commit.

# CHAPTER TWO

Felix brought us to the North End of Boston, with its narrow streets and brick buildings pushed together like some architect years ago had been deathly afraid of open space. Being with Felix the past few days, since we had driven down here from New Hampshire, I had gotten familiar with our temporary lodgings, but Felix drove by that brick building and went on for another two blocks.

I was going to ask him what was going on, but, through years of experience, I knew when to keep my mouth shut. His eyes narrow and his jaw tightens, and one can sense the energy coming from him while he's working. Now he backed into a narrow alleyway and waited, switching off the Cadillac's lights.

It was quiet. He shifted some in his seat. Leather squeaked. I kept my mouth shut.

A group of drunken college students stumbled by. One of them stopped and weaved his way into the alley, started fumbling at his belt and zipper. Felix said "Not on your life," and he lowered the window.

"Hey!" he called out.

The student raised his head, grunted something in return.

Felix said, "Pull it in, zip it up, or I'm coming out. And if I come out, your hands will be worthless for a month, and you'll be wearing an adult diaper. Got it?"

The student got it. He wandered back out to the street, moved away. Felix raised the window. He sat, silent, looking out the windshield.

"What's going on?"

Felix looked left, looked right, looked left again. "Don't know. Just got the feeling we're being followed."

"The cops?"

"Maybe. I don't know."

I kept quiet, gave him space. A few long minutes passed. "After years of being out there, doing what I do, you gain . . . a sixth sense, or a sight, or something like that. Nothing you can put your hand on, but you learn to trust it. Has saved my skin on a number of occasions."

"And you're feeling that now?"

He tugged at an ear. "That I am."

"But I don't see anything."

"Neither do I," he said. "But I feel something. . . ."

He switched on the headlights, put the Cadillac in drive, slid us back out on the narrow North End street. "Eh, probably nothing. I'm tired, you're tired, and it's damn late at night."

A few minutes later, he pulled up in front of our quarters. There was an empty spot in front of the four-story brick building. There was always an empty spot there, and when I had noted that to Felix our first night here, he had said, quietly, "Nobody in this neighborhood would dare to take it."

We got out into the chilly early morning air. Lots of lights out there, the hum of traffic, car horns and distant sirens. The street was jammed with parked cars, wet trash was underfoot, and, by the near alley, there was the strong smell of recently released urine.

Big-city life.

I hated it.

I wanted to be back at Tyler Beach, in my small hundred-year-old-plus home, deep in bed, listening only to the creaks of the old timbers and the gentle roar of the ocean waves crashing in, with no worries besides what I was going to have for breakfast the next day.

If I said something, I knew Felix would take me back right away. Tyler Beach was just about an hour away, and then we'd both be back where we belonged, instead of here, where we had to be.

We retrieved our respective pistols and then, from the back seat of the Cadillac, took out our duffel bags. Our first night here, after another long night of surveillance, I had been in favor of leaving our gear in the Cadillac instead of humping it up three flights of stairs, but Felix had instantly quashed that idea. "Not for a minute," he had said. "Leave stuff like that out in the car, you're leaving evidence. All it would take is some nitwit sideswiping or trying to steal the damn thing, and cops will be here, asking questions."

Now with duffel bags over our shoulders, Felix led the way and we went up some stone steps, and he unlocked the door. Dim light bulbs flickered in the stairwell, and we slowly went up the creaking stairs. Instead of the smell of urine and wet trash, there was the smell of spices and sauces.

On the third-floor landing, Felix unlocked another door and we stepped inside a very warm and cozy living room. There was a thick braided rug in the center, and two plush couches with lace doilies on the armrests. A light had been left on for us by the owner of this building, Aunt Teresa, a relative of Felix's who was no doubt fast asleep in her own room. We softly let the duffel bags down, for Aunt Teresa was quite the light sleeper, for which I couldn't blame her, since she was closing in on her tenth decade of life.

A small kitchen was on the other end of the living room, and there were two other small rooms, one of which was a spare bedroom, the other a sewing room. In a burst of generosity when we had first arrived three days ago, Felix had taken the sewing room and a fold-out couch. I think it was a positive comment on his character that he didn't readily seem to regret that decision, which was why I always let him use the tiny bathroom first.

When he was done I went into the bathroom myself. It had an old porcelain sink and a claw-footed bathtub. A small statue of Jesus was propped on top of the medicine cabinet.

Felix was already in his room when I got out, and I went into my lodging, closing the door behind me. I undressed and tossed my clothes on a simple wooden chair in the corner. I crawled into bed, switched off the light, and stared up at the ceiling. Even with the shade drawn, the outdoor light was illuminating everything inside, from the simple chest of drawers to the chair with my clothes on it, to the nightstand with another lace doily, and up on a small shelf by the door, a statue of the Virgin Mary. The statue was glow-in-the-dark, and her eerie light seemed to look right at me.

The bed was lumpy and old, and it had a musty smell. The pillow was too thick. I tossed and turned, tossed and turned, the sounds of traffic and horns still driving at me. I flicked the bedside lamp back on, reached over, and picked up a copy of yesterday's *Boston Globe*. I flipped through the pages, trying to get myself relaxed, and read the breathless stories about the upcoming presidential election and the usual distressing news from overseas. I then went to the editorial pages of the *Globe*, which typically had the most boring op-ed columnists on the planet, coupled with sincere letter-writers who railed against everything from the sales of bottled water to the military influence on kindergarten classes.

In the Metro section, which covered the area around Boston and its suburbs, there was a brief news item about the Falconer nuclear power plant and the continued investigation into the violence that had erupted during the last demonstrations. Two dead from gunshots from yet-undetermined shooters, several injured, and hundreds of thousands of dollars in damage to the power plant, which was still operating despite the damage.

I closed my eyes for a moment. Four days ago, I had been at the last Falconer demonstration, where members of the Nuclear Freedom Front had stormed through, and where gunfire had broken out, and where my dearest and oldest friend, Diane Woods of the Tyler Police Department, had been beaten nearly to death with an iron pipe.

As of now, from what I knew, Diane remained in a coma at the Exonia Hospital's ICU, just a twenty-minute drive from Falconer.

As of now, police and others were still looking for the Nuclear Freedom Front leader, Curt Chesak, whom I had seen with my own eyes pummeling Diane with an iron pipe.

And as of now, Felix and I had been trying to talk to BU History Professor Heywood Knowlton about his connection with Curt Chesak.

A police source had earlier told me that Professor Knowlton was friends with Curt and had supported him through his rise in the ranks of the NFF.

Our goal was to get to Curt before the police, and so far it had been a bust.

I thumbed through the rest of the paper and then tossed it back on the floor. A car alarm kicked off just up the street. I turned off the light and tried to sleep with a glowing Virgin Mary staring down at me, probably in disapproval for what I had in store for Curt Chesak.

Some draggy hours later, I joined Felix and his Aunt Teresa in the tiny kitchen for a brunch, which she had expertly prepared while she and Felix chattered at each other in Italian. Her kitchen looked like it could have been highlighted in the September 1959 issue of *House Beautiful*, with linoleum, an old-style white Frigidaire refrigerator with a big silver handle, and a skinny three-burner stove. Aunt Teresa looked a shade under five feet tall, with her gray hair tightly secured in the rear in a bun, bright brown eyes, and a wrinkled face and a quick mouth. She had on a long black dress with a yellow apron tied around her, and sensible black shoes.

But even in the kitchen's close quarters, she turned out a meal of strong black coffee, orange juice, fresh pastries, eggs, sausages, and oatmeal. I ate as well as I could while Felix sat across from me, and each time she came over to take away a plate or refill our coffee cups, she would gently caress Felix's shoulders or give him a kiss on the top of his head. I had on yesterday's shirt and khaki slacks, while Felix was making do in a blue bathrobe that had belonged to dear old departed Uncle Joseph.

Aunt Teresa came over and dropped three more links of sausage on my plate. She said something in Italian to Felix, and he laughed and said to me: "Aunt Teresa wants to know if a good-looking man like you is married."

"Go ahead, tell her the answer."

Felix replied and there was another back-and-forth, and Felix said: "Why, she asks. Haven't you found the right woman yet?"

I halted with my knife and fork. What a question. "I think I have," I said. "It's just that . . . well, circumstances. I'm in New Hampshire, and she's in Washington, trying to get Senator Jackson Hale elected president. Not sure what's going to happen when the election is over."

Felix translated that to Aunt Teresa, and then she stood there, glaring at me, and went into a long speech, waving a spatula around for emphasis. She went on and on, and I tried to keep up and look interested, and when she was done, she looked at Felix with emphasis and then stomped back to her stove.

"What was that all about?" I asked.

Felix picked up his coffee cup. "Aunt Teresa said you find the right person, don't let her go."

"Excuse me? I think she said a hell of a lot more than that."

Felix shrugged. "Just old family history. You don't need to know."

"But I want to know."

"Why?"

"Let's just say morbid curiosity. She seemed to have a lot to say."

Felix laughed. "Morbid. Good guess. Okay, she said you find the right person, you don't let them go. That in the years that God has put her on this earth, that her true love was her first husband, Peter, God rest his soul, whom she married in 1936 and who died in Anzio in 1944, God rest his soul and may the souls of the Nazis burn in eternity."

"That sounds—"

"Wait, I'm not finished. She said that she rushed into her second marriage, with Michael, who was a drunk and bitter man who chased women in the neighborhood and embarrassed her and his family, who beat her children. And then when her marriage to him ended, thank you Mother Mary, she was so lucky to find her sainted Joseph, who treated her as a princess and who raised her three girls as his own, God preserve him. And when he died, she went into mourning and never left it. So, young man, she says, she was lucky twice, but you may only be lucky once, and don't tempt the fates by ignoring this offering."

Felix picked up a napkin, wiped his fingers. I waited for a moment and said, "Is that all?"

"Pretty much."

"What do you mean, pretty much?"

"Let's just leave it at that."

So I finished my coffee and Aunt Teresa came back, picked up our plates, and when I tried to follow her to the sink, she shooed me back and gave me a slap to my hand. Felix laughed. "You'll learn, like the others, you don't mess with Aunt Teresa."

Something nudged at me, and I said, "Her second husband. Michael, the one who drank and beat her three children. She said that marriage ended. How? Desertion? Divorce?"

"Death," Felix said.

"Oh," I said. "That must have been rough."

"Sure was," Felix said. "Was years before I heard the real story."

"Which was what?"

Felix seemed to ponder that for a moment, and said, "All right. Family secrets revealed. Just don't let on that you know this, and don't let it affect your view of Aunt Teresa."

"Except for the fact she doesn't like help in the kitchen, I think she's an old sweetheart."

"Thanks, I'll make sure she knows that. Anyway, it was 1950, about four years after she remarried. Like she said, Michael was a creep. Drank too much, beat on her and the kids, and chased women all around the North End and beyond. He also managed to tick off some . . . independent businessmen who lived here."

"Your future employers?" I asked innocently. Felix always claimed that he listed "security consultant" on his 1040 tax return form every year, and I loved trying to get a rise out of him by poking holes in his so-called employment history.

"This is Aunt Teresa's story, not mine," he said, with a disapproving tone. "So here it was, summer of 1950, a scorching hot day, no A/C back then, just open windows, fans, and sleeping out on the fire escapes at night. Michael comes stumbling in about six A.M. or thereabouts, demanding breakfast, and Teresa says something like, well, you weren't here for supper last night, why should I make you breakfast? And in the kitchen, he cold-cocks her right in front of her three girls. She picks herself up, tells the girls to go back to bed and stay there, and they do. Michael sits his wide butt in that very same chair that you're sitting in, picks up his copy of the *Record-American*, and starts picking his races for Suffolk Downs."

Aunt Teresa was at the sink, singing some tune with a high, lilting voice.

"So while Michael is smoking a cigarette, picking the races, Aunt Teresa sets down a plate with bacon, toast, and two eggs over easy, and when Michael starts digging into his first meal of the day, Aunt Teresa steps behind him, grabs his hair, tugs his head back, and with her best kitchen knife she slits his throat."

"Tell me you're kidding."

He shrugged. "You asked, I told. And I never joke about family stories."

More singing from the old woman at the sink.

"What happened to her?"

"Short-term, she grabbed Michael's plate and ate her own breakfast. Didn't want good food to go to waste. Long-term, the police came by, local businessmen and others vouched for her good nature, and the charges eventually got swept. So there you go."

I wiped my own fingers on my napkin. "I get the feeling dear old Uncle Joseph was either very brave, or very loving."

"A bit of both."

Aunt Teresa came over, smiling, and spoke a rapid sentence. Felix said, "She wants to know if you need anything else."

I smiled up at her. "Not a thing."

## CHAPTER THREE

After breakfast, I gave Felix first crack at the bathroom, and then it was my turn, and I had to make do in the large tub with a hand-held shower fixture that had weak water pressure that barely dribbled on my hair and skin. Plus, since Felix had gone before me, the water had started off lukewarm and got colder from there.

I got dressed in my clothes from the day before, spent a second or two looking at the mirror, and then picked up my cell phone. No missed calls, no texts, no messages. I dialed a number from memory, where it went straight to voice mail, and after Annie Wynn's recorded voice warmed me, I said, "Just checking in. Off to work again. Hope you're hanging in there. Will try later."

Then I tried the phone of Kara Miles, Diane Woods's fiancée, and found that her phone was busy. I left a message with her as well, and then went out to the living room.

Felix was sitting on one of the overstuffed couches, reading that day's *Wall Street Journal*. He looked up. "What's the plan for the day?"

I sat down across from him. "The plan is . . . the plan is we're going to change things up."

"Fair enough. What do you have in mind?"

"We've been skulking around, planning to . . . entice the good professor to join us, where we'd have what the diplomats call a 'frank and open discussion.' I still want the discussion, but I'm tired of skulking around. I'm looking for a direct approach this time."

"Why not?" Felix asked, folding his *Wall Street Journal* in half. "So, when do you want to go?"

"Still have your laptop?"

"Unless Aunt Teresa's checking out Chippendale models, yeah, I still have my laptop."

"Let me do a little research, and we'll be on our way."

An hour later, Felix dropped me off at 226 Bay State Street in Boston, near Storrow Drive and the Charles River. The street was narrow and tree-lined, with a narrow grassy median strip with trees growing in the center. The buildings up and down the street all belonged to Boston University. He pulled the Cadillac to the side of the street. "Got your cell phone?"

"As much as I hate the evil device, yes, I do."

"Carrying?"

"Felix, I'm going on a college campus. What, you think I'll get assaulted in the faculty lounge?"

Two young coeds with long brown hair ambled by, stopped, looked at Felix, and then hesitantly regained their step. If Felix noticed it, he kept it to himself. Instead, he said: "You're setting to confront a guy who's supposedly helped and supported the low-life who's pretty much killed off your best friend. You better keep that in mind."

"She's not dead."

Felix sighed. "My friend . . . where she is and what happened to her, it might be merciful to let her go. Otherwise she has long decades ahead of her . . . not knowing who she is, not recognizing friends and family, and—"

"I've heard enough, thanks."

Felix said, "Yeah, I'm sure. Look, I'll be right out here waiting for you. Okay?"

I looked at the parking signs. "But you don't have a university parking sticker."

"No, but I got my winning attitude. What can possibly go wrong?"

The fall air in the city was so different from what I was used to. There was no smell of ocean, or autumn leaves, or seaweed and wet stones tossed up by my house. There was just the stench of exhaust and the continuous hum of traffic, punctuated by horns and sirens.

The sidewalk was made of brick, with attractive shrubs and plants at the base of the buildings, but to me it all looked too enthusiastic, as if some designer was desperately trying to soften the hard edges of this city.

I went up the steps to 226 Bay State Street, to a wooden front door with a large glass window. To the right of the door, bolted to the concrete wall, was a gold-and-red sign that said, in descending order:

226
BOSTON UNIVERSITY
AMERICAN
STUDIES
PRESERVATION
STUDIES

And underneath, in a much smaller typeface: RAMP AT REAR OF BUILDING.

I opened the door and went inside.

I meandered my way through the corridors, past wall decorations and bulletin boards with lots of flyers and posters pinned up. There were small clusters of students talking, and I could sense them checking me out as I went by. Some decades ago, I had been one of them, planning and hoping to change the world. Then I had left and gone to the place where I thought I *was* changing the world, and was then dismissive of the innocence and high thoughts of my college years.

Now I didn't have such complicated thoughts. Now I just wished these young people the very best, for what their supposed elders and betters were leaving them: lots of IOUs and trouble spots in the world that always flared up and never quite went away.

Outside the office of Professor Heywood Knowlton, a young man with a tan knapsack at his side was sitting on the floor, back up against the wall. He was busily texting someone with a pair of very dexterous thumbs, and he had a thin beard and very thick brown hair.

"Hey, buddy," I said.

He glanced up, still texting. Impressive.

"Yeah?"

"You have an appointment to see Professor Knowlton?"

"So?"

So far, so good, even with the one-syllable responses. I took out my wallet, passed over a fifty-dollar bill. "This is for you if you let me have it."

He looked confused. "You mean you want to take my appointment?"

"That's right."

He reached up, snapped the fifty-dollar bill from my hand. "Shit, bud, I would have done it for twenty."

The next generation gathered up his belongings and, with a wide smile on his face, trotted down the corridor.

I took his spot, leaning against the wall instead of sitting on the floor. Checked my watch. At the top of the hour, the door to Professor Knowlton's office swung open and a female student walked out, face clenched red, her knapsack clutched to her chest with both hands. She stifled a sob as she went past me.

After a second or two, I swung around and entered the office. It was large enough but cluttered, with a wide oak desk piled high with papers and folders. A window overlooked the street I'd just been on. Crowded bookshelves graced both walls, and in some of the spare wall space hung framed diplomas for Professor Knowlton, along with some interesting mementoes: a framed front page from *The New York Times* of August 8, 1974, stating NIXON RESIGNS; a copy of the famed Che Guevara print that has promoted the Marxist revolutionary over the decades by being used to sell everything from T-shirts to purses; and a photo of planet Earth, taken by one of the moon missions, with a caption stating DON'T TREAT YOUR MOTHER LIKE A TOILET.

Behind the desk a squat man sat, with a thick fringe of light brown hair about a bald head, eyeglasses perched up over his forehead, and a finely trimmed brown beard that was missing a moustache. He had on a black turtleneck, and both sleeves were rolled up. He was reading a stapled sheaf of papers when his glance shifted and took me in.

"You don't look like Don Oliphant," he said, his voice gravelly.

"I'm not, Professor Knowlton," I replied, stepping in front of his desk. "My name is Lewis Cole, and Don graciously allowed me to take his appointment."

He turned in his chair, dropped the papers on his desk. "Have a seat. You look too old to be a student, Mister Cole, so what brings you by today?"

I sat in a solid but comfortable wooden chair. "I was hoping I could ask you a few questions."

"For what purpose?" he asked sharply. "Are you a lawyer or a member of law enforcement, Mister Cole?"

"Worse," I said. "I'm a writer."

That brought a laugh. "What kind?"

"Well, freelance right now. I used to be a columnist for *Shoreline* magazine, based here in Boston."

"What did you write for them?"

"A column about the New Hampshire seacoast. Called 'Granite Shores.'"

"You said you're no longer with them. Quit?"

"Fired."

He tidied up some of his papers. "Economic problems?"

"Let's just say a personality conflict," I said. "I had one, and my editor didn't."

Another laugh. "Okay. So what kind of story are you working on?"

"Research, right now. About the demonstrations up at the Falconer nuclear power plant."

He frowned. "Nasty business."

"Certainly was," I said. "I was there in the crowd when Bronson Toles got shot."

He shook his head. "No, I meant the entire power plant up there being nasty business. Should never have been built. But the corporations and their enablers in the NRC and Congress swept aside people's concerns and had the damn place built. So nobody should have been surprised when the people finally spoke up and violence broke out."

"I think a lot of people were surprised, starting with Bronson Toles. And the other people who got killed and injured when the Nuclear Freedom Front folks stormed the plant site."

"That's what happens when you give poorly trained security personnel firearms. The innocents get killed."

"I think the forensics is still up in the air over who fired the fatal shots."

He laughed again. "Some writer you are, taking the company line. Don't worry, you won't be contradicted. Enough people will get the word, and the right paperwork will get shuffled around, so those who got killed actually committed suicide. Or some gunmen on some grassy knoll somewhere opened fire. But whatever it takes, the ones in power won't get blamed. It'll be just like the Little Big Horn rebellion back in 1976; scores of Native American activists were later found dead, and most of them supposedly died of exposure or suicide. I've read some of those autopsy reports. Funny how government doctors missed a bullet in the head when they diagnosed some woman activist as having died of exposure, and another one who was found in a bathtub with numerous knife wounds supposedly died later of carbon monoxide poisoning."

When I was in college, I wasn't too fond of professors who prattled on and on, and I found that my dislike hadn't gone away over the interceding decades.

"That's quite fascinating, Professor Knowlton, but I was hoping we could steer the conversation back to why I came here today. I also realize you only have a fifteen-minute block before another student comes knocking at your door."

He raised a hand. "My apologies, Mister Cole. Research, you said. For a freelance article, then?"

"That's what I'm hoping for. And I'm also hoping you could assist me in locating Curt Chesak, the head of the Nuclear Freedom Front. I'd like to talk to him about a proposed book project about the demonstrations at the power plant."

He said nothing and continued looking at me, and I looked right back at him. Finally he said, "You're certain you're not a law enforcement official?"

"Positive."

"Could I still see some ID, please?"

Feeling generous, I opened up my wallet, passed over my New Hampshire driver's license, as well as my official press pass, issued by the New Hampshire Department of Safety. He examined them both and gave them back to me.

"What makes you think I know anything about Curt Chesak?"

"I was led to believe that you were an associate of his."

"'An associate of his.' And who said that, someone whose dad worked for Senator McCarthy back during the Red Scare?"

"No," I said. "A source I know, a source I can trust."

"From the news accounts of what happened at Falconer, you must know that lots of cops are looking for Curt Chesak. Some of them have actually paid me a visit."

"Lucky you."

"Yeah, right, luck," he said. "And you know what I told each and every one of them? That even if I knew where Curt Chesak was—which I'm not admitting—I wouldn't even consider turning him in. Because he's a true believer, a fighter for the people, an organizer who has made a difference. To lots of people, he's a damn hero, and I'm not in the business of turning over heroes to the police."

"To lots of people, he's a damn thug."

Knowlton raised a hand. "Of course that's how the corporate-powered media are going to portray it, and—"

"I saw what he did," I said sharply, interrupting him. "I saw him at the Falconer plant site last week, where he took a length of pipe and nearly beat to death a Tyler police officer."

"Price of progress."

"The price of. . . ." I couldn't go on anymore. I wanted to reach across that academic desk, pick up his coffee mug, and crack it against his skull just to give him a taste of his blessed progress.

"Absolutely. The Tyler police officer who was allegedly injured by Curt Chesak wasn't a person anymore. He—"

"She," I corrected him.

"He, she, does it make a difference?"

"Makes a difference to some. Including me."

"Whatever," the professor said. "That police officer was more than just a police officer. She was a symbol of the corporate oligarchy that has been running this country for decades and, in the spirit of self-defense, what happened to her was a just response to oppression."

*Focus, focus,* I thought to myself. "So, when was the last time you saw Curt Chesak?"

A slight smile. "Not going to happen, sorry."

"But you do know him."

"I refer you to my earlier statement."

"Ah, even if you did know him, you wouldn't admit it."

"True, because you know, when it comes to—"

"Excuse me, I think you've misunderstood why I'm here."

"Oh?"

I stood up. "I'm not paying tens of thousands of dollars per semester to listen to stuff I can hear for free at 2 A.M. on Newbury Street, when the bars close."

His lips pursed and his eyes flared. "You can leave."

I headed for the door. "I don't need your permission."

Outside, I was hoping the air would freshen and cheer me up, but it did the opposite. The air was thick and oppressive, and the constant drone of nearby traffic seemed to burrow inside my skull, like a dull drill bit trying to fight its way through something unyielding. I got out on Bay State Street, looked up and down, and saw Felix's Cadillac at the intersection with Granby Street, partially parked up on a sidewalk.

But he wasn't alone.

Parked on the opposite side of the street was a dark blue Ford LTD with a whip antenna on its trunk. One man in a long black raincoat was standing by the open driver's door, while the other one was talking to Felix. To me they looked like cops. I wondered if they were ticked off by Felix's lack of parking etiquette.

I was too far away to hear what was going on, but I clearly could see that the discussion was quite animated, with lots of hand-waving and finger-pointing. Then Felix seemed to burst out laughing, and gently slapped the guy's shoulder. I started walking to Felix, feeling pretty good, all things considered, since Felix seemed to have the situation well in hand.

Felix turned and walked back to the Cadillac, both men shouted something, and Felix whirled around, crouching, pistol in hand, and shot at them both.

## CHAPTER FOUR

The sudden *boom!* of gunshots made me duck and hunker down behind an oak tree. Everything slowed down, like I was watching a movie and the projectionist had screwed up the speed of the film. The guy nearest Felix fell to the ground, rolled, and came up with his own pistol, shooting back at Felix.

Felix kept on firing, moving to take cover by the front of the Cadillac. Glass shattered on the LTD. The second guy ducked behind the open door of the LTD. More gunfire. The near guy grunted loud and fell back on the street. Didn't move. Felix was leaning over the hood and he popped out an empty magazine, quickly reloaded, kept up the firing.

I started moving, automatically reached to my side, found nothing.

Because someone stupidly thought he didn't have to be armed in such a safe area.

I had nothing to help Felix with.

But I kept on moving, as students and other folks ran away, screaming and yelling. Felix ducked behind his Cadillac. I didn't see him and got worried.

More gunfire.

A yelp from the second guy, who slumped into the driver's seat.

Sirens were screaming in the distance.

Felix popped up, went to the Cadillac, dove in and started up its engine.

I started running down the road.

Felix glanced back, saw me, and then drove away, making a sharp left onto Granby Street.

I stopped running, breathing hard, feeling like knives were slicing away at my lungs. The road was deserted. The LTD was still there, windows shattered, bullet holes in the door and the front fender, the left front tire sunk flat. The first guy shot was lying flat on his back, the other was still slumped over in the front seat.

I took a couple of deep breaths, turned, and started walking briskly away. Sirens grew louder. People were clumped at the end of Silber Way, looking down at the carnage on the other end of the street. I moved through them, not saying anything, not doing anything conspicuous, just wanting to get away as quickly and quietly as possible.

Two blocks away from the shooting, I took out my cell phone. I checked it and there were no messages, either voice or text. I turned and faced a building, phone in hand, like I was examining something important. I took the cover off, removed the battery and the SIM card. I broke the SIM card in half, kept all the pieces in hand. I strolled a few yards until I found a storm drain. I quickly knelt down, dumped everything down the storm drain, pretended to tie my shoe, and then kept on walking.

I suppose I was in shock. I was observing the streets, the people walking by and passing me, the sound of horns and sirens. I flinched as a white Boston police cruiser roared by, followed by another, heading to where I had just been. Everything seemed double-exposed, for what I was watching was overlaid by the sight of Felix and the other two men in a gunfight on a quiet college street just a few blocks away.

I kept on walking.

I ended up at Yawkey Way, adjacent to the most famous baseball park in America. Once again the Red Sox had not disappointed their diehard fans and had collapsed in spectacular fashion in August, leading to weeks of backbiting, gossiping, and some firings. So on this October evening, the lights were doused and pieces of scrap paper were the only things moving up and down the deserted street. I walked up to Gate A and stood there for a while, trying to ease my breathing, keeping my hands in my pockets.

Felix had season tickets to the Red Sox, and on those occasions whenever he invited me to a game, this was where we entered. Felix knew his way around Boston like he was the mayor of the damn place, and he had a secret parking spot near the park which meant it was only a five-minute walk to the game, going along with the thousands of people streaming in, most wearing Sox gear.

I looked up at the dark structure. Lots of fond memories from this place, opened up the year the RMS *Titanic* sank. Games lost and won. Beers and hot dogs consumed—Felix once saying "Still a great ballpark, but damn, they almost lost me when they started selling deli sandwiches here"—and it was nothing earth-shattering, but damn, it had been fun.

I started walking away.

My feet were aching something awful when I stopped again. I had hiked damn near halfway across the city, getting lost about a half dozen times, refusing always to ask for directions. Asking directions meant interacting with people, people with memories, and I didn't want anybody to remember me walking through Boston tonight.

Now I was in a semi-familiar neighborhood, with Italian restaurants and pizza joints and tourists and students milling about, looking for fun, food, and whatever else might come their way.

That third part worried me.

I took my time, walking along the narrow streets, until I reached the street where Aunt Teresa lived.

Looked quiet.

Looked calm.

Still didn't like it.

Nothing seemed out of place. Cars were parked up and down the street, there were college-aged men and women walking by, some were standing around, and. . . .

Standing around.

At one end of the block, a tall, muscular guy was sipping on a drink. At the other end of the block, another guy about the same size was gnawing on a slice of pizza. He was taking very, very tiny bites.

Both guys' heads were moving around, up and down the street, up and down the street. I walked into a restaurant, asked for and received a take-out menu, and walked away from Aunt Teresa's block.

Three blocks later, I dumped the menu in the trash.

At Park Street Station on the edge of Boston Common, I found a park bench, sat my tired butt down, took stock of the situation. I had about sixty bucks in my wallet and my credit cards. But using the credit cards was out of the question, at least for now. Felix and I had gotten a hell of a lot of attention, and I wasn't sure from who. All I knew was that Felix had felt threatened back at the college, and had responded rattlesnake-quick.

I shivered. I had a heavier coat for the autumn evening hours, but that coat was at Aunt Teresa's home, along with my other belongings. With cash, I could get on the T, head to North Station, and from there eventually catch the Amtrak Downeaster train that went north and eventually into my home state, and there to Exonia, home of Phillips Exonia Academy and the hospital where my friend Diane was barely surviving.

But what to do after that? Every other time I had gotten into a bind, I had always counted on my few friends to help me out. Paula Quinn, assistant editor at the *Tyler Chronicle*, was always there to dig up some obscure piece of information or give me a tidbit about local politics. But the last I knew, she was out in Colorado with her boyfriend—the town counsel for Tyler—taking a couple of weeks off after being hurt at that same anti-nuke rally in Falconer where the activist Bronson Toles had been shot.

Diane had always been Diane, but she was . . . she was out of the picture.

And Felix?

No joy. I had no idea where he had gone.

I rubbed my arms again, feeling the most alone I had in quite a long time. People kept on walking by, not as many as before, as the night lengthened and the air grew colder. Up to the left was Beacon Hill, home of the Massachusetts Legislature and the source of many a headline and criminal sentence, and behind me was the famed Boston Common.

I waited. I could make out the grinding sound of a T train rattling beneath me.

What to do?

I looked one way, and the other.

Traffic was thin.

I waited.

A car approached on Tremont Street, slowed, and then pulled in front of me, in a No Parking area. It was a bright red BMW sedan. The driver's side window rolled down.

Felix looked out at me.

I got up from the park bench, strolled over and around the BMW, opened the door, and sat down gratefully in the heated interior.

# CHAPTER FIVE

I fastened my seatbelt and Felix moved quickly into traffic. "You okay?"

"Feet hurt and my butt is frozen. And you?"

"Never finer. You dump your cell phone?"

"Quite dead," I said, adding, "Your aunt's place is under surveillance."

"Yeah, I know."

He stopped at a traffic light near Frog Pond. "What happened back there?" I asked him.

"I was waiting for you and those two pulled up. Showed me ID, stating they were FBI. Wanted to talk to me."

"Sweet Jesus, you shot two FBI agents?"

Felix tightened his hands on the steering wheel, made a sharp left turn. The BMW was a standard and he seemed to take a pure physical joy in working the clutch and moving the shift. His jaw worked and he kept quiet, and he quickly braked at another red light.

"Sorry," I said. "Spoke too fast. Spoke without thinking."

We waited at the light. It was a long wait.

The light turned green. Felix said, "I guess you damn well did."

Then we started moving again.

I kept my mouth shut. My feet were tingling with joy from not having to walk any more. Felix made another turn and we were on the Mass Avenue Bridge, heading into Cambridge.

"So I was parked there, waiting for you to come out. Then the LTD drove by, made a U-turn, parked across from me. One guy came out and walked over, wanted some identification. I politely asked him who he was. The guy said he was FBI, flashed me his ID. It didn't look right. The photo was slightly out of focus, print looked blurry, badge looked cheap. That was point number one. Point number two was when I asked him if I could take a closer look at the ID. He refused. Lewis, in my previous encounters with similar officials, they're always happy to show off their IDs. Makes them feel that much more important."

It was good to be in the warm interior of the BMW, good to be with Felix, good to hear him explain what had happened.

"So the first guy got closer in my face, wanted to know why I was at Boston University. I said I was there to meet a friend. What friend, he asked. None of your business, I said right back at him. Meanwhile, I was also keeping an eye on his driver, who was back at the LTD, standing behind an open door, giving him cover. And while this was all going on, I was evaluating."

We were now in the People's Republic of Cambridge. Luckily, the long-promised border and customs crossing had not yet been set up. "What do you mean, evaluating?"

Felix slowed down as we approached another red light. "Sounds spooky, hocus-pocus, all that crap, but in my line of work you develop a sense of what's going on. Learn how to sit in a restaurant. Know, when you're walking down a sidewalk, who might be a potential threat. Learn when to answer a party invite at some guy's house or stay home and watch basketball. And you know how much I hate basketball. But this sense, it's never failed me, not once. So I've learned to trust it."

"What was your sense telling you?"

"The whole thing was a setup," Felix plainly said. "The guy was too pushy, too demanding, too cocky to be an FBI agent. Plus his clothing and shoes, it just didn't add up. FBI guys like to dress flashy. He wasn't flashy at all. I talked to him for about two or three minutes, and by then I knew they were both fake. So I slapped him on the shoulder, told him good job, why doesn't he try out for summer stock theater next year, and I turned to walk back to my Caddy."

"Turning your back on them didn't seem too bright."

"Maybe not, but I had an advantage. The way I'd parked the Cadillac, I had a pretty good reflection from its side windows. When I was walking away from the gentleman actor, I saw him reach under his coat, grabbing a weapon. It was quickly going bad. I was either going to get shot right then, or they were going to drag me into the LTD and I was going to get shot later on. Neither outcome was appealing."

"You moved fast."

"I wasn't thinking, just reacting."

"Sorry again for second-guessing you."

"Apology accepted once again. And speaking of apologies, I'm sorry I didn't wait around for you. I only had seconds to get the hell out of there."

"Understood. Though I admit I was getting nervous after you didn't show up at Fenway Park or your aunt's place."

"Took a while to dump the Cadillac and pick up new wheels. Even with prep work, calls have to be made, people have to be paid off."

"Fair enough."

Felix made a series of turns and we went down a residential street. He pulled over and put the shift into neutral, left the engine running. "So, where now?"

"Off to Brookline," I said firmly. "To see Professor Knowlton."

"I take it you didn't get much joy from the professor?"

"Not a damn thing, except overpriced and undervalued opinions."

Felix glanced back at the rear of the BMW. "We're missing some gear."

"I think we can make do if we put our minds to it, don't you?"

Felix paused. "You really want to do this?"

"Do I have a choice?"

Felix shrugged, shifted into first and let out the clutch. "No, you've made that pretty clear."

He expertly drove us through the side and back streets of Cambridge, where we then passed over to Brookline. My feet were finally feeling like they were attached to a human, and after a couple more minutes of driving Felix got us to Professor Knowlton's neighborhood.

"Damn," Felix said.

"You said it."

We were definitely late.

Up ahead on the street, the place was lit up by flashing strobe lights from three fire trucks and two police cruisers. Rigid hose lines snaked their way across the road, and firefighters and police officers were doing their job as Professor Heywood Knowlton's house burned to the ground.

There was an all-night diner outside Brookline, on Route 2, where we stopped to have a meal. Not sure what kind of meal it could be called because of the time, but it made sense to refuel. We both had cups of coffee and Felix had an omelet stuffed with veggies, while I had scrambled eggs and bacon and hash browns. Felix looked at me with disdain and said, "Ketchup on eggs? Really?"

"Why not? Better than spoiling eggs with vegetables. Vegetables don't belong in eggs. They belong in salads or side dishes."

"Barbarian," Felix said.

"Just know what I like."

We ate in silence for a while, the other booths filled with late-night students, early-bird truckers, and a fair mix of whoever else was out and about at this hour of the night. When the plates had been cleared and the check dropped off, I said, "Your Aunt Teresa going to be okay?"

"Oh, cripes yeah," Felix said. "First of all, her neighbors will keep a good eye on her. Second, I really don't think someone's gonna pick up a lady her age and try to bring her in. And if they do, she'll start yapping at them in Italian, and if they get an Italian speaker in, then she'll start going at it with some sort of Sicilian dialect."

"Plus she's deadly with a kitchen knife."

"Only with relatives," Felix pointed out.

I picked up the check, thought for a moment, put it back down. "So what the hell is going on?"

"I'll remind you that I'm here as—"

"Yeah, advice and technical assistance." There was a sprinkling of toast crumbs by the end of the counter. For some reason it disturbed me, so I took a moist napkin and wiped it clean.

"So this what I think," I began. "Curt Chesak and the Nuclear Freedom Front . . . he's incredibly connected, or there are some serious types after his ass. But neither makes much sense. If he's connected, then who's pulling the strings? Anti-nukers and their friends? They don't have deep pockets, and the vast majority of them are peaceful. Their idea of being violent is writing snotty letters to the editor, or leaving anonymous postings on conservative Web sites. So that doesn't make much sense, that everything that's been thrown up against us has been from close friends of Curt Chesak. Unfortunately for us, and for him, Professor Knowlton was our only real connection to Chesak. With his house burning down around his ears, I don't think he's going to be seen anytime soon. Don't know if he was in that house or not, but he's certainly ticked someone off."

Felix picked up his coffee cup. "All right. Considering the reception I got at BU, then I'd say there are some serious types after his ass. Any theories?"

I wiped again at the countertop. "There were two guys with fake IDs at BU. I saw two other guys hanging out at your Aunt Teresa's place. Then you have the crew that burned down Professor Knowlton's house. That means at least six fellows with dark arts out there in the shadows, and they all need to be paid, to have logistical support, and to have backup. That's a lot of money, a lot of expertise."

"Maybe there are others out there like you, seeking revenge."

I made a face. "One person seeking revenge is a cliché. Two or more is just an incredible coincidence. I just don't know."

I made for the check again and Felix beat me to it. And as a man who knew his tradecraft, Felix paid the bill with a twenty and a five. No credit cards, no records.

"So what do you want to do now?"

"Beats me. You got any ideas?"

Felix said, "I want to check on my aunt."

"All right."

"And you?"

"Still planning to chase down Curt Chesak."

"Don't remember you having a boat called the *Pequod*," Felix said.

"That's a hell of a literary reference. Maybe you should be on *Jeopardy* or something."

He frowned. "Wouldn't pass the background check. So, while I'm checking in on Aunt Teresa, how are you going to find Chesak?"

"You got any suggestions?"

A shrug. "Whenever I've been stuck, sometimes going back to the beginning pays off."

"That's a hell of a suggestion, and I like it." I looked into my wallet. "But only if you can spot me some money."

Felix reached into his own wallet. "Have I ever said no?"

Several hours later, I emerged from a train in Exonia, the town directly next door to Tyler. I was tired, dirty, and hungry, the meal from the Brookline diner only a distant memory. From that diner, Felix took me to North Station in Boston, and with a cash advance, I got a one-way ticket on the Amtrak Downeaster to Exonia, home of the famed prep school, an obscene number of writers, and the hospital where Diane was. Felix had also slipped me my 9mm Beretta and said, "Be thankful there's no metal detectors on Amtrak."

It was well after midnight when I stepped into Exonia station, which was just a roofed-over portion of the platform. There was a parking area, a number of buildings, and a closed diner. A few cars were parked at the end of the lot. Two other passengers got out and quickly got in their cars and drove off.

Then a dark blue Ford sedan rattled into the lot, with EXONIA CAB on the side in yellow letters. I walked over and a woman driver peered out at me. She was smoking a cigarette and rolled down the window. "Where to?"

"The hotel near the hospital."

"Tyler Inn and Suites?"

"That's the one."

She frowned, and I said, "I know it's not much of a fare. Make you a deal: take me there and I'll pay double."

"And double the tip, too?"

"Of course."

"Mister, you got a deal."

I got in the back of the car and settled down in the seat. It was clean and smelled of Lysol and tobacco. She shifted and we left the parking lot, went up past a school and Catholic church, and made a left-hand turn. Within seconds we were passing through the old and impressive buildings of Phillips Exonia Academy, a prep school that's been teaching since 1765. There were a few lit Halloween decorations along the way. Usually Halloween is my favorite holiday, but not this year. I wasn't in the mood to celebrate anything fun or special about death or the spectral arts.

The driver had an all-news radio station on, which was broadcasting the latest poll numbers for the upcoming election between Senator Jackson Hale from Georgia and the current incumbent. The driver snorted at the news and said, "You follow this political shit?"

"Not as much as I used to."

"Then you're a smart fella, you are."

"Some nights, not tonight."

I had a pang of guilt. Annie Wynn. With my cell phone destroyed so whoever was out there couldn't trace my signal, I had no way to contact her, and my home number wasn't being answered either.

Through the center of Exonia, past a delightful bandshell that had two town hall buildings on opposite sides—an oddity, I know, but this was New Hampshire—and two traffic lights and turns later, we were at the Tyler Inn and Suites. After paying my driver, I wandered into the lobby, which was empty. I rang a bell on the counter and a yawning male clerk came out from behind, with a black goatee and slicked-back hair, and tattoos on the backs of his hands.

We had a bit of to and fro with me not wanting to use my credit card to pay or to guarantee the room. But I managed to give him the impression that my, quote, old lady, unquote, had kicked me to the curb—which explained my lack of luggage—and after slipping him a twenty, he slid across a keycard and said, "You take care, bro."

"You can count on it."

I went up to my room, got inside, and stripped and took a shower, and then collapsed in bed. Considering the noise level of the past few nights, I fell asleep within seconds.

# CHAPTER SIX

After getting dressed the next morning, I went down Porter Avenue and visited a nearby Dunkin' Donuts. Once upon a time, Dunkin' Donuts used to make and sell quite a variety of doughnuts; nowadays, they focus on specialty coffees, oddball sandwiches, muffins, and the random tasteless doughnut that gets shipped in from some secretly located bakery. Once upon a time I heard they used to make delicious crullers, but that might just be an urban legend. I got a black coffee with two sugars and a blueberry muffin and went up Alumni Drive to Exonia Hospital. The morning was crisp and bright, and I sat on a park bench, had my breakfast, and watched the stream of people coming to work. Most of them looked happy to be out and about.

Good for them.

When I was finished, I joined the good folks going inside and took the elevator up to the fourth floor, where the ICU and my best friend resided.

I breezed past the nurses' station at the entrance to the ICU, taking a left down the wide corridors. The rooms were large, with sliding glass doors and drapes. Nurses bustled about, and in front of Diane Woods's room her fiancée, Kara Miles, was standing, talking to a woman dressed in nurses' scrubs. Kara was shorter than me, with short dark hair and lots of piercings in her ears. She and Diane had had a semi-secret relationship until last year, when my quirky home state had legalized gay marriage. The two of them had a slight falling out during the anti-nuclear demonstrations at Falconer—Kara had been active in one of the peaceful protest groups, while Diane was doing her job and earning OT as one of the scores of cops at the scene—but engagement rings had been exchanged the day before the last protest.

The last protest, when Diane had been beaten by a steel-pipe-wielding Curt Chesak.

Kara spotted me approaching, excused herself from the nurse, and came my way. She had on jeans and a multi-colored knitted top, and I gave her a big hug as she kissed me on the cheek. "Oh, Lewis, so damn glad to see you."

I kissed her back. "How's she doing?"

"Not much has changed, which I guess could be called good news. At least she's stable."

"Can I see her?"

"Not for a bit. They're giving her a sponge bath, checking her dressings, stuff like that. Hey, let's talk."

Kara took my hand and led me to a tiny conference room. She moved with the self-confidence of a family member and patient advocate who knew her way around the ward, the staff, and the bureaucracy. The room had a small settee, a phone, and two chairs, and she left the door open as we sat down.

She took a breath. "She's been stable, and the swelling in her brain has gone down. She's still in a coma, but . . . but we're hopeful. What else can we be, Lewis? Doctor Hanratty said that if the swelling decrease continues, and there are other signs of improvement, you know. . . ."

Kara choked up, looked away. I squeezed her hand, and she squeezed my hand back. "I'm the first visitor of the day?"

She grabbed a tissue from a nearby box, wiped at her eyes. "You sure are. There's been a constant stream of cops coming in, day after day. Just to spend a few minutes, of course, but damn, it's something to see all those cops line up to visit her, even if she doesn't know they're in the room."

"I've read that some coma studies say patients can hear what's going on, no matter how deep the coma."

"That'd be great." Then she giggled. "Then Diane heard something naughty the other day."

"What's that?"

"Oh, two days ago, this woman came in, just before the end of visiting hours. Real pushy woman, had on a dark blue power suit, leather briefcase, took control of the room. Know what I mean?"

"I've both met and worked for the type."

"She said she was from some law enforcement support council, wanted to come in and introduce herself, evaluate Diane. I asked her what for, and she said that her group had financial resources to support Diane once she was either discharged or transferred to another facility. Something to supplement her regular insurance and disability. I said that was great. She said she had some paperwork that needed to be filled out, and would I be a dear and go down to the first-floor cafeteria to retrieve it, since she left it on one of the tables."

"Really?"

"Truly. You can imagine what I said to that. Then she got huffy and said, well, if the proper paperwork wasn't filled out, then Diane wouldn't be eligible for compensation under the plan. And I told her what she could do with the paperwork, and where she could shove it, and then she stalked off. I remember her stiletto heels making a hell of a racket on the tile floor when she left."

I didn't like what I was hearing. "Did she tell you her name?"

"Dickerson. Yeah, a Miss Dickerson. Don't remember her first name."

"She leave a business card?"

"No."

"Remember the name of the charity?"

She slowly shook her head, frowning. "No, it was a mouthful. Something like the Blue Line Support Council for Police, or the Badge of Blue Support Agency . . . Lewis, is something wrong?"

I took a breath. "Did she come back the next day with the paperwork? Or call you to set up an appointment?"

"No. Hey, what's wrong?"

I was glad that with the open door, I could see the entrance to Diane's ICU unit. "Tell me, Kara, how friendly are you with the Tyler cops?"

"Those that know me and Diane, pretty good. What's going on?"

"Bear with me, just for another moment. Who's the highest ranking cop you know?"

"That'd be Captain Kate Nickerson."

"All right, this is what I want you to do. When we're done here, you call Captain Nickerson, and you tell her that you believe somebody came by the other day who wanted to do Diane harm."

"Shit. . . ."

"You ask the Captain if she could set up some off-duty Tyler cops to provide guard service for Diane. They'll have to work with hospital security. But from now on, no more visitors to Diane unless you or a staff member can vouch for his or her identity. Okay?"

Kara leaned out, to also look at Diane's room. Her voice quavered. "You mean that woman that came in, she was going to . . . she was going to do something bad to Diane?"

"Maybe, maybe not. Perhaps she came in to do what she said she was there for, to get some paperwork signed. Maybe she got ticked off by you, stormed out, and got in a car accident, so she never came back."

Kara looked back at me. "Or maybe she was here to pull Diane's plug."

"Or maybe I'm being paranoid."

"But why? Why would someone want to kill Diane?"

"Somebody tried to do it at the protest a couple of days ago."

"But that was part of the protest, random, with all those people coming in and fighting the cops."

"Surely was," I said. "But let's just play along with my paranoia. Make the call, and have Captain Nickerson work with hospital security."

The door to ICU slid open, and two nurses emerged. Kara stood up and both nurses smiled to Kara, like they were telling her it was all right to go in.

"Won't that kind of protection . . . won't that cost a lot of money?"

"I imagine the Tyler cops will do it for free," I said. "If not, send the bill to me."

Kara let me go into Diane's room first, a courtesy I'm sure so that I could look and react at seeing Diane without being watched by Kara. Something deep and cold burrowed inside of me when I saw her still form on the bed. A white cotton blanket was pulled up almost to her chin. IV tubes ran into her wrists. A tube was taped about her mouth, and a ventilator raised her chest up and down. Her short brown hair was a tangled mess, and her eyes were shut. The wounds on her face were covered with bandages, and the bruises were turning yellow and green. Her face was swollen, like it had been injected with some sort of fluid.

Kara came up behind me, slid her arm into mine. "Hard to believe, but she's actually looking better."

"Glad to hear that."

"Doctor Hanratty said sometime tomorrow they're going to take the tube out, see if she can breathe on her own."

"I'll keep my fingers crossed."

"Please do."

We stood there quietly, listening to the hiss and whir of the ventilation system doing its work, the beeps and buzzes coming from a number of monitors. Kara said, "What are you up to, Lewis?"

"Just visiting a friend, that's all."

She squeezed my arm. "You don't think Diane has told me tales about you over the years? And this is the first time you've been by in days? Which means you've been busy. And if you've been busy, you've been up to something."

"I've been working."

"What kind of work?"

"The work that leads me to Curt Chesak, who did this to Diane."

She squeezed my arm again. "Hold on. I've got something to give you. I'll be right back."

Kara bustled her way out, and I was alone with Diane. I stepped forward and rubbed the top of her hand, took in her injuries, her medical support, the whole dreary mess.

I bent over, kissed her cool and dry forehead, then I moved my mouth down to her right ear. "Diane . . . I'm doing everything I can to make it right. You can count on me. And whatever happens . . ." and something dry and hard seemed to catch in my throat ". . . I'll look after Kara. I promise."

I stood there, wiped at my eyes, and turned around as Kara came back into the room. We both walked out into the hallway.

"Here, this is for you," she said, handing over a white business envelope to me. "A state police detective came by and told me to give this to you."

"Did he leave a name?"

"No, but he said you'd know who it was from."

"Really?"

"He said unless you've had a lot of experience with state police detectives lately, you'd know."

Of course I'd know. Detective Pete Renzi of the New Hampshire State Police had been the lead investigator in the assassination of Bronson Toles last week, the anti-nuclear activist who had been murdered by his stepson to prevent him from giving away thousands of hours of old tape recordings that could have made millions for Toles, his wife, and his stepson. Instead, Toles wanted to give all the money away, and that charitable thinking had led to his death.

And irony of ironies, most of the tapes had been destroyed in a fire intentionally set by a former columnist for *Shoreline* magazine.

Renzi had also been the detective who had clued me in to Professor Knowlton and his connection with Curt Chesak of the Nuclear Freedom Front.

I tore open the envelope. Inside was a white sheet of paper, no letterhead, just one line of type, centered in the middle:

*Lewis, trust me on this, leave it alone.*

Really?

I folded up the sheet of paper, put it back into the envelope, shoved it in my rear pocket.

"Everything okay?" Kara asked.

"Nothing I can't handle."

She smiled. "You're a damn slab of granite, Lewis, aren't you? Able to do everything."

"Some days more than others. Look, can I ask a favor?"

Her eyes filled up. "Absolutely."

"Wondering if I could borrow your car. And maybe your condo."

She stared at me for a moment, retrieved her purse, and came back with a set of keys. She tugged free two keys and passed them over. "Use both as long as you want. I don't expect to be moving far from here."

"Thanks."

Kara took my hand and led me back to the small room we had been in earlier. She turned and said, "You're still working, right? Still looking for that Curt Chesak?"

"That I am."

"And what do you plan to do once you find him?"

I let a second or two pass. "I really don't want to tell you, Kara."

She nodded in understanding. She kissed me one more time, whispered, "You get him, Lewis. You get him."

## CHAPTER SEVEN

At the parking lot of the Lafayette House on Tyler Beach, I easily found an empty parking spot and maneuvered Kara's Subaru to a halt. It was mid-morning and clouds had roared in from the west, making the day both look and feel gray and cold. The Lafayette House is one of the few surviving New Hampshire grand hotels from the end of the nineteenth century, multi-story with a number of Victorian-style turrets and a long wrap-around porch, and a perfect lawn with a view of the slate-colored churning Atlantic.

I sat for a long while, staring out at the ocean, thinking and juggling things. Before me was Atlantic Avenue, also known as U.S. Route 1-A, and on the other side of the road was a large yet narrow parking lot. Being off-season, the lot was mostly empty. I considered that a good sign. I swung around and saw no one on the porch, no one sitting in the white Adirondack chairs on the perfect lawn.

I got out of the car, zipped up my coat. The wind was steady, biting. I walked briskly down the driveway, jogged across Atlantic Avenue, and then started walking north, on a very narrow sidewalk. I looked to my left and then my right, like I was a tourist from Omaha seeing the ocean for the very first time. After striding about fifty yards or so, I made a quick descent to the right, stepping onto the Lafayette House parking lot. At this end, there were a number of large boulders, blocking the end of the lot, save for one area where a rough dirt lane was visible.

My own driveway.

I walked down the bumpy, not-very-well-maintained road, as my home came into view. It was about a hundred and fifty years old, and it started out as a lifeboat station for the U.S. Lifesaving Service, then junior officers' quarters for the Samson Point Artillery Station—now a state park—and, before it came into my possession, belonged for a number of years to the Department of the Interior.

For the past several years, the old house with the weathered siding and nearby sagging garage had been more than a home to me: it'd been my safe harbor, and I was so very, very happy to be back.

This wonderful feeling would last about another thirty seconds.

When I unlocked the sturdy front door and stepped in, it was all wrong. Hard to describe, but walking into my house quickly reminded me of a movie I had seen last summer with Diane Woods. At first the movie had seemed fine, but after just a few seconds, it was quickly obvious that the projectionist needed to slightly focus the film.

That's what was going on here. When I stopped and looked around, everything seemed to be in its correct place, but no, everything was just slightly askew. The old Oriental rug in the center of my living room. The position of the couch, two chairs, and the coffee table. All had been moved and put back in their places, but not exactly.

My house had been tossed, and tossed by experts.

I trotted upstairs to my office and my bedroom, saw the same evidence of my safe harbor being violated. I quickly gathered up a few things and ran downstairs. I ran outside, closed and locked the door, glanced back at my home, and started up the driveway.

Then I stopped.

The driveway was the quick and safe way back up to the parking lot and Atlantic Avenue.

Instead, I turned around, started scrambling over boulders the size of a Mini Cooper, taking the long and rough way back.

It was a good choice.

⁂

Walking back toward the Lafayette House but from a different direction, I saw one and then two dark-blue Chevrolet Suburbans roar up Atlantic Avenue and then turn into the once-empty parking lot of the Lafayette House. One Suburban went bounding down my driveway, and the other one veered and blocked the driveway entrance. I kept on walking, head down, hands in pockets, trying to look like some guy out for a mid-morning walk, not having much of a care in the world.

I came up to Kara's rusting Subaru, once again smiling inside at the peace signs, anti-nuclear stickers, and one sticker that said something like IT WILL BE A GREAT DAY WHEN SCHOOLS HAVE ALL THE FUNDS THEY NEED AND THE AIR FORCE HAS A BAKE SALE TO BUY A BOMBER. Sure. Tell that to Air Force pilots working lumbering bombers on patrol to defend their nation, said bombers having been built when their grandparents had been dating.

I got in the Subaru, calmly put the key into the ignition, started it up after three tries, and then exited the parking lot, heading south.

The condo unit that Diane and Kara lived in was about fifteen minutes away.

I took thirty minutes.

Those thirty minutes weren't wasted. I spent them driving, backtracking, and sitting for a few minutes in parking lots, looking about me. Nobody seemed to be following me; but then again, nobody had been in my house, but my presence had obviously alerted a ready-response team that came roaring in about ten minutes after I had unlocked my door.

That meant staffing, that meant money, and, above all, that meant a lot of patience.

And smarts.

So the lack of cars following me meant nothing. A GPS unit of some sort could have been tagged on the Subaru's bumper, or some sort of stealth platform made up to look like a seagull was now floating above me, taking real-time photos and data acquisition.

Maybe I was being paranoid, but so far it had been paying off.

I made one more stop at a tiny grocery store, picked up a copy of that day's *Tyler Chronicle* and *Boston Globe*, and got to Diane and Kara's place.

They resided in Tyler Meadows, a set of condominium units built right up to Tyler Harbor. I parked the Subaru and took in the view, and my chest ached at seeing the concrete structures and lights of the Falconer nuclear power plant on the other side of the harbor and a wide expanse of marshes. That's where it had all started, less than a week ago.

And something else bothered me. Out in the harbor were some fishing vessels, and one lonely sailboat, sail furled, at anchor. The fishing boats belonged. They would go out any time they could, all fall and winter, to make their catch. But the sailing boat didn't belong. The name of the sailing craft was the *Miranda*, it belonged to Diane Woods, and it should have been hauled out by now.

Lots of things were being left undone.

I walked over to the entrance to the condo unit where I had spent lots of time over the years, for brunch or a quick lunch or some lengthy dinners. I unlocked the door, closed it behind me, and went up the short staircase to the first floor. It opened up into a living room that had an adjacent kitchen and dining area with a grand view of Tyler Harbor. I sat down at the round oak kitchen table and sat there for a bit, just thinking, brooding.

So many memories here, of lots of laughter and long conversations and the occasional cross word, as Diane's professional life sometimes got mixed up in my oddball personal life. But through it all, our friendship had deepened, had grown, and had gotten to this point.

I unfolded the papers but could not read them. I looked over at the living room and saw the photos of Diane and Kara, sharing their moments together, and photos were up on the refrigerator, some curling over magnets holding them up. The place was musty and smelled of old cooking scents and soap and perfume.

I looked around again, stood up and folded the papers together, put them under my arm. My original goal had been to stay here for a while, lie low, think things through and try to figure out what the hell to do next.

But I didn't belong here. It belonged to Diane and Kara. Though I was sure they wouldn't think so, I felt like an intruder, a stranger.

I looked once more at all the photos, seeing the smiling faces, wanting to see them in my mind's eye instead of the drawn face of Kara and the unconscious face of Diane.

Then I left, making sure the door was locked behind me.

After a couple of quick errands, I drove back to the Tyler Inn and Suites in Exonia and, still having the upset spouse look on my face, I managed to get my room for another night while paying just cash. In my room I stretched out on the bed, started going through that day's *Boston Globe*.

I went through the first section.

Then the second section.

And the last section, the sports pages.

I shook my head. Went back to work.

And then I found it, in a tiny paragraph buried deep within the Metro section.

UNAUTHORIZED MOVIE SHOOTING SCARES BU

Unbelievable.

I had to read the story three times before it sank in.

The shootings on Bay State Street near buildings belonging to the Boston University campus were officially reported as a student filmmaking project gone awry. Two BU students were being held in custody, names not yet made public. Quotes from witnesses about how realistic the entire episode had been, with shot-out windows, two people being shot, blood everywhere. "Even though they should have gotten the right permits and made the right notifications, whoever did this deserves an Oscar," said Harry McDermott, twenty, a BU student.

I folded the paper shut. Went to the other side of the room, went through a plastic bag with the cheery blue Wal-Mart logo on its side. I removed a disposable cell phone, read the directions, powered it up, and made a phone call to Massachusetts. It was answered after one ring.

"Yeah?"

"Looking for Tinios."

"Yeah?"

"Give him this number, all right?"

The man hung up on me. I put the phone down and paced the room, thinking things through. I looked at the *Tyler Chronicle*, which had a recap of last week's bloody events at the Falconer nuclear power plant. There were four photos on the front page. The largest showed Curt Chesak, face masked, among a group of protesters, holding up a police helmet in celebration after ripping it off Diane's beaten face. Three smaller photos, with a headline over them saying: THE DEAD AT FALCONER. Two were of an older man and woman, who had been shot and killed by persons unknown at about the same time Diane Woods was being beaten nearly to death. The third was of someone I had met a couple of days prior, a John Todd Thomas, who had been a student at Colby College up in Maine. John had brought me to an encampment belonging to the Nuclear Freedom Front to meet Curt Chesak, and he then disappeared, his body being found later in the nearby marshes, a gunshot wound to his head.

THE DEAD AT FALCONER.

The other two were a man and a woman, both active in the NFF, one from Massachusetts, the other from Pennsylvania. He ran an organic food store. She worked in a knitting collective. And John Todd Thomas originally came from Arlington, Virginia, a place I once had known extremely well.

The ringing of my new phone startled me. I looked at the incoming number, saw the ID was being blocked. I answered it by saying "Hello," and a man on the other end said, "What's up?"

I sat in one of the two chairs in the room in relief. Among the numerous things Felix and I had gone over before embarking on this little adventure in justice was setting up a procedure to contact each other, using a middleman that Felix trusted and had used many times before. Even though the phone number I used said it was in Massachusetts, there was no guarantee the man lived there. Felix said he was a genius with the intricacies of the phone system, and when he was eleven or twelve he'd had a pitch-perfect whistling ability that enabled him to fool the phone system, to make free long-distance phone calls.

"You okay?"

"Hanging in there."

"How's your relative?"

Felix said, "No change, thankfully. But she's off to Florida for a while. Good for her bones and other things."

"Glad to hear it."

"And you?"

"Things are getting more interesting."

"Do tell."

"Did you read the *Boston Globe* today?"

"Haven't gotten to it," Felix said.

"Check out the Metro section. Seems a couple of students were filming a movie near the Boston University campus. Lots of gunfire, bullets flying, bodies on the street."

"The hell you say," Felix said, both surprise and admiration in his voice.

"Page B-2, News Briefs," I said. "Check it out. You know what this means, don't you?"

"I've been around, I don't need a picture drawn."

Felix's tone was pretty calm, a feeling I didn't share. "All right, no drawn picture, but Felix, we've just entered the world of my former employer."

No answer from the other end. I knew Felix was considering what I had just said; and to emphasize my point, I added: "Just so there's no confusion, I don't mean *Shoreline* magazine and my crazy editor, Denise Pichette-Volk. I mean before that."

"Before that" being as a research analyst for an obscure section of the Department of Defense, which I had left years ago after the people in my section were all killed—except for me—in a training accident that could have embarrassed many a corrupt soul in our government.

I could hear Felix breathe. It was a damn fine cell phone.

"Well, how about that," he finally said.

"Remember our little discussion back at the diner? About the number of men we've run up against since we went to Boston?"

"How could I forget? You put ketchup on eggs, remember?"

I pressed on. "You add the logistics and financing that you need to support that effort, and then you add on the ability to fake a news story about the shooting back at BU . . . we're talking government agencies here."

"Ours or theirs?"

"Somebody's, that's for damn sure."

Outside my room, I could hear someone vacuuming the hallway. Any other time, I would find that incredibly irritating. Right now, I found it incredibly soothing.

Felix said, "You be extra careful, then."

"What? No warning from you about stepping away, backing down, letting everything just settle out?"

Felix said, "They hurt your friend. I wasn't going to insult your intelligence."

"Thanks."

"I'm going to be tied up for another day or three, getting Aunt Teresa out and down to Florida. You going to need anything?"

"You beat me to it," I said. "Yeah, I'm going to be doing some out-of-state traveling. I need a photo ID and a credit card to match. Plus some cash. Can it be done?"

"How long do you need it for?"

"Just a couple of days."

"Yeah, it can be done. Where are you now?"

I told him where and my room number, and he said, "Okay, it'll be arranged. But what do you have planned?"

"You said something earlier about going back to the beginning."

"Yeah. I remember."

"I'm going back to the beginning, and then some."

I brought Kara's Subaru back to the Exonia Hospital parking lot and then took the elevator up to the ICU. At the entrance to Diane's room, a muscular-looking young man was reading a copy of the *Union-Leader* newspaper out of Manchester, the state's largest city. He had on jeans and a flannel shirt, and on display at his right hip was a holster with an automatic pistol.

Despite all that had gone on earlier, I felt happy at seeing him. I slowly approached him and he quickly folded his newspaper and put it in his lap.

"Help with you something?"

"I'm looking for Kara Miles."

"And you are?"

"Lewis Cole. I'm a friend of hers and the detective sergeant."

He stared me up and down and said, "You got ID?"

"Sure do. Let me get it."

I moved slowly, went to my wallet, slipped out my New Hampshire driver's license. I suppose I could have also passed over my press card, issued by the N.H. Department of Safety, but since I was no longer employed by *Shoreline*, I didn't want to be accused of doing something illegal.

The police officer gave my license a quick scan, grunted, handed it back. "So it is you, and you're one lucky fella. There's four names on a list of people allowed to visit who don't work at the hospital, and you're one of them." He motioned with his left shoulder. "Kara's in there with the detective sergeant. You want I should get her?"

To do what? To tell her about the faint outlines of something dark and monstrous that had been stirred up out there, that was after me and her and Diane and no doubt others?

I passed over the keys to Kara's car and condo. "Give these to her, if you don't mind. Tell her thanks, that I've made other arrangements."

"Fair enough. Anything else you'd like to say?"

"Officer, I'd love to, but I just don't have the time."

Sometimes in my off moments I like to think that maybe the Greek or Roman gods of old are still at work up there, sort of like a little immigrant grocery store going up against the current Walmart Supercenters of organized religion. Their activities by nature get drowned out, but every now and then they poke up, like they did tonight when the God of Irony—whoever she or he was—sent me a signal with the arrival at the Tyler Inn and Suites of a cab the front desk had called for me. Like before, it was a dark blue sedan with the yellow letters EXONIA CAB stuck on the side.

The window rolled down. The same cloud of cigarette smoke. The same driver from the other night.

"Oh, it's you," she said.

"Try to contain your enthusiasm."

She took a hefty drag from her cigarette. "What, you need to get over to the train station again? Why the hell don't you just walk it? Couldn't be more than a mile."

I reached for the door handle. "Maybe I just like your company."

"Hah."

I opened the door, said, "A different place this time. How does Durham sound?"

Her tone brightened. "Mister, Durham sounds just fine."

To get to Durham from Exonia meant traveling through two small New Hampshire towns, and my new best friend kept up an entertaining chatter as we proceeded. Even in this day and age, there were dairy farmlands and wide-open fields, and it was good to look at the red, gold, and yellow of the fall foliage as we approached Durham. My personal driver talked about the weather, about the snotty prep-school kids in Exonia, her aching hips, and how her husband George was adjusting to his new artificial knee—"and thank Christ the V.A. eventually said it was a service-related injury, otherwise my grandkids would be paying off that bill when we're both dead and gone."

Downtown Durham consisted of the post office, a couple of beer-and-pizza places, and a tidy downtown with two-story brick buildings. The UNH buildings were mostly brick and marble, and when I was dropped off near a main intersection with lots of college students walking briskly along, my driver asked, "You need a ride back?"

"I do, but I don't know how long I'll be."

She passed over a creased business card. "Call me."

I glanced at the card. "Maggie, I appreciate it, but like I said, I don't know when I'll be done."

Maggie shrugged, put the car into drive. "What, you think my dance card is full for the rest of the day? No worries, pal, okay?"

She drove off, and I thought: no worries.

I wondered what that felt like.

## CHAPTER EIGHT

I walked a ways and sat on a stone wall, across from a dormitory called Congreve Hall. Like most of the surrounding buildings, it was brick with white windows and black shutters. Students walked along the concrete sidewalks, singly and in groups, most carrying knapsacks or book bags. I eyed them carefully as they walked by. There were times in this nation's storied past that college students had had the luxury of studying in a safe bubble of fun and higher learning, only worrying about being popular or getting good grades, or getting the best education possible.

We were no longer in that special time. Nobody said anything as they passed by, but everything was off. Out there in the alleged real world, men and women with decades' worth of experience in manufacturing, computers, and marketing were desperately snapping up entry-level jobs, leaving nothing behind for the hundreds of thousands of kids graduating each year. And of those graduating, "jobs" sometimes meant unpaid internships, moving back home, and looking with deepening dread at the payment book for their tens of thousands of dollars in student loans.

I'm not sure if I felt pity, or envy, or what. So I just sat there and ran things through my mind, from the note from Detective Renzi telling me to drop the matter, to the *Globe* story blithely writing about a movie shoot going awry, to those strong men hanging around Aunt Teresa's apartment in the North End.

A lot to keep me occupied, which was good, because a couple of hours passed before the young woman I was looking for showed up. Her name was Haleigh Miller, and I had met her during the Falconer nuclear power plant demonstrations a few weeks back. She had befriended me when I covered the protests for my previous employer, *Shoreline* magazine, and she had also managed to hook me up with meeting Curt Chesak back before the violence erupted.

And speaking of violence and friendship, she had also been the girlfriend of Victor Toles, arrested last week for murdering his stepfather, local anti-nuclear activist Bronson Toles, with a skilled sniper shot to the head. Victor didn't like his stepfather's plan to sell valuable demo tapes of up-and-coming music acts to support his charitable causes. The stepson and his mom wanted to do something else with the money, like live in luxury for the rest of their lives.

An old and understandable conflict.

I stood up as Haleigh came closer, and she spotted me and stopped on the paved pathway.

"Oh. You."

"Yeah, it's me," I said. "I won't take much of your time. Just need to ask you a couple of quick questions."

Her face sagged, like the muscles and tendons there had suddenly lost their ability to keep things in place, and for a moment it seemed like she was about to burst into tears. She sniffled some and said, "Shit, okay, can we sit for a second?"

We went back to the stone wall and sat down and I asked, "How are you doing?"

"Stupid question. Ask another."

"What about Victor?"

A shrug. "Haven't seen or talked to him since that . . . since that day."

Ah, yes, that day, when I'd visited Victor and his mom at their residence, discovering there that Victor was the shooter, and where Haleigh had stood up for her man by slugging me in the head with a softball bat. I had been trapped in a basement for a while, until I managed to escape and overpower Victor, and also managed to burn most of the valuable demo tapes.

"Some day. What news of him?"

"Arrested and charged with Bronson's murder, and his mom's trying to get a defense fund going with her old leftie friends."

"Just the one murder?"

"Isn't that enough?"

"Probably," I said.

"Any more questions? I've got a paper due tomorrow and haven't even started researching it."

"A week ago, when I asked to meet up with Curt Chesak, you came through. I was probably the only reporter in the area who got an interview with him before the demonstrations went violent."

"And before he beat the crap out of that Tyler cop."

"That Tyler cop happens to be my best friend."

"Oh. Sorry, I guess."

"So here's the deal. You had to talk to somebody in the movement to set up the interview. I want to know who he or she is."

"Why?"

"You're an intelligent young lady, Haleigh. I'm sure you can figure it out."

"So you want to find Curt Chesak."

"That I do."

"Why not let the cops find him first?"

"Haleigh, you really don't want to know any more."

She seemed to consider that. She kicked at some of the colorful leaves on the ground, her head lowered. She lifted her head. "You . . . you had a choice, last week, to let the Tyler and state police know about me and Victor. You didn't do it. You said you were doing it for my Air Force dad, so he wouldn't have to worry about his daughter from the other side of the world."

I kept quiet. Let her think it through. Haleigh sighed. "Ever since the protests, none of my so-called friends want to have anything to do with me. They think that since I was with Victor when he killed his stepdad, like I should have known, like I should have prevented it. All this talk about fellowship, about togetherness, about standing as one against The Man . . . so much bullshit. I can't believe it, Lewis. I still can't believe it."

"Sorry you had to find that out."

"I guess that's part of growing up, eh?"

"Some would say that."

"Sure," she said. "So I say to hell with sticking together. The guy you're looking for is a college instructor, from the Philosophy department. Name of Ken Marvel. Active in Chesak's group but real quiet, in the background, almost invisible."

"Thanks for telling me."

Haleigh grabbed her knapsack, stood up. "And he's a real prick. I know about him because he tried to hit on me one night when he was having some beers at the Stone Chapel, trying to bring Bronson Toles over to the dark side of the anti-nuclear movement. I hope you have fun with him, Lewis, I really do."

It didn't take much work, but I found out what I could about Ken Marvel. Like Haleigh said, he was an instructor at the school's Philosophy department, which meant he didn't have tenure and served semester to semester at the university's pleasure. I couldn't find out much about him in the large digital library called the Internet, but I did find that he lived in Lee, a small town adjacent to Durham, which was home to college employees, a few farms, and a mix of locals.

Getting there proved to be a challenge, since my Ford Explorer was still at my home on Tyler Beach and unreachable. But fortunately enough for me, this part of New Hampshire had a transit system consisting of brightly colored buses usually operated by college students looking to help pay for their tuition.

It took me about thirty minutes to get to Lee by finding the right bus to take, and I had a turn of good fortune when it turned out that one of the bus stops in Lee was at a service station that was only about a ten-minute walk to his house, 10 Oakland Road. The road was a typical New Hampshire back country road, single lane with no yellow line painted down the center, and definitely no sidewalk, guard rail, or streetlights. I strolled on the dirt shoulder, checking the mailboxes, until I finally came to number 10, which I found just as the sun was starting to set. The driveway leading into the woods was dirt.

No name on the mailbox. Not unusual. This was, after all, the Live Free or Die state.

I started down the driveway, keeping to the side in case a car or truck came bouncing along the narrow dirt lane. Pine trees and brush grew close to the edge of the road, which allowed me cover in case I was spotted.

But I went down there with no problem, going about a hundred feet to where the road widened to a dirt turnaround before what's known as a double-wide, a pre-fab trailer, that was dumped here on a concrete slab. Lights were off inside the single-story home with black-shingled roof, and there was a sudden burst of barking. Two dogs emerged from doghouses, secured by long lengths of chain, and they snapped and growled in my direction. I wasn't sure what breed they were, but they looked thin and mangy. The areas around their doghouses were worn-down dirt, with empty food bowls and water bowls scattered before them.

The dogs barked some more and, feeling like living on the edge, I talked low and soft to them and walked forward. One and then the other sniffed my hands, then whined and flopped in the dirt. I squatted down and rubbed their heads, butts, and bellies, and in a few minutes I think I made two new best friends.

"Where's your alleged master, guys, huh? He coming back home soon?"

One licked my hand, and the other one licked himself in a private place. Then they panted in appreciation, and I got up.

"Sorry, guys. If I had a treat or two, I'd pass it along."

It was getting darker. I pondered my options, stepped back and into a stand of birches, and took out my cell phone. I checked the time. Not too early, not too late.

So what to do?

Something I hadn't done in a while.

I dialed a phone number with a Washington, D.C. area code.

The phone rang and rang and I was anticipating sliding into voicemail, when I was pleasantly surprised by a woman answering. "Hello, this is Annie."

"Hey, Annie, it's your faithful New Hampshire correspondent."

A soft laugh that still had the ability to make me tingle. "Why, as I live, breathe, and scramble for votes, it's the mysterious Lewis Cole. Didn't recognize your number on the caller ID. Have a new phone?"

"I do."

"What happened to your other phone?"

"Somebody broke it in half and dumped it in a drainpipe in Boston."

"Anybody you know?"

"It was me."

Another soft laugh. "Sounds like a story to me. What are you up to now, hon?"

"If you really want to know. . . ."

"Of course I want to know," and there was the barest hint of impatience in her voice, a hint I long ago had learned to recognize.

"Currently, I'm standing alone in a bunch of trees in Lee, staring at an empty house, being kept company by two dogs who look like they got a bath last year."

"Are the dogs dangerous?"

"Nope. They're chained."

"And are you waiting for someone?"

"Always waiting for someone."

"I see. Haven't heard from you in a while. You still hunting?"

"That I am, Annie."

She sighed. "And how long is the hunt going to last?"

Hearing her sigh made me tighten my grip on the cell phone. "Until it's done."

"Or you give up."

"No, until it's done."

"Or you're hurt. Or arrested. Or something worse."

"Tell you what, let's change the subject. What are you up to?"

"Nothing so exciting. Just trying to elect a good man president."

*Yes*, I thought, *a good man with a bad wife*. "Anything new on that end?"

"Nothing I can share," she said.

"Ah, who's keeping secrets now, eh?"

A pause on her end, and I sensed I had gone too far. She sighed once more and said, "I know it's been a while, but you know how D.C. works,

Lewis. Knowledge and secrets are the coin of the realm. And I don't know who might be listening in . . . you know how it is."

"I sure do."

"Lewis. . . ."

"Yes, dear."

"We need to talk."

"That's what we're doing now, isn't it?"

"No, we're chatting. Big difference."

Headlights appeared at the end of the driveway, along with the sound of a car engine. "Sorry, Annie. I've got to run."

"We still have to talk."

I stepped back, concerned I'd be seen. "I know, I know, but I've got to run."

"Oh. The hunt continues?"

"It sure does."

A touch of sharpness again in her voice, crystal-clear even though she was hundreds of miles away. "Nice to know you're dedicated to something."

Then she clicked off.

So did I. And put the phone away.

The dogs started barking again as a dented and rusty Nissan pickup truck rolled in and came to a halt. A tall guy carrying two plastic shopping bags stepped out, and the dogs increased their barking. "Shut the hell up!" he called out. "I'll feed you in a minute, for Christ's sake."

He walked up to the double-wide, unlocked the front door, and went in. He bustled around inside for a few minutes, while his dogs kept on yelping, and then there was a sudden *flick* as an outdoor floodlight came on. He came out again, bearing two metal bowls with dry dog food in them. He appeared to be in his early thirties, gaunt, wearing blue jeans and a tan down jacket. His hair was thin up forward and was pulled back in the rear in a ponytail. He was talking to himself as he dropped a bowl in front of each dog and then went back inside. I gave him a few minutes to recover from his exertions, and then I walked up to the front door. No doorbell or doorknob, so I just hammered on the door.

"Hold on!" came the voice. He opened the front door, left the storm door closed. "Yeah?"

"Ken Marvel? UNH instructor?"

"So far, so good. Do I know you?"

"Nope. The name is Lewis Cole. I'm a freelance magazine writer, hoping I could ask you a few questions."

"What kind of magazines?"

"*Shoreline,* for one," I said, which wasn't much of a lie.

"Never heard of it. Any other magazines I might have heard of?"

"That's the one."

"Sorry, not interested."

He slammed the door.

Well.

I wondered what kind of philosophy he taught at UNH, and doubted his students were getting their tuition's worth.

I banged on the door again. And again he opened it up. "When I said I wasn't interested, that meant you could leave."

"But *I'm* still interested. Doesn't that count for something?"

"Doubt it. What the hell are you working on?"

"A story about the anti-nuclear demonstrations at Falconer."

"Never heard of it," he said, and slammed the door once more.

I opened up the storm door, knocked once more. The main door flew open, and his eyes widened in quick surprise as my right hand snapped out, grabbed his shirt collar, and pulled him forward to me. I stepped aside so he flew out the door and down the steps, where he hit the ground with a satisfying thud.

I turned around and sat on the steps. He called me a name or two—nothing original, which lowered my appreciation of him as an educated individual—and he rolled over and came right at me. I gauged his approach, and as he got to the steps I quickly lifted up my right leg, braced myself, and he ran right into my right foot, at a particular angle above his knees and below his waist that definitely got his attention.

A few moments passed as he curled up on the ground, rocking back and forth, looking about the same shape and intelligence as a jumbo shrimp.

I got off the steps and walked over to him. "Sorry I was so direct there, professor . . . or do your students call you instructor? Or Mister Marvel?"

Through gritted teeth, he said, "They call me Ken."

"Wow, that's very forward-thinking of you. Getting down with the students, sharing and discussing issues of the day."

"You bastard. . . ."

"Nope, my birth certificate says otherwise. But I will admit I'm in a foul, foul mood." I squatted down on the ground, carefully keeping a good distance away from him. "You see, I'm trying to locate a single bit of information, and after lots of travel, bad food, and so-so sleeping accommodations, I've come to you. My mistake was thinking that you and I could have a civilized discussion, perhaps come to a mutual understanding and respect of each other's positions, and then go on from there. But when you came at me full of attitude, well, the part of me that's not the better angel of my nature emerged. My apologies."

His hands fell away from his private parts. His breathing eased. He got up and into a sitting position. "You sure move fast for an old guy."

"A compliment and insult in one sentence. I'm sure you fit right in at the Philosophy department."

He ran a hand across the bald part of his head. "Yeah, but there's no future there. No future in anything in higher education that doesn't produce good little worker bees and consumer bees. Plus I'm an instructor, which means no tenure, lots of hours, and minimal pay. And the tenured ones, no matter which department they belong to, they live in that special ivory tower where they've managed to quickly pull the ladder up after them."

"We've all got problems, don't we. Look, I'm looking for some information about the anti-nuclear demonstrations. I get that and I leave."

"Maybe I'll call the Lee cops, have you arrested for assault."

"Maybe you will, and I'll say it's all a misunderstanding, with no witnesses. To be terribly self-promoting, I'll drop a name or two in law enforcement that will cast suspicions on you and make me look like the citizen of the year."

He rubbed at his head again, moved his legs around. "So what are you looking for, what information about the demonstrations?"

"I take it you were involved with them?"

"Damn right I was. We've got to stop the madness of—"

I held up my hand. "Please. I was there for a number of days. I know all the talking points. You were with the Nuclear Freedom Front, right?"

"Sort of. Knew some people there, worked with them."

"Good. Because I'm looking for Curt Chesak."

"Why do you want to know where he is?"

"Let's just say I'm from the Publishers Clearing House prize patrol and leave it at that."

"No," Ken quickly said.

"No, what? No, I don't know where Curt Chesak is living, or no, I'm not going to tell you?"

His expression hardened. "Just no. Take it any way you like."

I made a point of sighing. "Fair enough. No hard feelings, eh?"

I stood up and extended my hand, and he took my hand and I helped him up, and then I kept on helping him up as I pulled him, tripped him, and then pushed him to the ground. I got on his back and deftly undid my leather belt, and in a few seconds I had him secured by the wrists. A lot more cursing ensued—again, nothing particularly original; I guess a mind is a terrible thing to waste—and near the doghouses, I found some lengths of rope. In a few minutes, I had my belt back, and I had a very unhappy college instructor under my control.

"Wasn't it Plato who said philosophy is the highest form of music?" I asked. "Not sure if I have the ear for music or philosophy, but let's see what I can do."

## CHAPTER NINE

I moved around his cluttered yard, discovered a lawn chair, which I brought back. Late-fall insects were battering themselves around the spotlight, and the dogs, having eaten their fill, were lying down, watching me and their supposed master.

Lawn chair before him, I sat down and said, "What's with the dogs?"

"What about them?"

"Why do you keep them outdoors like this, all chained up? Very medieval, don't you think?"

"I hate the damn things. Why should I have them in my house?"

"Then why do you have them?"

He spat at me, missed. "I don't have them. They belong to my damn ex-wife Melissa, and every week she promises me she'll come here and pick them up. Damn bitch is in California now . . . how in hell is that supposed to take place?"

"You're a college instructor, Ken, I'm sure you'll figure it out." I crossed my hands in my lap. "Here's the situation. I want to know where Curt Chesak is. From your replies, I have a pretty good idea you know where he is."

He said I should perform an impossible sexual act upon myself. I said, "I've heard worse. So here we go. I want that information, and I'm prepared to wait a very long time for you to give it to me."

Ken said something rude again about my parentage. I said, "Words, professor. Just words. Haven't you taught your students about the origin of the phrase 'sticks and stones'?"

His breathing quickened. "What are you going to do, torture me?"

"Nope. Learned a long, long time ago that torture results in poor intelligence results. People will say or do anything to escape torture. I'm not going to touch you at all, Ken. Not one bit."

I crossed my legs and looked at him. He looked at his house, his ex-wife's dogs, and then to me. "So what the hell is going on here?"

I held my hands out. "So we wait. I'll wait here, and you'll wait there on the ground. It's going to get colder. Your circulation will start to fail. You'll get thirsty, hungry, and any bathroom needs you have will need to be taken care of where you lie. I might get up, stretch my legs, wander into your open home to see what I might scrounge for food and drink, and maybe come back out here and keep on sitting with some blankets to keep me warm. I might turn off the floodlight so I can get some star-gazing in. So that's what's going on, Ken."

Another explosion of words sent my way, involving my parentage, my sexual habits, and certain barnyard animals.

I said, "Again, I've heard worse."

He gave up about three hours later. "Please," he whispered. "Please."

"You know the deal."

"Curt . . . a real fucking mystery man . . . came in and, depending on who you talked to, either was from Boston or L.A. or New York . . . smart, wicked smart . . . but after he joined the NFF, went from being a grunt to the guy running the joint. . . ."

"Why is that?"

"Who the fuck knows . . . he just had this . . . knack . . . of running things . . . and money, he had lots of money . . . always in cash . . . we need camping gear, no prob . . . cell phones . . . no prob. . . ."

"Where did the money come from?"

"Nobody knew that either."

"What about Professor Heywood Knowlton? From BU?"

"Gave him chops . . . introduced him around . . . vouched for him . . . I got the feeling he brought Curt to other professors in other colleges. . . ."

One of the dogs got up, walked in a circle, urinated, and sat back down. "You said he was a mystery man. What sort of clues did you figure out?"

"I'm so damn cold. . . ."

"I need to know more."

He coughed. "Don't know if this means anything . . . couple of my girl students . . . they were in love with him . . . him being a bad boy and all . . . they cooked for him, cleaned, probably boffed him. . . ."

"Very sweet. Go on."

". . . one night, one of the girls came to me . . . she was doing his washing . . . found some papers stuck in his pocket. . . ."

"What were they?"

"Didn't make sense. . . ."

"Doesn't have to make sense. What were they?"

"One was a boarding pass . . . from Boston to Dulles . . . the other was a scrap of paper, a phone number or something . . . written on hotel stationery, located in Crystal something or another."

"Crystal City? In Virginia?"

"Yeah. . . ."

"So what was the phone number for?"

"Huh?"

"Come on, Ken, you're a smart fellow. You tell me you weren't curious, you didn't give that number a quick dial?"

He coughed again, kept quiet. By then I was sitting with two wool blankets over my legs and torso. I held up one of the blankets. "So close, Ken, so very close."

". . . a bunch of lawyers. A law firm. On K Street in D.C. . . . you know who lives there. . . ."

"I do," I said. "Lobbyists. The name of the firm?"

"I don't remember . . . the receptionist spoke so fast . . . but O'Toole was one of the names . . . I know that . . . O'Toole . . . God, please, please. . . ."

I got off the chair, gently rolled him around, tried to undo the knots. I couldn't do it. His struggles and the cold had tightened the knots, so I went into his house and his dirty kitchen, came out with a serrated steak knife, and cut away the ropes. He yelped and I spent quite a few minutes, rubbing his wrists and ankles, helping him get the circulation going again. When

I thought I had made progress, I wrapped him in the two wool blankets and sat him up. I also tossed the steak knife into the woods.

"So long, Ken," I said. "Sorry this all took place."

"What," he spat out, "you're apologizing now? You expecting me to accept that?"

"Not for a moment," I said. "What happened to you was my responsibility, my fault, start to finish. I regret every second of it."

I started walking up the driveway. He yelled after me. "But why? Why do you want Curt so bad?"

Over my shoulder, I said, "He hurt a friend of mine, put her in a coma, practically killed her."

His voice raised in a screech. "This? You did this to me over a friend?"

"I did," I said. "And if you had any friends, you just might understand that."

He yelled some more and I kept walking, exhausted. When I was out of eyesight and earshot of the not-so-good professor, the enormity of what I had just done to him over the past few hours struck me. I slowed my walking, stopped, and, with a massive cramp and heave, bent over and vomited into Ken's driveway. Not much came up, not much at all. It's been said that more often than not, people feel better after throwing up, after expelling whatever was bothering them.

Not tonight. I felt empty and my mouth tasted foul, and what was bothering me refused to leave.

Back to the service station I walked, and in a dim light from the closed building I saw the bus schedule and saw that it had ceased service for the evening. I looked up and down the road and saw no headlights. Lee is a lovely small town, but I doubted there was a motel room within walking distance. I took out my cell phone, made a call, and then put the phone away. I waited. I put my hands in my coat, walked around the small parking lot of the service station. A half moon was shining. A wind came up and leaves skittered across the road. Some distance away, an owl hooted.

I seemed far away in time and place from the crowded demonstrations near the ocean some days back, with the scent of pepper gas and tear gas in the air, the crowds of people chanting, trying to break into the power plant perimeter, and that dark, cloudy, rainy day when a dedicated group did get in, burned a few buildings, and where two of the demonstrators ended up shot dead.

Adding to the murder that had taken place a couple of days earlier.

I paused in my walking. A car roared by, didn't stop. I thought of other things, of police being pushed back at that last demonstration, of seeing Diane Woods being pushed up a slight incline, all alone, trying to defend herself, falling back, Curt Chesak upon her, wielding a lead pipe which he brought down again and again, eventually holding up her police helmet in triumph.

Remembered a lot of things. Started getting cold. Kept on walking around.

Headlights. The car slowed down and it was a rattling blue Ford sedan with EXONIA CAB on the side. Window rolled down, and the older woman inside said, "You again?"

"We've got to stop meeting like this."

"Only if you stop paying. Hop in."

I got in the rear, and she turned around in the lot and headed back out. "Exonia?"

"Yes."

"Tyler Inn and Suites?"

"Yes again."

We drove on for a few minutes. "You know my name is Maggie. What's yours?"

"I'm Lewis."

"Lewis, may not be any of my business, but what the hell's going on with you? You seem to be a guy without a car, but you dress and speak all right, have all your teeth, smell good. So you're not a loser."

"Maybe I just don't like to drive."

"Hah," she said, turning well through a sharp curve. "This ain't Boston or Cambridge. Public transport sucks. Way I see things, only losers don't have cars. Guys like you, if your car is in the shop, maybe you get a rental, maybe borrow a car from a friend."

"Good observation. You always been a cab driver?"

Maggie laughed at that. "Used to work as a secretary in the Manchester police department. Retired and decided not to sit on my ass all day and get my brains sucked out by the TV, and take care of my alleged better half. This gig gets me out and about, meeting people, stuff like that. Besides, I love to drive."

I folded my arms, looked out the side window. Should be getting back to Exonia in about ten, fifteen minutes.

Maggie said, "Sorry. Asking too many damn questions. All you're paying for tonight is a ride, that's it."

I said, "You see a lot of justice there on the Manchester streets, working for the police?"

"Sometimes. Not all the time. But at least they were trying. What, you trying to get justice done?"

"I am."

"You a cop, or a P.I.?"

"You know any cops or P.I.'s who get shuttled around in a cab?"

"Can't say I do. So you're keeping a low profile."

"That I am."

"Anonymous cab, staying at a hotel, paying in cash . . . must be some serious justice you're looking for."

"It is."

"Family or friend?"

"Friend."

"Who is he?"

"She," I said. "She. And she's the finest woman I know."

"Wife? Girlfriend?"

A sharp tang of . . . guilt? Anger? For I realized what I had just said, and knew I was so glad Annie Wynn wasn't there to hear it.

"Just a friend."

She glanced back at me. "That's one hell of a friend you got there, Lewis. And you need any more transport, I'm your gal. And despite my loud mouth, I know how to keep secrets."

"Thanks, Maggie."

## CHAPTER TEN

In the morning, after a restless night at the Tyler Inn and Suites, I had a cup of coffee for breakfast and walked up to the Exonia Hospital. Back to the ICU, and another cop was sitting guard outside Diane's room, and Kara Miles was standing next to him, talking. The cop was yet another bulky guy with short hair, and Kara patted his shoulder as I approached, and he visibly relaxed.

Kara looked tired. No surprise there. She had on sneakers, gray sweats, green T-shirt, and a gray hoodie sweatshirt. I gave her a quick hug and smelled stale coffee and grease.

"Lewis, so good to see you."

"Same here. How is she?"

Slight shrug. "Bit of excitement last night . . . it looked like she was responding to some outside stimuli, or whatever they call it. I was talking to her and her eyes opened. Just for a moment or two. God, I was so excited. But the doctors said it might have just been an unconscious reaction."

She quickly grabbed my hand, squeezed it. "But she's in there. I know she is. She's hearing everything . . . I just know it. And later today, they're going to take her off the ventilator, see if she can breathe on her own."

"Can I see her?"

Kara released my hand. "Go ahead. I'm sure she'd be glad to hear your voice."

I slid open the door to her room and stepped in. Nothing much had changed; there were still plenty of get-well cards, balloons, and floral bouquets crowding a shelf near the window. I went over to Diane, sat down, held her left hand. The usual gear and equipment was over her, bleeping and blooping. She was still breathing via a ventilator, white tape across her mouth holding everything in. Her face was still bruised and bandaged, and I reached up and gently traced an old scar on her chin, where a long-ago fight with a drunken male in the booking room had scarred her when she was just a patrolwoman.

"When you finally get your lazy carcass out of here, think of all the stories you can spin about your new scars," I said. "Impress the town manager and the selectmen. Maybe get you a raise one of these days."

*Thump-thump*, and the *hiss* of the respirator.

"I got Kara's back, no worries there. Even if you're in rehab for a couple of years, or longer, I'll watch over her."

*Thump-thump, hiss.*

"Remember when we first met, about six months after I moved in? My place was a dump, belonged to the Department of the Interior. Given to me as a bribe to keep my mouth shut for my service at the Department of Defense. I hired a local woman to clean the joint for a few months, especially while I had to wait to get the windows replaced. All that beach sand blowing in, getting into the clothes and bedding. Mrs. Martin. Nice woman, but her nephew had scammed her and had taken all her savings."

*Hiss, thump-thump.*

"She told me the Tyler cops couldn't do much, because his name was on the savings account. But Mrs. Martin was so upset . . . so I talked to her nephew and pointed out the error of his ways. Never told you this because I hated to admit it, but he was living in a condo in Porter. I was talking to him on his balcony and . . . well, I gave him a good view of downtown Porter. Upside down. Me holding on to his ankles . . . which was a hell of a feat, since I wasn't feeling the best. But he paid up, and you heard about that, told me to leave police work alone. And I said it wasn't police work, it was community activism . . . and it went on from there, didn't it."

*Thump-thump, hiss.*

"I'm off for a while. Tracing down some faint leads." I stroked her hand. "Tell you the truth, I'm pretty much scared out of my wits. I'm going someplace . . . someplace I've tried to forget, someplace I've put out of my mind. But I've got a job to do, and a promise to keep."

I got up, kissed her forehead. "I love you, Diane. So very much."

Then I walked out.

I met up with Kara as she was returning from the nurses' station with a cup of coffee. "Talk to you for a sec?"

"Absolutely."

We went into the same small room as before, and she sat down with a sigh. I sat down across from her. "I'm going to be away for a few days."

"All right."

From my wallet I took out a creased business card, passed it over to her. She gave it a glance and raised her eyebrows. "A lawyer? In Boston?"

"That's right. If you don't hear from me in a week, I want you to call him. Tell him I've been absent for seven days. He'll know what to do from there."

Her eyebrows went up a bit higher. "Not sure I like the sound of this, Lewis."

"Sorry to put this on you at this time, but there's nobody else in the area I can rely on."

"But your friend. . . ."

"She's in D.C. Trying to elect a president."

She took the business card and carefully slipped it into her hoodie's front pocket. "What are you telling me? Where are you going?"

"You don't want nor need to know."

Kara chewed for a moment on her lower lip. "You're going someplace bad, someplace dangerous."

"You could say that."

"Why?"

"You know why."

"But the cops. . . ."

"The cops are good at what they do. But sometimes there are . . . circumstances where they can't go or do anything. I don't have those restrictions. And I'm going to see this one through, no matter what."

"You're talking in riddles."

I got up. "I'm talking the only way I know how. Sorry, Kara. Remember, seven days."

That evening, I was at South Station in Boston, a transportation hub in the southern part of the city. In my continuing trend to explore transportation options in my neighborhood, I had taken a bus from Newburyport, Massachusetts, to Boston. Trains, cabs, and buses left South Station and went throughout New England and the Northeast. In the big lobby I sat on a wide wooden bench and watched the people eddy and flow about me. A soft black duffel bag was at my feet, my 9mm Beretta was in a shoulder holster on the left for easy access. I had a concealed-carry permit for the state of Massachusetts. I didn't have carry permits for the several states I was about to pass through, and that didn't bother me a bit.

Eventually one man broke away from the crowd and sat next to me. Something tight around my chest lessened.

"Good to see you, Felix."

"The same."

"How's your great-aunt?"

"Off to Florida a month ahead of schedule. She put up a hell of a fight, but I figured out a way to get her to leave early."

"What did you do?"

"Told her that her retirement village was holding a fundraiser for wounded troops from a nearby base, and that they needed her lasagna recipe. So off she went." He handed over a thick business-sized envelope. "Loan, ID, and credit card as requested. We'll pass on the official paperwork."

"Thanks. How are you doing?"

He stretched out his legs, crossed them at the ankle. "Hell of a thing. We still got guys with sharp eyes hanging out in the North End, and my place in North Tyler is under watch as well. Over the years, you and I have been involved in some shadowy work, have gone up against some bad guys and gals. But this time . . . you know the phrase 'stir up a hornets' nest'? Man, you've stirred up a whole goddamn colony of nests."

"So I have. Sorry about that."

"Not a problem. Part of the life I chose, years ago. Dealing with angry insects and associated creatures."

The P.A. system issued some sort of gibberish that sounded like Olde English on crack. Felix said, "The question I have is, how are you doing?"

"Working. Snooping. Going places."

"Like D.C.? You told me plenty of times that you would never, ever go back there. So what's changed?"

"Circumstances."

"Meaning you found something linking Curt Chesak to something in D.C."

"Yes."

"Something connecting him to your past life?"

I kept quiet, put the bulging envelope in my soft carry-on bag.

Felix said, "You want some company?"

I couldn't believe he had just said that. "D.C.'s not the North End. Or New England."

"What, you think I can't handle myself against hired goons from the Feds?" he asked, exasperation in his voice. "First of all, I've been dodging Feds most of my life. I'm used to it, and they haven't caught me yet. Secondly, I've had other hard men after me, plenty of times, whose weapon of choice was either an ice pick through the ear or two in the hat. So I think I can do just fine in D.C."

"Have to do this one alone. I have to move fast, have to think quickly on my feet . . . and it might not end well."

"So I just hang out up here?"

"You just hang out up here. If you don't hear from me in a week, do me one last favor and check on Kara Miles, up at the Exonia Hospital."

"Diane Woods's S.O. What do I do?"

"Whatever she asks. All right?"

Felix leaned over, offered a hand. I gave it a firm shake. "All right. You can count on me."

"Always have."

He stood up. Fingered the zipper on his jacket. Looked over at the crowd, then at me. "You be careful out there among the English, pal."

"You can count on it."

Felix looked at me one last time. "You carrying?"

"I am."

He shook his head in dismay. "Sorry to hear that."

"Sorry that I'm carrying?"

"No," he said, finally zippering up his coat. "No, not that. You see, Lewis, there was a time when I could tell you were carrying. You were so conscious of the fact that you were armed that I had no problem seeing through you. But now I can't tell. Which means you've changed, and not in a good way."

He turned, and I lost him in the crowd.

## CHAPTER ELEVEN

Nearly twelve hours later, the next morning, I got off a Greyhound bus at the company's terminal in Washington, a few blocks north of Union Station. I was stiff and felt grimy and greasy after spending so many hours sitting down or dozing. The bus had lumbered its way down the Northeast corridor, and it was full of people either like myself—wanting no official record of their travel—or those who couldn't afford anything quicker, like a train or airplane. There were a crying baby or two, an old man who snored loudly, and a couple of soldiers going home on leave, still wearing their camos. They kept to themselves and stared a lot out of the windows as they passed through the country they had sworn to defend.

I strode out to the street, which had a lot of traffic and taxicabs backed up. Eventually I got in the back seat of a Diamond taxi with an older African-American male driving. He had on a cloth jacket and cap, with a beefy arm and hand draped over the steering wheel. I got in, and he murmured, "Where to?"

I handed him a fifty-dollar bill. "If you don't mind, just drive around, show me the sights. It's been a long time since I've been here."

He grunted, put the cab into drive. "I'll see what I can do."

Over the next half hour, I sat in the rear of the clean cab as we drove around the city, passing Capitol Hill, the Supreme Court building, the National Archives, and the Smithsonian along the Mall. The Air & Space Museum, the Museum of Natural History . . . so many beautiful buildings with beautiful and historical objects within. The monument park to World War II veterans, then a swoop and drive past the Jefferson Memorial. The Washington Monument, the reflecting pool, and Old Abe, staring out at the Union he had sacrificed himself to save.

And a drive at a distance from the White House, once upon a time called the People's House. Lots of memories and thoughts and melancholy swirled through my mind in that taxicab.

At a stoplight, my quiet tour guide swiveled around and said, "You satisfied?"

"Pretty much."

"We could go across the river, check out the Pentagon and Arlington National Cemetery if you'd like."

"No, I would very much not like," I said. I passed over another fifty-dollar bill. "How about a motel or hotel that's near D.C., safe and clean and reasonably priced? Can we go there?"

He deftly pocketed the bill. "We can do that."

A few minutes later, he pulled into a small lot adjacent to a two-story motel called Lincoln Arms, just on the edge of D.C. "This will suit you just fine, mister."

"Thanks," I said. "I owe you any more?"

He laughed, a pleasing sound. "Shit, man. No, we're doin' fine."

"Feel like earning a bit more?"

"Why the hell not?"

I opened up the door. "Come back in an hour, all right?"

"You payin', I'm comin'."

"Thanks."

An hour later, I was back outside, freshly washed, shaved, and dressed, wearing a nice fall uniform of slacks, shirt, tie, and blue blazer. My Bianchi leather holster kept my 9mm Beretta in place. Right on the dot, the Diamond cab pulled up and the driver looked me up and down and said, "Man, you clean up nice."

"Thanks, that was my plan."

Back into the cab, and he said, "More monuments, museums?"

"How about a cesspool?"

That made him pause. "Plenty of places to choose from."

I gave him an address on K Street. A chuckle from him. "That's a good choice."

In the K Street area of D.C., my guide drove around and found an empty spot to park for a moment. The buildings here were large, some fairly new and built with clean stone and glass. He kept the cab idling, looked around him. He suddenly spoke. "My boy came back from Afghanistan last year. Body didn't have a scratch but something's going on inside of him, know what I mean?"

"Yeah, I do."

"He's not crazy, mind you. He's just changed . . . real, real quiet. Used to go out clubbing, hanging with his boys . . . now all he wants to do is sit in his bedroom and read. That's all he does, read old, old books, about spaceships and trips to the moon, and he eats three meals a day and sleeps twelve hours a night. He's back, but not really back."

I didn't know what to say, so I kept my mouth shut. He sighed and I slipped over two twenties. He waved the two bills up at the gleaming buildings. "Think anybody who works there has a boy like mine?"

"Not for a moment."

"Don't think that'll change anytime soon, right?"

"Afraid not."

Another sigh. "We can dream, I guess."

I liked my cabbie but I also liked keeping things quiet, so I walked two blocks until I got to the address I was looking for, that of Munce, Price & O'Toole, Professional Associates. Before I made the long bus ride down to D.C., I had spent a few minutes at the Tyler Public Library, using one of their computers to do research on Munce, Price & O'Toole. And my research came up pretty thin. They had been in business for nearly two decades, were considered one of the most influential lobbying firms in the capital, and had a range of interests from agriculture to energy to pharmaceuticals to arms dealers and about everything else in between.

What I couldn't find out was who they specifically represented. Their client lists were very confidential and, unlike other lobbying firms whose reach exceeded their grasp, they rarely made the pages of the *Washington Post* and *The New York Times*, and in those appearances there was never any mention of scandals, arrests, or payoffs.

Meaning they were either very lucky or very good, or a combination thereof.

On this part of K Street, the buildings were a mix of old eight-story brick buildings, next to eight- or ten-story newer office buildings. There were four lanes of road in the middle, two local lanes on either side, with median strips and lots of trees. The sidewalks were quite busy with well-dressed men and women, striding along, doing their business, most of them with cell phones pushed up against their ears. So much power, so much money, so much wrong. For decades, both parties had declared this particular street the source of all evil in government, but neither had done very much about it. It was like two sets of mechanics, facing a car that wouldn't start, with one set insisting that a new windshield would make it all right, with the other set equally insisting that four new tires would do the trick.

I missed the address of Munce, Price & O'Toole and had to circle back to find it. It was a simple glass door with gold lettering. I tugged open the door and walked into a lobby.

A small lobby.

A *very* small lobby.

It had a light-blue luxurious carpet, indirect lighting, and a curved counter where a receptionist sat. She was in her late twenties, early thirties, and excuse my old-fashioned observation but she was drop-dead gorgeous. A mane of blond hair that was expertly done, soft red lipsticked lips, and a clinging black dress that showed off a very taut and curvy body. She had a wide smile as I approached, and she was wearing a Bluetooth headset in her left ear.

Before her was a telephone that struck me as very odd. There was no keypad, no buttons, nothing. Just a handset. To her right was a plain wooden door that had the firm's name in gold letters, along with a door-knob with a keypad lock.

"Good afternoon, sir, how can I help you?" she asked in a soft Southern voice.

I looked around, took the place in. Another very odd thing: no coffee table with magazines, no comfortable chairs or couches for clients or salesmen to cool their heels.

Munce, Price & O'Toole looked like a very tightly wrapped place.

I showed her my press pass, issued by the N.H. Department of Safety, which had my name, photo, and the name of my former employer, *Shoreline* magazine. I held it for just a second or two, long enough for her to recognize it as a press pass, and hopefully not long enough for her to memorize my name.

"I'm working on a story about different lobbying firms in Washington and what their clients feel about deep-sea fishing rights."

Her smile didn't change a bit, but her voice seemed shaky. "Deep-sea what?"

"Deep-sea fishing rights. Haven't you heard about the fishing quota controversies in the Northeast?"

"I can't say I really have, sir."

"That's my point. More people need to know about these issues, and I'm looking for information about possible lobbying actions that your firm has conducted. Is there a spokesman I can talk to?"

The receptionist quickly regained her composure. "I'm afraid there isn't."

"Really? Nobody to interact with the news media?"

"Our firm rarely interacts with the news media. We find that our clients prefer it that way."

"How about community outreach?"

"We don't do community outreach."

"Oh. Well, can you tell me which clients may have an interest in deep-sea fishing rights?"

"I'm afraid I'm not in a position to help you."

"But what kind of clients do you have?"

"I'm afraid I'm not in a position to help you."

"Really, I mean, can't you tell me—"

A quick buzz on her phone. She toggled something and nodded, speaking into her Bluetooth. "I see. I see."

Then she looked up at me, widened her smile some. "You know, Mister. . . ."

"Smith."

"Smith," she said. "Someone's coming right now who might be able to help you."

"I'm sure."

I turned and got the hell out.

I was about ten feet down the sidewalk when I realized my earlier mistake. The place looked quiet, small, and non-threatening. All of which were quickly proving to be false. I was certain that when I'd walked into that lobby, I was being observed and recorded, both by sound and vision. Plus I wouldn't doubt that there were hidden metal detectors or X-ray devices around the doorframe through which I'd gone.

Which meant to someone sitting in a room, deep in the building, that an armed man was in the lobby, asking lots of probing questions. Hence the call to the receptionist, to encourage her to keep me in place.

I got to the corner, glanced back. Two men had emerged from the doorway of Munce, Price & O'Toole, one breaking left, the other breaking right. They strode quickly and purposefully.

So did I. I went down and crossed the street, dodging through traffic, all of the drivers no doubt conducting the people's business, and I got a barrage of honking horns for my trouble. Another glance back.

There. An alleyway behind the building hosting Munce, Price & O'Toole. Two more men emerged. Their heads swiveled as they scanned the streets, and then they were looking at something in their hands.

Another good guess. Print-outs of my face, from hidden cameras in the lobby.

I kept on moving, trying to keep the fast-moving pedestrians between me and the sharp eyes of the wolves trying to pick up my scent. I had no illusions. If those men or others were to catch up with me, all it would take would be a long-distance Taser shot, or some sort of device to shoot a projectile with a nerve agent, or something else equally impressive to drop me. A few seconds after that, I would be bundled into an unmarked van or an ambulance, and then I would be gone. I'd probably end up in a basement or a lonely farm somewhere, about to receive an interrogation from folks thinking waterboarding was just a passing fad. I could try to get a shot off first at my pursuers, but who would I shoot? The guys following me, or people about me who might be working for the same employer?

My pace picked up. I went past a Starbucks and a number of other buildings with open, inviting doors.

But those invitations were all traps.

I couldn't chance ducking in someplace, to be cornered.

My hand was under my coat, on the butt of my Beretta.

Still moving.

Was that a shout?

Still moving.

A horn blared.

Honked again.

Another shout.

I spared a half-second glance to my right.

A Diamond cab was pulled to the side, with a familiar-looking driver.

A set-up? An ambush? Could I trust him?

I went to the cab's rear door, opened it up.

I was tired of being paranoid.

He was accelerating before I even had the door closed, and made a sharp left corner, blasting through a red light, causing a screech of brakes and another blast of horns. I caught my breath and looked out the rear window. None of my pursuers seemed to be after me. Even then, my driver took no chances. He made a couple more turns before we were traveling at a steady pace along J Street.

"Thanks," I finally said.

"Glad to be of service."

"How the hell did you end up there?"

I could see his strong shoulders shrug. "You're a man who likes passing around the green. I like guys like that. So I figured I'd hang around the neighborhood for a while, see if you needed another ride."

"Oh," I said. "Is that all?"

A chuckle. "The way you asked me for a place. Most folks ask for a joint near the Metro station or the monuments or museums. You just wanted someplace close, clean, and inexpensive. Means you were here on a job. But most guys I ride, if they're on a job, someone else is paying the freight. So this is something personal for you . . . and the way you moved, way you kept quiet, don't think you were applying to the State Department or something like that."

I settled back into the seat. "Good observations."

"Spent many years in this man's Air Force, looking at radar screens. I was trained to look at things, m'man. And when you got out of my cab a few minutes ago, I told myself that you were going into harm's way, and I'd better be around to scoop you up if you come out of a building at a fast pace."

I looked at his license, caught his name. "Thanks, Frank. I really appreciate that."

He pulled up at a stoplight. "So how did the job go?"

"Managed to apparently piss off some people."

"Means you're doing something right."

"Thanks for the compliment." I wiped at my forehead. It was cool and dry. First real big surprise of the day.

"What kind of job are you up to, anyway?"

"Trying to make things right for a friend."

"Male or female?"

"Female."

The light changed. We moved ahead. "Hah, I think I know what you're saying."

"And you'd be wrong. She's not my wife or my girlfriend. Just . . . best friend I've ever had."

"She in trouble?"

"She may be dying. And I'm looking for the guy who did that to her."

The back of his neck tensed up. "Then go get the fucker. Where do you want to go next?"

"Nearest Metro station will do."

"You sure? I don't mind driving you to your next place, if it's part of your job."

"I appreciate that. But those bad guys . . . they might be waiting for me at the next stop. You were lucky once, Frank. I don't want you to be unlucky the next time."

He turned to me. "You could let me worry about that."

"Yeah, but there's your son, right? He needs you."

Frank took a turn. Up ahead I saw the familiar sign for the Metro. "There's that. All right, good luck, whatever you're doing. You seem like a good guy. Make me happy to see the good guys win one for a change."

"Me too."

## CHAPTER TWELVE

Nearly thirty minutes later, I was in the Commonwealth of Virginia, walking along a residential street in a very pricey suburb of Arlington. All the homes looked like their value was about equal to the amount of money I've made in my life, and they were set far from the street. They were made of brick or wood, several had horse pastures in the rear, and as the sole pedestrian on the street I felt very much out of place.

The one I was looking for was numbered 119, and it was a huge Colonial-style home, white with black shutters, with an attached three-car garage. The landscape was carefully manicured and set, and there was a brick walkway up to the door. Oak trees and pine trees decorated the yard. I paused and gave it a good long glance.

I strolled up the brick walkway to the front door. It was wooden, carved, and it looked like something out of a sixteenth-century Bavarian carver's workshop. There was no doorbell, just a knob in the center that I spun and spun. I could hear a rough tingling noise come from within.

I stood back. Adjusted my clothes. Wondered how shabby I looked.

The door opened up. A man about twenty years older than me stood there, wearing khaki pants, loafers, a white turtleneck, and a navy blue buttoned cardigan. Half-sized reading glasses were perched at the end of his prominent nose, and his white hair was trimmed quite short. In one hand he had a copy of *The Economist* magazine, and he looked attentive, yet so very, very tired.

"Yes?"

"Lawrence Thomas? Lawrence Todd Thomas?"

"Who are you, if I may ask?" he asked, his voice soft.

"My name's Lewis Cole. I'm a journalist from New Hampshire. I'm here about your son, John Todd Thomas."

He pursed his lips, shook his head. "I'm afraid I have nothing to say to you."

"Mister Thomas, please, I really think—"

"Good day, Mister Cole."

The door started closing, and I said: "Except for his killer, I'm the last one to see your son alive."

The door halted.

Opened back up again.

His eyes were watery. "Then do come in, please."

The inside of the house was large, clean, and quite ordered. The carpets were Oriental, the furniture was wood and old, and there were lots of books and framed photos. On one coffee table was a framed photo of the man's son, John Todd Thomas. The photo was in color, it showed him at his college campus in Maine, and a black mourning ribbon was placed across a corner of the glass.

As Lawrence padded into the living room, he said, "Do have a seat. My wife Frances . . . well, she's upstairs, and I prefer her to stay there. I do intend to listen to you, but whatever information you share, well, I do intend to protect Frances. I'm sure you understand."

"Yes, I do."

"I'd offer you coffee or tea, but even after retirement I still haven't gotten the hang of our kitchen gear. So how about a bottled water?"

"That would be fine."

I gingerly sat down on the edge of a couch that looked like it had been lifted from an Early American furniture display at the Boston Museum of Fine Arts, and gave the room another look. There were black-and-white wedding photos of Lawrence Thomas, with a young woman who was no doubt Frances. More photos of their only son, as a Cub Scout, Boy Scout, Little Leaguer, and soccer player. I recalled the young man I had met over a week ago up at the Falconer nuclear power plant, when he had escorted me to visit Curt Chesak of the Nuclear Freedom Front. Soon after he had escorted me, he had been shot to death in the salt marshes around the power plant, and for a few long hours I had been a suspect in his murder.

Lawrence came back, carrying two bottles of Poland Spring water. I got up and he handed one over, then cocked his head. "I have an idea we'll be discussing things of a sensitive nature . . . so perhaps we should go to the rear garden."

"That would be fine."

I followed him out of the living room, to a short hallway and a small room that had floor-to-ceiling French doors. He opened up the near door and I followed him out. There was statuary and a water fountain, and small shrubs and plants that I couldn't recognize. He walked a few yards, past some hedgework, until we came to a stone bench. He sat down with a sigh, stretched his legs. Before us was a small pool, with lily pads and orange fish lazily swimming about. We both unscrewed the tops of our bottles and I took a satisfying swig.

He did the same, looked down at the pond. "This was one of John's favorite places, this little pond."

"I can see why. It's quite beautiful."

"True, and John would spend hours here, on his knees, looking at the water, the fish, the frogs and crayfish. He often begged me to get bigger and better fish, like Japanese koi, and I always refused. It didn't make sense to spend ten or fifteen dollars for a fish that might end up in the belly of a raccoon or a Great Blue Heron."

He took a tiny sip of his water. "Days like these, you look back in regret, think of all the times you said no, all the times you said later, son, all the missed ball games and recitals and events . . . it makes one feel very, very old. Are you married, Mister Cole?"

"No, I'm not."

"I envy you, then. For not having that special terror of being a parent, of worrying about your only son, of seeing him grow up with skinned knees and broken arms. At some point, after he's gone through the temptations of high school and the chances of injury that come with a driver's license, you expect that the odds are now in his favor. That he will grow old and marry and bless you with a fine daughter-in-law and grandchildren . . . and in the space of one depressing late-night phone call from a place you've never heard of, it's gone. It's all gone."

A jet glided overhead, heading to Reagan or to Dulles, airports named after famed Cold Warriors. I watched the fish at play. "What kind of fish are those?"

A short laugh. "Standard issue goldfish. Five dollars for a plastic bag of a couple dozen. You toss them in the water and you can forget about them. They eat what they eat, they reproduce, and in the winter they burrow in the mud. That's why I found them so attractive." He turned a little on the bench. "Tell me about the last time you saw John."

"I was doing a story about the anti-nuclear demonstrations at the Falconer nuclear power plant. There were two factions in the protests. The smaller was the more violent of the two, the Nuclear Freedom Front. I made an arrangement to interview the head of the NFF, Curt Chesak."

Lawrence nodded. "I'm familiar with the organization and its leader. Do go on."

"I was escorted to a hidden site in the nearby woods where the NFF was camping out. I had an interview with Chesak. My escort in and out of the camp was your son."

He lowered his head, put a hand to his forehead, like he was trying to hide whatever emotions were playing across his face. "My son . . . a good boy, though we did disagree about politics. Most fathers and sons do, don't they. His mother and I weren't thrilled with the schooling he was missing, volunteering for that . . . group. But he was headstrong, my boy."

Lawrence raised his head. His eyes were red-rimmed. "Was he good at what he was doing? Was he well? Was he proud?"

"Yes to all three," I said. "He was smart, he knew what he was doing, and he did it well."

A nod. "Thank you . . . if I may. . . ."

"Go right ahead."

"We've not heard much from the police in your state. Do you know anything about the investigation, or its progress?"

This was about to get interesting, and not in a good way. I looked over at the pond again. "Some."

"And?"

"You might not like hearing what I have to say."

"I think you underestimate me, Mister Cole."

"All right. At first police believed that your son had been shot by Victor Toles. Victor earlier had assassinated his stepfather, a prominent anti-nuclear activist."

"Really? Why? Was he opposed to his father's actions?"

"Yes, but not involving nuclear power. It involved money, lots of money."

"And why would he have killed my son?"

"When your son escorted me out of the camp, Victor showed up and took me away instead, sending John back to the site. A few minutes later, Victor tried to shoot me in the marshes near the campsite. I managed to escape and later, slogging around in the marshes, I heard another gunshot, the one that killed your son. I thought it was Victor, shooting your son to cover up the fact that he had tried to kill me. Now, I doubt it."

"Why?"

"Because Victor Toles is under arrest, and he's only been charged with one killing, that of his stepdad. No one's been charged with the murder of your son."

He slowly nodded. "All this I pretty much know, except for your part in it. All right, is there more?"

"There is. Curt Chesak led the demonstrators who broke into the plant site, where two demonstrators were killed and a number of police officers were seriously injured. I think Curt killed your son, Mister Thomas."

"Why? Why would that . . . man kill my boy?"

I took a deep breath, looked right into the older man's eyes. "Because I believe he found out that your son was working for you and the CIA."

# CHAPTER THIRTEEN

Lawrence stared at me, and whip-snap, his arm flew out and he slapped me across the face. It stung, it was a surprise, and I bit my tongue in the process, but I kept my place on the stone bench.

"You . . . how dare you say that?" he asked, voice shaking. "What the hell gives you the right to say anything of the sort? My God, what a fantasy . . . that I worked for the CIA. Where did you get such a bullshit story?"

"From your son."

"He never said such a thing!"

"Unfortunately for you, he did, when he was bringing me into that campsite, not letting me know where it was located, and when I complimented him on his tradecraft. He said he'd learned everything he knew from his father. And when I saw his obituary a while later, it said that you were retired from government service. A rather bland description, but one that fits one who used to work for the CIA."

I wanted to rub my left cheek, but I kept my composure. "Just so you know, I wasn't always a journalist, Mister Todd. A number of years ago, I worked at the Department of Defense."

"Not impressive," he replied. "Tens of thousands of people have worked at the DoD. What did you do there? Something impressive, like toilet paper analyst? Parking-lot guard? Late-night housekeeping?"

"I was a research analyst with a group within the Defense Research Agency called the Marginal Issues Section. I worked there for nearly a decade."

His eyes narrowed. "What was your clearance level?"

"What difference does it make? It's been such a long while, I'm sure the classification levels have changed at least a half dozen times. But I'll tell you it was high enough."

A pause. "When did you leave?"

I told him.

"Why did you leave, Mister Cole?"

"Medical discharge."

"Really? What did you do, cut your finger on a letter opener? Have a water cooler drop on your foot?"

I stood up. "No. One day my section and I were in a remote part of one of the Nevada testing ranges, doing a field exercise. We got lost. We traveled into one of the testing ranges, where we were exposed to a biological agent that was illegal under a number of arms-control treaties in place at the time. Everyone except for me was killed. In exchange for keeping my mouth shut, I was pensioned off and sent away."

"Mister Cole, I—"

"I came here, hoping to share information, perhaps reach some sort of arrangement where you and I could seek the same person responsible for murdering your son, and for nearly murdering a friend of mine. But if you'd rather sit on your bony ass and insult me, then I'll leave."

I turned and started up the walk.

"Mister Cole . . . please. Do return. My apologies."

It was a struggle, but I turned. I went back and sat down.

"My apologies as well for striking you . . . for, if truth be told, I should be striking myself."

"All apologies accepted."

He attempted a wry smile. "And my ass isn't that bony."

"Duly noted."

He turned some and looked at the pond, folded his arms. "Whatever conversation we have over the next several minutes never happened. Clear?"

"Oh, yes, it's clear. I remember the drill."

"Well, in case you don't remember all of the particulars of the drill, here's something else you should know. This part of my garden is under constant electronic jamming. If you have some sort of recording device or transmitter on you, nothing will be recorded."

"I thought you were retired."

"Retired, but not stupid." He wiggled his feet and said, "And you're certainly not stupid. What brought you to the theory that my son was working for me?"

"Because your son was killed in a location near where Curt Chesak was residing. Because Curt Chesak has a taste for violence. Because Victor Toles has not been charged with your boy's death. And because Curt Chesak is somehow connected to a D.C. lobbying firm that apparently has its fingers in a lot of interesting areas."

Boy, did that get his attention. He sat straight up and said, "Tell me more."

"Your turn," I said. "I've passed along a few chunks of information. Do me the honor of returning the favor."

"Fair enough," he said. "You were right. My boy . . . my poor dear boy . . . he wasn't really working for me, or the Agency, you understand. It was all quite informal. Whatever information he had on Curt Chesak, I asked him to pass it on to me."

"Why?"

"Because the man's an enigma, that's why. He's like that idiot that showed up in Mexico a few years back, Subcommandante Marcos or something like that. Guy wore a ski mask to preserve his identity, supposedly was this revolutionary, was going to organize the Mexican peasants and overthrow the evil oppressors, blah blah blah. You know how we knew the guy was a phony? When all these Hollywood types hiked into the wilderness to show their solidarity with him and the working class. A real revolutionary wouldn't have let those bozos within a hundred miles of him and his troops. Of course, if those Hollywood types really wanted to show their solidarity, they'd give away about eighty percent of their fortunes to the oppressed and still have enough to live on quite comfortably."

"Sometimes the obvious solutions escape people."

"That should be put on a bumper sticker somewhere. Anyway, that was the same thing for Curt Chesak. We wanted to know who he was, where he came from, and how he came to lead a violent anti-nuclear protest organization."

"And who was backing him?"

"Of course. Don't be stupid. It's beneath you."

"What have you found out?"

He shook a finger at me. "Your turn."

This give-and-take reminded me so much of my previous career that it almost made me nauseous. I pressed on. "The lobbying group is Munce, Price & O'Toole. Very little on the Internet. Their clients include foreign governments and industries, including agriculture, military, energy, pharmaceuticals, and the like."

Lawrence rubbed at his chin. "I don't know about them, but I'm sure I can find out. All right, time for your question."

"Where did you work at the Agency?"

Another slight smile. "Nothing too glamorous. An economics desk. Not really where you'd expect James Bond to be sitting, am I right?"

I kept quiet for a moment, but only a moment. "You and your former co-workers . . . you guys were concerned about what was happening at Falconer."

"Good point."

"Nuclear energy supplies about twenty percent of the electricity in this country."

"Another good point."

"If current or future nuclear plants are closed or delayed, that means replacement power has to come from someplace else. Domestic or foreign. So if you were some sort of . . . collective that wanted to increase your market share, you might do something like fund and support a militant group that would disrupt one of your competitors."

Lawrence put his hands up, gave me a slow clap-clap-clap. "Nicely done, Mister Cole. Too bad you're not still at the DoD, or with my Agency."

"Not going to happen."

"Why? Still bitter about what happened to you in Nevada?"

"No, I can't stand the hours."

That brought a slight smile. "True . . . and number-crunching at the CIA can be dull indeed."

"So why are you involved? And not the FBI?"

"Because economic terrorism isn't as sexy as cyberterrorism, or actual terrorism. That's what the FBI is concerned about, and rightfully so. But a functioning, healthy economy . . . without it, this planet will go very dark in a very, very short time. And it wouldn't take much. A short-term oil embargo. A real nasty computer virus. Some refineries off-line. A few low-yield nukes with the right EMP effect. My God, and are we prepared? Not in the least. Hell, libraries are burning books now because everything's stored electronically. But what happens when the electronics fail? Collapse. Utter and final collapse."

I didn't have anything to add at the moment, and he put his chin in his hand and brooded. "So we bend the rules against the use of CIA assets in-country. We go around asking for favors, asking for friends . . . even asking for relatives, God help us, to give us information and data. Anything and everything, so we can get a handle on what's going on out there and who's paying for it."

He used both hands to wipe at his eyes. A couple more mournful minutes passed, and his voice strengthened. "Are you a student of history?"

"Most history," I said. "Not very good when it comes to Far East or African history. I know my limitations."

"Good for you. So many don't. Do you think if you were able to go back in time and talk to a random Roman citizen in the second or third century, that they would realize they were a citizen of an empire in decline?"

"No, they wouldn't. They were too close to it."

"Yes, they were, weren't they. Oh, they'd mutter about the barbarians, the corruption, the high taxes, but they would still be convinced that they belonged to the most powerful empire on earth. They would still be thinking that, right up to the time Rome was sacked, the aqueducts dried up, and the harbors were destroyed. You know, the Romans were able to make these wonderful artificial harbors; but centuries later, their descendants would see nothing about them but harbors that would trap and sink ships. From one port to the next, fatal harbors, never to be repaired or used again."

For the last few sentences he stared across at the garden again, and he said, "Anything more you can offer?"

"Yes," I said. "There are other interests out there. I've encountered them a few times."

"Really? That's fascinating. Do let me know."

"I found out that Chesak was backed by a professor of history at Boston University. I went to interview him, he had nothing to tell me, and when I left his office some men posing as federal agents attempted to detain a . . . friend of mine."

"What kind of friend?"

"Security consultant."

"Ah, a wise idea. Were they successful in detaining your friend?"

"No. Shots were fired. I saw the two men fall. Their vehicle was shot up. There were dozens of witnesses. The next day, the *Boston Globe* reported that the whole incident was a student-run film project gone awry. Later that same day, the BU professor disappeared and his house burned down. My own house is under surveillance."

He rubbed at his chin. "Fascinating."

"Seemed mostly terrifying at the time."

"Yes, yes, of course. So what does that tell you, former analyst Cole?"

"You tell me. Any chance they were your guys?"

"Hah! I wish . . . but still, who knows. Do I have to remind you that our previous work was trying to find truth in a wilderness of mirrors?"

"No reminding necessary."

"So maybe it was another section in the Agency. Or any one of a number of agencies covered under the government. Or contractors . . . when you have slippery work that needs to be done, without wanting to leave a clear trail behind, you use contractors. Or foreign interests . . . or foreign interests using domestic contractors. So many possibilities."

Another jet flew overhead, once again seeking a safe landing. "So, where do we go from here?"

Lawrence turned to me, eyes red-rimmed. "Do you have a suggestion?"

"I do."

"Then tell me."

"You might not like it."

"Try me."

"When it comes to who's involved, I don't care."

"What do you mean?"

"Let me make it clear. As to who's involved, who's behind it, who's paying, I don't give a crap. I want Curt Chesak. I get the feeling you want him too. So that's my only focus."

Lawrence slowly nodded. "You said he hurt a friend of yours. Do tell me more."

"When the protesters in favor of violence finally breached the fence the last demonstration day, Chesak led the way. He and some others ambushed a couple of cops. One of them was my best friend."

"Name?"

"Detective Sergeant Diane Woods."

A tilt of his head. "Girlfriend? Fiancée?"

"No. Just the best friend I've ever had."

"How is she doing?"

"She received serious head injuries. She's in a coma. She may die."

Lawrence seemed to consider that. "When you say you want Curt Chesak, what do you mean, exactly?"

"I want to find him, talk to him, and then kill him. That's what I mean. Exactly."

A smile creased his old face. "Would you care to stay for dinner, Mister Cole?"

Despite the fact that I was in a mourning household, dinner was fine indeed, and Lawrence took care of the bulk of it. His wife Frances was a thin blond woman with an engaging smile who had on gray slacks and a light blue sweater, with gold jewelry on her tanned wrists and neck. One had only to look at her eyes when she was quiet to see the sadness that was now living there. Our meal was grilled steaks, brown rice, and a mixed salad, with a bottle of Cabernet Sauvignon. Lawrence introduced me as someone who had retired from government service on a medical leave, and our conversation revolved around the weather, the upcoming election, and what kind of winters Virginia had versus New Hampshire.

With coffee and cake and a bit more conversation, Frances led me upstairs to the spare bedroom. "This used to be John's, before he . . . before he left for school." She opened the door and the room was plain, with a bed and a colorful quilt on top of it, a writing desk, a bookshelf, and a closet door. There were no photos or certificates or trophies or anything else that announced that this room belonged to an only son.

"It looks fine, Frances, thank you," I said.

Her hand idly traced the doorknob. "Are you married, Lewis?"

"No"

"Any children?"

"Not a one."

Her hand still worked the shiny doorknob. "One always expects that your child will long outlive you." She brought her hand up, squeezed it with the other. "It's a special type of hell, to be a parent who must bury her boy."

Frances stepped out in the hallway and quickly walked away.

Alone in the room, I opened the closet door, looking for hangers for my clothes. There I came upon John's clothes, neatly hanging in rows, and below that, plastic bins of his possessions. I stared for a moment, thinking about a young life now gone, just tidied up and placed in the closet, with the door sadly closed behind it.

I closed the door and left my clothes on the writing table's chair.

The bed was comfortable and the sheets were clean and crisp. I stretched out and tried to relax. It was hard to do. Lots of thoughts and possibilities were racing through my mind, like the proverbial hamster running its wheel that went nowhere. I looked up at the ceiling, thought of the young man I had met just last week, a young man who was in college and was so proud and sure of his beliefs and his future.

I rested my head in my hands. I had been like that, once, in a time and place that seemed as far away as the Great Depression or the Civil War. In my college days, I had been active in student journalism, had covered great protests and assemblies over the nuclear freeze at a time when it seemed terrifying that a former Hollywood actor was now our president. The debates were over silos, throw-weights, arms limitation, and insurgencies in Central

America. And before I slid into my chosen career as an activist journalist, I took a very different route, being co-opted by The Man, joining the system of oppression organized by the oligarchy patriarchy.

Or something like that.

And less than six months into my job in the DoD, I quickly learned that my four years of college, save the time drinking and dating, had been pretty much a waste when it came to learning what was really going on in the world.

I shifted some in the bed.

The poor boy who had once slept and dreamed in this bed, well, at least he didn't live long enough to see his illusions shattered.

Not much of a silver lining, but it was the only thing I could come up with.

During the night, I had some sort of nightmare that I thankfully forgot when my eyes opened up. The sheets and blanket had been tossed to the floor, and I moved as quietly as I could, bringing everything back to where it had been.

I froze, now in bed. There were murmurs and soft crying from a room down the hall.

I lay very still.

The night turned out to be so very long.

# CHAPTER FOURTEEN

In the morning Lawrence made breakfast, tea and toast, and apologized for the thinness of the meal.

"Frances had a rough night," he explained. "So I'm letting her sleep in."

"I'm afraid it might have been my fault."

He buttered a slice of toast. "How's that?"

"I had a bad dream last night. Moved around a lot in the bed. I think that might have awakened Frances."

He kept on buttering his toast.

"And I think . . . maybe the sound of me moving around in your son's bed, that might have disturbed her. Brought back some memories. Maybe . . . some hope."

Lawrence took a bite of his toast. "Yes, you're correct. She poked me in the ribs, half-asleep, telling me that rascal John was trying to sneak back into his room. That I should go to his room and check him out, to see if he had been drinking. Then she realized what she had been saying. And that was that."

"Sorry."

"No more sorrys," Lawrence said. "So what now?"

"Got one last appointment to keep, and then back to New Hampshire."

"Do you think Chesak is still up there?"

"Don't know where the hell he is," I said. "But I intend to keep pressing and pressing."

"Doing what, then?"

"Sometimes you press and poke, you get a reaction. That reaction can prove to be useful. It can lead you to places, to people. That's what I intend to do."

Lawrence nodded, got up from the table, went to a door that seemed to lead into a cellar. I finished my tea and toast, and then he came back up, holding a cell phone in his hand.

"This is for you."

"Already have a cell phone."

"Not like this one," he said. "This one is shielded and encrypted. Your standard cell phone can easily be triangulated with the right equipment and the right agency, such that you can get a caller's position within a certain number of yards. This one, however, is quite black and untraceable."

I took the phone. "It's already pre-programmed with my number," Lawrence said. "You get anywhere, you have more information, you pass it along. If I come across anything of interest, I'll pass it along as well."

"You got a deal."

A sharp nod. "I didn't know about Munce, Price & O'Toole and their connection with Curt Chesak until you showed up. For that, you have my thanks."

"Fair enough. But I want to make something quite clear before I leave here with this very cool James Bond phone. I've said it before and I'll say it again. You and your friends in the Agency might want to scoop up Curt Chesak, interrogate him, find out who's paying him and why they're paying him. My interest in him is more medieval. Do you understand?"

"I do."

"So if there's going to be a conflict between the Agency's wishes and my wishes, you can guess who's coming out on top."

Lawrence sighed. "As a retired yet active member of this nation's intelligence community, I'm horrified at what you're saying. As a father who's lost his son, you have my full and total support."

I went through the phone's features one more time, and Lawrence said, "You said you have an appointment. Here, in Arlington?"

"Nope. In D.C."

"How are you planning to get there?"

"Walk until I find a cab. Then get to the Metro station."

Lawrence shook his head. "No. I'll arrange for a ride."

"I don't think that's a very good idea. I don't think you want a record with a cab company that I was picked up here."

He started gathering up our meager breakfast dishes. "You think just because I'm retired, I've gotten stupid all of a sudden? I have friends, I have previous arrangements. I'll have a car and discreet driver ready to pick you up in a few minutes." He went over to the sink. "May I ask where's your appointment?"

"At the election headquarters of Senator Jackson Hale."

That got his attention. "What, you intend to volunteer?"

"No."

"Confess all?"

"Hardly. No, I'm going to see a friend of mine."

He put the dishes in the dishwasher. "Former DoD co-worker?"

"No again. She's a close friend. Girlfriend, I suppose you could say."

"But you live in New Hampshire."

"I do. And I intend to stay there."

"Does she want to go back to New Hampshire after the election?"

I stood up from the table, new phone in hand. "Not for a second."

He smiled. "Now I know why that's your last appointment."

My ride was a black Lincoln Town Car, and my driver was a cheerful Nepalese man who proudly told me that he had once been a Gurkha soldier, serving in the Royal Gurkha Rifles, and that Lawrence had once saved his life at some remote outpost in Afghanistan. His name was Suraj Gurung.

At a traffic light he turned, grinning. "So ever since then, I am in Mister Lawrence's debt. Especially since he arranged for my family and me to come here, to this blessed land."

"Mister Lawrence is lucky to have you at his side."

Suraj chuckled. In the front seat of the Town Car was a copy of that day's *Washington Post.* He reached underneath the paper, pulled out a long, curved knife called a *kukri.* "Many Taliban have felt the kiss of this, and if anyone attempts to harm Mister Lawrence, they will get a sweet kiss, indeed."

I was dropped off on M Street, at an impressive office building that had a huge banner stretched across the lobby entrance: HALE FOR PRESIDENT CAMPAIGN HEADQUARTERS. I went down the street and purchased that day's *Post* from a kiosk, and then slowly walked back to campaign headquarters. I took my time. I slowly went up the sidewalk and down, and then, on a return trip, my patience paid off.

Two black limos rolled up and a group of serious-looking men and women in power suits bailed out. I resisted the urge to make a serious circus clown car reference. Half of them were talking on cell phones, and the other half were talking to each other, hands and arms flying. They went through the double glass doors, and I fell in step behind them. They skirted past a security desk, flashing badges, and they didn't hesitate as they approached a bank of elevators. A uniformed security guard—a young female—waved us all through.

So much for D.C. security.

With the aid of cheerful campaign workers who were no doubt impressed with the newspaper I was carrying and my age, it took just a couple of minutes to find Annie Wynn's office, which was an impressive office indeed. When I had first seen her at work for Senator Jackson Hale of Georgia, it had been a frigid January in New Hampshire with lots of snow and ice. Her office back then had been a battered surplus battleship-gray desk, jammed up against a host of others in a rented space that had once been a clothing store in downtown Manchester. The phones would always be ringing, voices would be raised, and trash barrels were overflowing with pizza boxes and Chinese takeout food containers.

Now she had a private office, with expensive-looking furniture, leather chairs, a couch, a credenza, and piles of newspapers and briefing books. I sat down on the couch, looked out the window which had a jaw-dropping view of the office building across the street. The whole floor was neat, with nary a pizza box to be found, and the phones had low ringing chimes that seemed to gently ask you to pick them up.

Yet there was still a sense of energy to the people out there in the other offices and cubicles, a grim determination to fight these last few weeks to elect their man president. I recalled my father, years and years ago when I was in high school, talking about the last presidential candidate who had seemed to enjoy it all, Humphrey, the former V.P. from Minnesota. A "happy warrior," my father had said, the very last of the breed.

I took in the office. A television set that was muted, showing CNN, and a computer monitor. No photos, no mementoes, nothing personal in here that said it belonged to Annie Wynn, formerly of Massachusetts, who spent a lot of time in New Hampshire.

Her voice, coming down the hall: ". . . and tell Eddie to bump back the caucus meeting to two P.M. The Senator's BBC interview is going to run over, I know it. And get me the latest numbers from Colorado, and damn it, I don't care what they say, I want a better sampling this time!"

She breezed in, dumped a set of black briefing books on the table, and turned to me, cell phone in hand.

Her hand lowered. Her face showed shock, but still looked pretty good. Pretty damn good, in fact. She had on black high-heeled shoes, black hose, and a dark gray skirt cut just above her knees. The blouse fit her curves nicely and was ivory with lots of collar and lace, and her fine auburn hair was curled around at the base of her neck in some sort of braid. I was pleased to see she was wearing a gold necklace that I had bought for her last summer at a crafts fair up at Sunapee, New Hampshire.

"Annie," I said.

She shook her head. "Lewis, what the hell are you doing here?"

I stood up. "Nice to see you, too."

She bit her lower lip, closed her eyes for a quick moment. "Sorry, it's been one of those months." Now she smiled and I went to her, and we hugged and kissed, and the touch and smell of her made it suddenly seem all right.

Still smiling, she went around and sat behind her desk, and I sat across from her on a fine black leather chair. "You bad boy, how did you get in here?"

"I walked."

"Past security?"

"Apparently so," and she shook her head.

"Sorry," she said. "Not a laughing matter." She picked up a pen, scribbled a note, and then said, "Dear one, why didn't you tell me you were coming?"

"It was sort of a last-minute trip," I said. "Some business to take care of down here."

"Really? You told me you'd never, ever come back to D.C. Even to visit. Must have been something pretty important to get you out of New Hampshire."

"Important enough."

"So when are you going to take care of your business?"

"Already done."

"Let me guess. Your quest to make everything right for your Diane Woods?"

"That's right."

"Guess I do know you, huh?" she asked. "So, when did you get to town?"

"Yesterday morning."

Another "oh," followed by "I see. So I was last on your schedule, then?"

"No," I said, "I was saving the best for last."

Her face was impassive on that one. More than ever, I felt out of sorts, out of place. Annie looked at her calendar and said, "Lewis, I'm already late for a status report, and I'm booked solid for the rest of the day, not even time for dinner. But maybe cocktails at eleven tonight, if things aren't too crazy."

"No, I've got something to say, Annie, and it shouldn't take long."

She leaned back in her chair. "Funny, I have something to say too. You first."

I looked into that sweet, adorable face that I had spent so many long and delightful hours with, from cross-country skiing along deserted trails near the Atlantic Ocean, to trips to Fenway Park and gourmet meals at hidden restaurants in the North Shore. Hikes in the White Mountains and late nights watching old movies on TCM, and long, luscious, and soul-fulfilling hours in bed.

I took a breath. "I'm sorry, Annie, it's not going to work. The two of us. This is your town now. Some time ago it was mine. I belonged here.

I thrived here. But those days are long gone. I've been here less than two days, and I feel like I'm going to jump out of my skin, or that some car is going to run me down on Pennsylvania Avenue."

I paused. She stayed quiet. I went on. "But I can't ask, I can't hope, I can't expect you to head back north when the campaign ends. You've already told me that the Senator has promised you a future here, on his senate staff if he loses, on his presidential staff if he wins."

"So glad you remembered," she said, voice dry.

"You belong here now, Annie. Not me. So it's not going to work."

She slowly moved her pen around in a circle on her desk. "So you think it's over."

"Considering the few encounters we've had these past several weeks, and the quality of our conversations, I can't see it being anything else."

My mouth had dried out, my heart was slowly and heavily thumping along, and I waited.

Annie looked out the window, looked back at me. "Once again, you've led the way, my friend. As much as it pains me to say so, you're right. It is over. And I just haven't had the time or the guts to take a look at it."

She made another rotation of her pen, looked up. "Still friends?"

"Forever, Annie. Forever."

Her phone started ringing, and a young man with a pained expression on his face rapped at the side of the door. "Annie, Mister Geers is really getting impatient."

"I'll be right there."

I got up and the young man stepped out, and I leaned over the desk and gave her a kiss. She smiled when I pulled back, but she hadn't really kissed me in return. "There are some things of yours, back at Tyler Beach," I said. "I'll box them up and send them here, if you don't mind."

A quick nod as she gathered up her papers and briefing books. She still ignored her ringing phone. "That'd be fine, Lewis, but as you can see, I'm already late."

"No problem."

I started out of the office, recalled something and turned. "Annie, what were you going to say?"

Her head was still bent down. "What? What do you mean?"

"When I got here, you said you had something to say to me. What was it?"

"Oh." She raised up her head, briefing books and binders clasped to her chest. "Yes, sorry. I was going to ask if you'd do me a favor. But . . . it's not that important anymore."

"Go ahead, Annie, say it."

"Well. . . ."

"Please, tell me what you were going to say."

Again, she bit her lower lip. "The thing you're doing for Diane. The man who hurt her. Your hunt for Curt Chesak. Please stop it, will you?"

It felt like my heart had slowed right down, my blood now the consistency of cold molasses.

"What did you just say?"

"You heard me. This obsession on finding Curt Chesak. Please stop it. You're making waves, Lewis, waves that can get the wrong people pissed off enough to hurt you, me, and the Senator. So stop it. Please. For me."

I looked behind me and up and down the adjacent wide hallway, suddenly wondering if hard-eyed men with dark suits and earpieces were coming my way.

But so far, the coast was clear.

"Annie?"

"Yes?"

"You know what I said right back then, about being friends forever?"

"I do."

I walked out her door. "Forever just ended."

## CHAPTER FIFTEEN

The bus drive back to Massachusetts took about the same amount of time as before—twelve hours—but as I brooded and thought and brooded some more, it seemed to take twice as long. I napped and drank water or fruit juice, my stomach too tightly wrapped to accept any food. We stopped twice for refueling and rest stops, and I had to force myself to get off the bus and walk around to stretch my legs. The trip to D.C. and Arlington had been fruitful, even though the fruit had been bitter indeed. Probably a cliché; so sue me.

Our last stop was outside Hartford, and after I returned to my seat, I noticed a young man and his pregnant wife come up the aisle. He was in BDUs and his black hair was cut high and tight. He was in his twenties and his wife looked to be in her teens, and she had a shy smile as she followed her soldier husband onto the bus. The driver was still inside the station, completing some paperwork.

There were two empty seats, one behind the other, right next to me. Their companion seats had been occupied by two young men, bearded, wearing cargo pants and black fleece jackets. Bottles of designer water and bags of snacks were next to them on the empty seats. At the previous stop, the two of them had come in together, laughing and joking. The soldier stopped and looked at them, murmured something, but he was ignored by both young men. Each of them had iPod earphones in, they were reading *Maxim* and *Rolling Stone*, and their heads were slowly bobbing up and down in time with their secret tunes.

Feeling generous, I gave the two seated men about fifteen seconds, and then I stood up. The soldier looked me over and I gave him my best older guy smile. "Just a sec, just you wait."

I leaned down, tapped the near guy on the shoulder. He glanced up at me, frowned, went back to his music and magazine. I gave him a harder tap, and he looked up.

"The fuck you want?" he said, taking one of his earbuds out.

"Nice to meet you too," I replied. I motioned to the soldier and his wife standing in the aisleway. "How about being a sport, move up one seat, let the corporal and his pregnant wife sit together."

"How about minding your own fucking business?"

He moved to replace his earbud, but I was quicker. With my right hand, I grabbed his beard, tugged him forward. He yelped. With my left hand, I took the wire to his iPod and quickly wrapped it around his neck, started twisting it as I also twisted his beard. He gurgled and started waving his arms.

"Tell you what," I said. "When I let you go, you can move one seat forward and sit next to your pal."

I tightened the beard and the iPod wires a bit more. His face colored. "Or you and I can see if that emergency exit behind you really does work, as I toss your ass out on the pavement. Can I get an amen?"

He nodded once, twice, thrice.

I let him go, stood up.

"Fair enough." I stepped back and the guy, his face red and his nose dripping, bustled out of the seat, grabbing his belongings as he did so. The soldier and his wife backed down a few feet, and when the way was clear, they sat down together. The soldier gave me a knowing glance, and his wife ignored me and just kept her adoring gaze on her husband.

I took my seat, let out a breath. Wondered what Annie Wynn was doing at this very moment, and decided not to think about that anymore.

At North Station in Boston, I sat for a few minutes on one of the long wooden benches, just catching my breath. People in a hurry moved around, to and fro, and I tried to organize my thoughts, which were dark and disorganized indeed.

Curt Chesak.

Hell, I wasn't even sure that was his name.

But I knew who he was, and what he did.

He was a hired gun, hired to raise hell, to be an *agent provocateur.* Soon after my last view of him at the Falconer nuclear power plant, beating the proverbial crap out of Diane Woods, my chase of him had resulted in a gunfight outside Boston University, the disappearance of a BU professor, said professor's house burning down, and a fair number of well-armed and sharp-eyed men keeping an eye on Aunt Teresa's house in the North End and my own house at Tyler Beach. Not to mention the story of the BU gunfight being spun into a story for the *Boston Globe* about a student filmmaking project gone awry.

So who were they? Contractors working for a federal agency? Contractors working for a foreign government—take your pick of any unstable oil-exporting country out there—or a foreign intelligence agency? Or maybe for some transnational corporation?

Too much to think about.

I rubbed at my hands, thought longingly of a meal that hadn't been wrapped in plastic and a wide comfortable bathroom that didn't bump and sway in the traffic.

Still too much to think about.

So stop thinking.

I smiled slightly.

So stop thinking already.

I flashed back to my first weeks working at the DoD as a research analyst, when one of my now long-deceased instructors had forcefully told us young 'uns, as she had said, not to think above your pay grade. Meaning, as she pointed out, if your job was to research and prepare a report on the latest variant of the Soviet SS-18 intercontinental ballistic missile and its guidance system, then do the goddamn report. Don't think about any impact on arms control treaties, about the future threat of war, or the current nuclear offensive capability of the United States or the USSR.

Just do your goddamn report.

So there you go.

I didn't care who was paying Chesak or why they were doing it.

I just wanted to find him.

After getting my ticket for the Downeaster to take me back up north to Exonia, I gave Felix Tinios a call. He picked it up after four rings and said, "Yeah."

A signal. Things were not well, which was why he answered the phone the way he did.

"You okay?" I asked.

"Been better."

"You where you said you'd be?"

"Had to go someplace else. Didn't work out."

"How's the other part of the equation?"

Slight laugh. "Looking for a knife."

"Glad to hear that."

"Got anything for me?"

"Nope."

"Anything you need?" he asked.

"Not at the moment."

"Gotta go."

He hung up. I put the cell phone back in my coat pocket, feeling cool, feeling uncomfortable. Felix had been going to take his Aunt Teresa to her winter haven in Florida after the BU shootout, and obviously the long reach of whoever was in Boston had managed to reach the Sunshine State and was nipping at Felix's heels.

Just another signal, as if I needed one, of what I was up against.

And I had lied to Felix just now. I sure as hell needed him here, and not thousands of miles away. I needed his muscle, his street smarts, and his resources as I went up against the well-armed shadows that were protecting Curt Chesak.

Then my phone rang, and I felt sweet relief course through me.

Had to be Felix, calling me back, telling me all was well, squared away.

I dug out my phone, saw that the incoming number was blocked.

Good ol' Felix.

I answered the phone. "So, things improving?"

Another voice answered instead. "Beats the hell out of me," the man said. "I understand you're looking for me."

I literally could not believe who was on the other end of the phone.

"Lewis? It's Curt Chesak. How's it going?"

I had to press my phone hard against my ear because my hand suddenly started trembling. "Curt Chesak? For real?"

He laughed and I had no doubt it was him. He said, "In the flesh, my friend. In the flesh."

"I'm not your friend."

"Just being polite."

"Then be a sport and, speaking of in the flesh, why don't you stop by, have a chat? Maybe we could have a cup of coffee or something."

Another laugh. "Lewis, sorry, that's not going to happen."

"So, why the call? To gloat?"

"Oh, no, no, I'm too professional to gloat. No, the reason I'm calling you is to politely ask you to stop sniffing around and asking questions."

"Gee, you know, Curt, I sort of quit my job last week, so I have a lot of free time on my hands. And I find you so very fascinating."

"Then you have good taste. But trust me when I say this, Lewis: keeping after me is going to end badly."

"As badly as Detective Sergeant Woods? Or John Todd Thomas? And those other innocents shot at the power plant? Sounds like something you would do, doesn't it. Shooting two protesters to raise a fuss."

"Just doing my job," he said. "Like you used to do, back at the Pentagon."

"No comparison."

"Oh, really? So tell me, Lewis, when you were in the bowels of the Pentagon, doing your research tasks for the higher-ups, isn't it the truth that some of the work you did was used in targeting? Mmm? Helping those with the fingers on the triggers send a Tomahawk cruise missile to some tents in a desert, or helping certain troops go into Bolivia or Colombia to take out a village or two? How many innocents perished because of your job?"

"Still no comparison," I said, feeling my voice rise. "I was working under the direction of lawfully selected personnel, under the direction of a legally elected government."

Another laugh. "Perhaps I can say the very same thing."

"Oh? Is it confession time?"

"Not hardly," Curt said. "If I was one to blab, it would sort of kill my employment opportunities."

"Funny you mentioned kill. That's been on my mind for a while."

"Oh, Lewis, please. Stop talking nonsense. Your time has passed, and I thank you for your service. It's my time now. There are huge forces at play out there, moving around, settling scores and preparing for the next half-century. You were a pawn once, and now I'm in the same place. Doing what I can, making money, just muddling through."

"Sounds like you have a real self-esteem issue, Curt. Leave me out of it."

"I would love to leave you out of everything. So why not do me the favor of stopping your activities, then, and we'll both be on our separate ways? What you're doing is stirring up attention and notice, in lots of different circles, and that has to stop."

"You forgot to add one more thing."

"What's that?"

"The 'or else.' It's part of the rules. You issue a request, you tell me to fulfill the request, 'or else.' So what's the 'or else'?"

"The 'or else' is that you won't like the end results. Like a certain missing BU professor. Or those bodies at Falconer. Or a vegetable at the Exonia Hospital."

My heart wasn't racing along, it was moving glacier-slow, one heavy *lump-lump* at a time. "Then why the warning? Why not just take care of me and remove me from the board?"

There was quiet for a bit of time, such that I thought he had hung up. He spoke again, and his voice had a sense of concern in it. "Trust me, I've been under a lot of pressure from my employer . . . supervisor . . . whatever the hell you want to call them, to do just that. But you know what, Lewis? I like you. I like you bunches. When we had that conversation back in

Falconer during the demonstrations, at that disgusting campground, you came in full of piss and vinegar and attitude. Before you, I had a few other news media interviews and by God, they came in with their kneepads, ready to kiss my ass or do even more. They were convinced that I was working for the poor huddled sheep out there, that I was on the cutting edge of some societal revolution. Those loons missed the 1960s and the Pentagon Papers and Watergate, and by God, here I was, to make them feel oh, so very special."

"How did you not laugh, knowing what you knew?"

A chuckle. "Yeah, that was something. They would have croaked if they knew who I was and who was paying me. But you came along, not ready to kiss anything, and you didn't take any of my carefully pre-planned bullshit. Nope, hell, you even lectured me on the background of *Führerprinzip*, of a strong leader who is infallible. God, I almost reached over and kissed you for that. The first real intelligent conversation I'd had in months. You know how hard it is to show enthusiasm when some pimply longhair who isn't old enough to drink wants to lecture you on how algae will solve our energy problems?"

"Poor you. Almost makes me feel sorry, except for the woman and the men you killed, and what you did to my friend."

"Can't you just put that aside, Lewis? Show some respect? From one pawn to another? Please?"

"Tell you what," I said, my heart rate now kicking up several notches. "I like you, Curt. You have a way with words. You know how to flatter, plead, and make me feel so special. Let's get together, real soon, and swap war stories. What do you think?"

A cold voice. "You're mocking me."

"Like I said, Curt, I'm sensing a terrible self-esteem problem from you."

"I gave you a chance. So here's the deal. Agree to stop right now or I'll finish my job, hurt you bad. Got it? Do you agree?"

"Take this for what it means," I said: "Not on your life."

And I hung up on him.

I got the shakes for a few minutes and then heard my train being called, and I hustled down to the platform and just made it, settling into a comfortable seat that had a nice view of northern Boston as we headed out. But my mind wasn't on the view.

He was going to finish the job.

He was going to hurt me bad.

Pretty easy to figure out what he meant.

I got my cell phone out, tried Kara Miles.

Went straight to voicemail.

No time to waste on leaving a message, hoping she'd pick it up.

"Sir?"

I called the Exonia Hospital switchboard, asked to be connected to the ICU.

A burst of static, and then nothing.

Lost cell coverage.

"Sir?"

Went back to the phone, my fingers feeling as thick as sausages, pressing down the keys.

Still no service.

"Sir!"

I looked up. A sharp-faced woman was staring at me from an opposite seat, wearing a khaki jacket, khaki slacks, sensible black flat shoes, and a multi-hued terrycloth bag at her feet.

"Yes?"

She pointed to a sign. "This is a no-cell-phone car! Can't you read?"

"I can read," I said. "This is an emergency."

She turned, sniffed loudly. "That's what they all say."

So many responses tumbling through my mind, no time to choose one.

*Focus.*

Dialed the number to the Exonia Hospital again, and this time it rang through to the switchboard. I asked for the ICU and, after a few seconds that seemed to last a few hours, the phone was picked up.

"ICU, Eva speaking."

"Eva, this is an emergency. My name is Lewis Cole, I'm from Tyler, and I need to speak to Kara Miles, right away. She's the partner of Diane Woods, a patient there."

Eva, God bless her, didn't waste my time, didn't ask me questions, didn't demand to know more.

"I'll put you on hold. I'll get her."

There was soft music that seemed better suited for a slow-moving elevator, and then there was a satisfying click and Kara's voice: "Lewis, what's going on?"

"Kara, listen to me, and please don't waste time, all right?"

"If you're trying to scare me, you're succeeding."

"Good. I just got a phone call from Curt Chesak, the—"

"The guy who tried to kill Diane? What did he want? Where is he? Did you call the cops?"

"Kara, shut up."

"Lewis—"

"Kara, somebody is coming to kill Diane. In a very few minutes, if not sooner. Is there a Tyler cop there, guarding Diane's room?"

"Yes."

"Do you know him?"

"What?"

"I said do you know him, do you recognize him, have you ever seen him before today."

No answer. Had I been cut off?

A slow response. "No . . . he said he was new to the department. Said he hoped Diane would get better . . . said it was a shame what had happened to her."

"Kara, when we're done, I want you to call Captain Kate Nickerson and get her to send some cops over from the Exonia police, and then have her send a couple more off-duty cops from Tyler. Then have Eva, the ICU nurse, have her get hospital security up to Diane's room. I don't want that rookie within ten feet of her, all right?"

Even with the lousy cell phone connection, I could tell she was weeping. "Okay . . . okay, I get it. How do you know someone's coming to kill Diane?"

"Because Curt Chesak told me so, that's why."

I hung up, sat back in my seat, wondered why the train was moving so damn slow.

The sharp-faced woman across the way with the sensible shoes frowned at me again.

"That seemed to be one very long emergency," she pointed out with a cutting tone in her voice.

"Sorry," I said. "I was thinking locally, acting globally."

Puzzled, she said, "What?"

"Exactly," I said.

## CHAPTER SIXTEEN

As we passed through Newburyport with our next stop Exonia, I cursed myself for being as stupid as those recommending back in 1960 that we nuke the Russkies and get it over with, and I fumbled around in my luggage. I took out the special cell phone that Lawrence Thomas had given me, a day and several hundred miles earlier. I pressed the SEND button and waited.

It was picked up on the second ring. "Thomas."

"Lawrence, this is Lewis Cole."

"Yes?"

Even with the provenance of the phone, I still wanted to be careful. "Recall that person we were talking about? The one with the mutual interest?"

"Of course."

"He talked to me some time ago."

His voice was sharp. "In person?"

"No. Via cell phone."

"Did you get anything actionable?" His voice was still sharp.

I had to flash back to my previous career, wasting precious seconds. Actionable intelligence: a piece of information that could be used to break a code, identify a covert site, or locate a suspect.

"No," I said. "But you need to tell me something."

"Proceed."

"When you gave me this cell phone, you talked about being able to track and trace a call. Can you track where Curt Chesak was when he made that call?"

"Do you have his incoming number?"

"No. It was blocked."

"I don't think so."

I pressed on. "You don't think? Does that mean there's a possibility? Is there some way you can trace a phone call that came in to my cell phone, even without knowing the source number?"

A slight hissing of static. The woman across the aisle was giving me a look, like she was wishing me to choke on a free-range cheeseburger or something.

Lawrence said, with hesitation, "I don't know. Maybe. I haven't been retired that long, but so much can change so quickly when it comes to technology."

"Can you find out?"

"I damn well will. I'll call you as quick as I can. Where are you now?"

"About ten minutes away from Exonia, New Hampshire."

"What's up there?"

"Someone I'm trying to save."

"Then get off the phone and go do it, Lewis."

Good advice. I hung up.

At Exonia I didn't have a lucky arrival. My friendly taxi driver Maggie was nowhere to be seen. I fumbled through my receipts and such and found her business card, but the phone rang and rang with no answer. My aislemate who had a longing for cell-phone-free train cars strode by me and got into a Prius. I wasn't about to ask her for a ride, because I didn't want to be hectored for the next several minutes or, worse, be made to apologize for what I had done.

At the far end of the parking lot, I saw a woman approach her parked Volvo, and then looked away. Wasn't about to work, not with night approaching. I went over to the diner and inside, where two young men were working at a small island counter. Magazine racks stretched off to the right, and there was a small grocery aisle to the left, and seating for the diner was behind the two young men, both bearded, wearing T-shirts commemorating musicians I had never heard of.

"Excuse me, guys," I said. "I need a ride to the hospital."

One head snapped up. "You sick or something?"

"No, I just need to get there."

The guy on the right said, "Exonia cab can pick you up. Payphone's out back."

"No one's answering the phone."

The other guy laughed. "Bet Eric's on duty right now, and he's sleeping something off. Poor bastard's working three jobs, trying to keep his house."

From my wallet, I took out a ten-dollar bill. "The hospital's only a couple of miles away. Any chance one of you can give me a ride?"

They were quiet at seeing the ten-dollar bill, and I put another down on top of it. "Twenty bucks. Less than ten minutes. What do you say?"

The one on the right slipped the money away. "Sounds like you've got an emergency."

I said, "You know it."

The guy's name was Peter, a decent sort who drove a Toyota pickup truck and who blasted through a changing traffic light near the hospital so I wouldn't have to wait. He drove right up to the entrance and surprised me by offering his hand, which I shook. "Hate going to the hospital," Peter said. "Either you're dying, or they're doing their best to kill you."

I got out of the truck. "And I'm trying to make sure they don't do both."

A quick stride through the lobby, and then an elevator took me to the ICU floor. I could hear a jumble of voices as I went through the wide double doors. There was a gaggle of men and women clustered around the nurses' station. I saw two uniformed security officers, a cop from Exonia, another cop from Tyler, and a few others in civilian clothes. Lots of raised voices. I spotted a very tired-looking Kara Miles, and she saw me. I put a finger to my lips and motioned her over. She nodded in understanding and went past the crowd and into the family room we had used before.

I went in, closed the door, gave her a quick hug. We sat down across from each other. "How are things? What's going on?"

"You were right," she said. "That cop wasn't a cop."

"Diane?"

"He never got into her room."

My chest felt a lot lighter. "Tell me more."

She shook her head. "I don't know how he knew that I was suspicious of him. After I made those phone calls when I got off with you, I went out and tried chatting with him, just to pass the time until the other cops arrived. But . . . he noticed. Somehow he noticed. He just smiled, got up, said he had to get a cup of coffee. Then he left. The Exonia police showed up about two minutes later, followed by some additional Tyler cops."

"What did you tell them? Did you tell them you got a call from me?"

She rubbed her hands together. "No. No, I didn't want to bring you into it. So I just told them I felt uncomfortable about the officer keeping watch on Diane's room, and they didn't ask many questions."

"Do you know what happened to the cop who was supposed to be here?"

"Captain Nickerson said he was found in his apartment. Unconscious and bound. He's en route to the Porter Hospital. Lewis, how did the fake cop know that something was up?"

"The good ones make excellent poker players. They can sense your emotions, your fear, what's going on with your expression. Don't beat yourself up. Just be happy he's not here."

She slowly nodded, her hands still rubbing.

"Diane," I said. "How's Diane?"

"They took her breathing tube out. She's breathing on her own."

I almost broke out into a wide smile, but stopped while keeping a look on Kara. "What's wrong, then?"

"She's got pneumonia. They're hopeful they caught it in time . . . but with someone in her shape, it can be very, very serious." Kara wiped at her eyes. "Oh, shit, Lewis, what am I going to do?"

"What you've been doing, day after day," I said. "Staying here. Keeping witness. Talking to her."

After we talked for a few more minutes, she wanted to get a drink, and I followed her out of the small family room. The crowd of people around the nurses' station had gotten smaller, but a man in a dark gray suit emerged from the group and crooked his finger at me.

New Hampshire State Police Detective Pete Renzi. He had been the lead detective on the Bronson Toles murder case a number of days ago, and he was also the one who had left me a note that told me to "leave it alone."

I suppose I could have left *him* alone and scurried out of the hospital. But he had helped me during that chaotic time, when demonstrators were clogging the streets of Falconer, when violence was in the air, and when the Falconer police had arrested me and had planned to charge me with the murder of young John Todd Thomas.

Renzi had gotten me freed, had helped me.

I owed him that.

So I walked right over.

"Can I help you, Detective?"

"I doubt it," Renzi said. "But you can try."

We went back into the same family room that Kara and I had just used, and he closed the door. We sat down opposite each other. He looked me up and down and said, "No offense, Lewis, but you look like crap."

"None taken. Ask you a question?"

"Sure, I'll give you first crack."

"What are you doing here?"

"I was in the area, heard there was a fracas involving Detective Woods. So here I am."

"And here I am," I pointed out. "A hell of a coincidence, don't you think?"

A slight grimace. "What, you think I came here because I was sure you'd show up?"

"Sure. A good opportunity to remind me of that sweet letter you sent my way a few days ago, the one where you said, quote, Lewis, trust me on this, leave it alone, unquote. Care to elaborate?"

Renzi carefully said, "You're a reasonably smart fellow. Do I need to spell it out?"

"You said a minute ago that I look like crap. For the sake of argument, let's say I'm feeling like crap and thinking like crap. So yeah, spell it out, Detective. What's the 'this' I should stay away from? Seeking justice for Diane?"

He squirmed some in his seat. "Justice will be done."

"Really? How far along are you in arresting and prosecuting Curt Chesak?"

"The case is still under active investigation."

"Again, how far along are you in arresting him?"

He let out a breath. "The case is still under active investigation. That's all I can say."

I shook my head. "That's not good enough."

"Lewis, it's going to have to be good enough."

"Or what? Going to threaten me with arrest? For doing what, exactly?"

"No, no threats. Nothing bad is going to come to you from the New Hampshire State Police. That I can promise."

"But that leaves a lot of other interested people out there who might want to do me harm. So what's going on?"

He shook his head. "That's the best I can do."

"The best? Really? Detective, one of your fellow members of the thin blue line is in a coma, not more than fifteen feet away from us, and you're giving up? Just like that?"

Renzi's face colored. "I'm not giving up. Not for a moment."

"The hell you aren't. Otherwise you'd be here telling me to keep at it, no matter what."

"Keeping at what? Being the lone knight, the Don Quixote, chasing a goddamn windmill? Let it slide. Help Diane and her partner. I know justice will happen. One way or another, justice will happen."

"What? Curt Chesak will get his hands slapped? Sent away somewhere? Get Gitmoed? Is that what someone told you, or told the Colonel of the State Police to tell you? 'Don't worry your pretty little head over the Chesak case, Detective. Higher-ups will resolve this matter so you don't have to dirty your hands.' Is that what happened?"

He stood up. "When the time comes, you'll remember this talk."

"I hope not."

Renzi slammed the door open and went out into the area by the nurses' station. Kara was sipping a cup of coffee with Captain Nickerson of the Tyler Police Department and another cop, and as I was going over to see what was new, my cell phone rang.

I picked it up. No caller ID. One of the nurses glared at me, and I ducked back into the family room, answering the phone as I closed the door behind myself.

"Yes?"

"Cole," came Curt Chesak's voice, low and chilly. "Remember our last call?"

"How could I forget someone so charming and sociopathic?"

He said: "You didn't agree to stop with your actions. So I did what I had to do. So if you don't stop now, at this moment, it'll be a bullet to the back of the head. Got it?"

I looked at the closed door, the ICU and Diane Woods just beyond it.

"What the hell have you done?"

"You were warned. Next time will be a visit from Mister Remington."

He hung up. I thought for a moment.

Chesak said he had just done something.

What?

I started frantically dialing a number on my phone, willing my fingers to be accurate and not to fumble.

The phone rang and rang and rang.

Each ringing of the tone cut into me.

A voice answered. I nearly slid out of the chair in relief.

"Yeah?" It was Felix.

"You okay down there?"

"As well as could be expected. And you?"

"Hanging in there."

"Would love to chat but it's not going to happen. Sorry. Okay?"

"You got it."

I hung up the phone, almost dizzy with what had gone on these past few minutes.

"Lewis, old boy," I said to myself, getting up, "when this is all done and over with, you're going to spend a month doing absolutely nothing."

I stepped back into the ICU area. Kara was moving to me, away from Captain Nickerson, who had a cell phone pushed against her right ear. Kara stopped in front of me, lip trembling, tears in her eyes.

I couldn't move. Couldn't breathe. Couldn't do much of anything.

"Oh, Lewis, I'm so sorry."

"What is it? Is it Diane? Is it?"

A sharp shake of her head. "No, nothing's changed with Diane."

"Then what is it?"

"Oh, Lewis, I'm so very, very sorry." She caught her breath. "Captain Nickerson just got the news. Your house is on fire."

# CHAPTER SEVENTEEN

Not much of a memory of getting to Tyler Beach from Exonia. Remembered borrowing Kara's Subaru again. Remembered a short length of time on the highway to the beach, Route 101.

There was a traffic jam on Route 1-A, also known as Atlantic Avenue, up by where most of the hotels and cottages thinned out. It was one lane of traffic and, after putting up with the long crawl, I pulled into the parking lot of the Lafayette House, trembling with fearful anticipation of what I was going to see next.

From the parking lot of the Lafayette House, I first noticed the smell of wood burning, then the low rumble of the pumper trucks from the Tyler Fire Department at work. There was a lawn in front of the old Victorian hotel, and in the summer white lawn chairs and wicker furniture were spread out so guests could sip their expensive drinks and watch the ocean at play.

Not much furniture today, just a few guests huddled in small groups watching the smoke billow up. Not much of a view, just the smoke billowing up, so I went down the lawn and dodged through the traffic. A fire hose had been stretched from the Lafayette House across the road, with lengths of lumber on either side so vehicles could slowly drive over the hose without damaging it.

I went into the hotel parking lot, the smell of smoke stronger, the engine noises louder. A fire truck from the Tyler Fire Department was parked at the top of my dirt driveway, another fire hose snaking its way down to the fire. Smoke was rising up hard from my house. Two Tyler cops were keeping the onlookers at bay, and I went to the left, scrambled up on some rocks, looked down, and, for the third time in my life, my heart was broken.

The shed to the right of the house was gone, a pile of burned timber and roof collapsed on top of my destroyed Ford Explorer. Flames were billowing up from the center of my house, going through the near windows. A trio of firefighters pushed ahead, spraying hard with a hose. Smoke and steam rose up. They backed away. Two firefighters rushed forward, axes in hand, and broke open the front door. With oxygen to feed on, the flames and smoke grew wider and larger. But now the firefighters had access, and hunkered down, they blasted in with their fire hose. I thought of my television and fireplace and collection of books and old Oriental rugs on the first floor, how the smoke and fire and water were burning, staining, and soaking everything.

My hands were shaking. I put them together. A crashing sound as the sliding glass door on the second floor, where my bedroom and a small deck were located, blew out. Flames roared out like a torch.

The second floor. My office. My books. My computer. The few mementoes I had from my parents, my high school and college years, even my years of service at the Department of Defense. Prized photos of my parents, the memory of the first time my heart had broken, when I got news one late night at a college dorm that their iced-over commuter plane had rolled over at night and plunged into a cornfield in Indiana.

And another few prized photos, of Cissy Manning, my co-worker from the DoD, a woman who had agreed to share her life with me years back, and who had been dead for such a long time, killed with the other members of my intelligence section, where I had been the sole survivor.

The second time my heart had broken.

All now gone.

More smoke and steam rushing out of my bedroom.

Nothing more to see here.

I got off the rock, back to the ground, and walked away from the smoke and fire and memories.

I took a room at the Lafayette House, as far away as I could get from the fire scene. Down there were police and firefighters and arson investigators, but I wasn't going to talk to them, not at all. I was able to get a room without using my credit cards, through a sympathetic desk clerk who recognized me as a regular customer of the hotel's little gift shop, where I occasionally purchased my daily newspapers.

The room was tidy and small, and it overlooked the rear parking lot and a wide expanse of salt marsh.

I sat on the edge of the bed, conscious that whatever I had left for baggage was in Kara's Subaru, and that my clothes reeked of smoke, the molecules of the smoke having begun their life in my clothes or books or memories. I supposed a shower was in order, and maybe the hotel's laundry, but that all could wait. From my coat pocket I took out two cell phones, put them both on the bed. The one on the left was the one Felix had given me, and the second was from Lawrence Todd Thomas.

I picked up the second one, pressed the send button. As before, it was picked up on the second ring.

"Thomas."

"It's Lewis Cole."

He got right into it. "I'm waiting to see if my . . . contacts can do a better refinement of their current analysis, but I'm not hopeful. So far we know he's in your state, in Belknap County."

"A good start, I guess. That leaves out nine other counties. But I need to tell you, I just got another call from Curt Chesak."

"When?"

"About a half hour ago."

"A half . . . thirty minutes? You've waited thirty minutes to call me? What the hell are you doing up there in New Hampshire, Cole?"

A lot of things, I wanted to shout back at him, especially watching the home I loved, filled with memories and possessions, burning to the ground.

But I caught myself before I said it.

For how could I balance my loss of a home with his loss of a son?

"No excuse," I said. "Got to you as soon as I could."

He took a breath. "All right. I'll see what I can do. The technology is above my pay grade, but I'm sure one more call from Mister Chesak will help narrow the search."

"Glad to hear it."

"And once I get you that information, what then?"

"Then it's done."

I waited for a reply, and he said, his voice now concerned, "You okay, Lewis?"

"No worries," I said. "I'll be waiting for you to get back to me."

This time, I hung up on him.

I woke up startled, the sound of a phone ringing. I had fallen asleep on the bed, clothes still on, and I fumbled on the nightstand, picking up the phone, groggy from the short night's sleep. Dial tone.

I had answered Lawrence's special cell phone. No word, then.

Only one phone left. I grabbed it by the fourth or fifth ring, dread in my heart, wondering if it was Curt Chesak.

"Hey," a male voice said.

But it was someone else.

"Hey yourself."

It was Felix Tinios.

"What's up?" he asked.

Such an open-ended message. "Lots, but it can wait."

"Up for a meal?"

I sat up. "Sure."

"You know that place you took me for my birthday last year? I mean, not that place. The other place."

"Sure, I remember. What time?"

"That time, minus seven."

"See you."

"Great."

I got up, stripped off my clothes and opened a window. I draped my clothes over the window, hoping the air would remove the worst of the smoky stench. Then I took a long shower and thought through a number of things.

Once I was dressed, the phone rang yet again, and this time it was the room's phone. I picked it up, and the sympathetic desk clerk from earlier said, "Lewis? There's someone down here who wants to see you."

"Who is it?"

"She says she's a reporter from the *Tyler Chronicle.*"

Paula Quinn. A lover from some time ago, a sweet friend, and someone who had nearly gotten killed the day Bronson Toles was shot. She had been standing next to him when the shot blew off his head, and later, the same shooter—Victor Toles—had tried a second time to kill her.

A rough couple of weeks, ending up with her pledging her undying love for me, and then going on a trip with her boyfriend out West.

This rotten day was going places I hadn't even imagined.

"Tell her I'll be right down."

Paula was waiting for me in the lobby area of the Lafayette House. Her blond hair had been layered short in an attempt to hide her ears, which didn't quite work, and it also managed to highlight her pug nose. She had on a knee-length black coat and she looked troubled, reporter's notebook in her slim hands as I came over to her, a digital camera hanging from her shoulder.

"Oh, Lewis," she said, and she came into my arms for a very long and warm hug. When we stepped apart, she said, "Your poor, poor house. . . ."

I could only nod. She touched my cheek. "How are you doing? I see you haven't shaved in a while."

"Not that great. At some point I'm going to have to go across the street and survey what's left . . . if anything. Guess I should have packed a razor before I left."

"Do you know what happened? How it started?"

"Not a thing. I was in Exonia, visiting Diane Woods, when I heard about the fire."

"I just saw a guy arrive from the State Fire Marshal's office before I came in here," she said. "You want to go over and see him?"

"Not right now."

Her eyebrows raised at that. "Not right now? Why not?"

"I've got something else going on. Look, what's across the street isn't going to leave any time soon."

"But don't you want to know if they think it was arson or accidental?"

I didn't say anything. She eyed me. "You already know, don't you?"

"Paula, you look great. How was your trip with the town counsel, Mister Spencer?"

A flickering smile. "Did me lots of good. And please, his name's Mark. You're allowed to say his name."

"Gee, thanks, I'll remember that."

"I tell you, we had a great, great time. Both of us. Him away from the town hall, me away from the newspaper. It was good to just be out there in Colorado, the two of us, with all those mountains. Did some skiing, visited some ghost towns, just relaxed. Now, good job on changing the subject, Lewis, but your house. You already know what happened, don't you. Was it arson? Who could it be? I mean . . . oh."

I glanced around the lobby to see if we were being watched. The lobby was covered with a colorful rug with comfortable chairs and settees, and a fireplace on the other side had a cheery little flame. Yeah, nice little trapped cheery flame, right where it belonged.

Paula said: "Before I left on my trip, you said you had something to do. Something about finding the guy who beat up Diane Woods. That's what's going on, isn't it?"

"Is this Paula Quinn my friend asking me, or Paula Quinn assistant editor of the *Chronicle*?"

"By asking that," she said, voice sharp, "you're making an assumption that I'm not here as your friend."

"I'm asking that," I replied, "because I need to do something, and I don't need the publicity, and Paula, I cherish you and what we have and all that, but my house is burning down at this moment, and I'm not in the best of moods."

She slowly nodded. "Sorry."

"No apologies needed. So you're doing better?"

She smiled, lifted up her left hand, wiggled the fingers. I spotted the ring.

Something both sweet and sour went through me. "Congratulations, Paula. When's the blessed event?"

"Next June."

"Am I invited?"

"Stupid question. Of course."

"Well, I'm thinking about the town counsel, I mean, Mark. I don't think he cares that much for me."

She leaned over, kissed me on the cheek. "I do, and that's what counts." There was a pause, and she said: "I need to tell you something. The day the sniper tried to shoot me at my condo, and when I hid out at your house, I said some things."

Paula certainly had, I recalled, telling me that she had always loved me, and that she was my true love, and she was saying those things right up to when her boyfriend—now fiancé—had come to my house to pick her up.

"You were scared. You were in shock. I understand."

She seemed relieved. "You okay?"

I shook my head. "About that, yes. About my house and everything else, no."

That earned me another kiss on the cheek, and I went back up to my room, and she went back outside to the story.

# CHAPTER EIGHTEEN

When I finally left the Lafayette House, I drove out of the parking lot and did my best to avoid the scene across the street. People were still gathered around the rock knoll, looking down, and there was still some smoke drifting up, but I tried to keep my eyes on the road. I next made my way to Manchester, and the usually fifty-minute trip took nearly an hour and a half, because I went along some back roads and state roads, avoiding the major east-west highway that runs from Tyler to Manchester. The good thing was that I was driving Kara's rattling Subaru, which meant it probably wasn't carrying a tracking device. The bad thing was that with all the political bumper stickers attached to the rear, I was about as visible as an NRA member at a vegan convention.

In Manchester, the state's largest city, I pulled into a neighborhood along the banks of the Amoskeag River, where huge brick mill buildings more than a century old had been converted into artists' lofts, condos, office space, and restaurants. I checked my watch. Exactly noon. I parked at the far end of one long mill building, where the end unit hosted Fratello's Restaurant, a grand Italian place that attracted a lot of the professionals who worked in the nearby renovated office spaces.

Last year, Felix and I had ended up here for a promised birthday dinner that had taken an odd turn. We were supposed to go to a small Italian eatery down the road in Bedford that had gotten rave reviews in the local newspapers, and when we got to the place, it was closed with a sign outside saying the owner/chef had unexpectedly become ill. Later, the owner/chef of that tiny Italian eatery was found at Logan Airport. In his car. In the trunk.

Felix had just shrugged his shoulders at the news and said, "Some people take their olive oil very seriously."

So that day we had gone up to Manchester, and that dinner at Fratello's had been a good one, with lots of delicious food, wine, laughter, and memories, but I had no illusion that today's lunch would be as much fun or as memorable.

I went into the entranceway, and there standing by the hostess stand was Felix, who was talking to a young woman with raven hair and a snug red dress, who kept on pressing menus against her impressive chest as if trying to cool them down.

Felix turned to me, smiled. His skin was darker than usual, and he was finely dressed in a dark blue suit, light blue shirt, and red necktie. The coat had been expertly tailored to hold whatever weapon he was carrying this afternoon, while I made do with my Harris tweed.

A snug handshake, a slap on the shoulder. "Good to see you," he said. "And what's with the facial hair? You forget to shave or something?

"Good to see you, too," I replied, and it was true, it did feel good. For the past several days, it seemed like Felix was the only one who knew who I was and where I was coming from. I rubbed at the bristle on my face and chin. "Truth is, I've been running so far and so fast, shaving's been taking a back seat."

The hostess came up to us but reserved her gaze for Felix. "Speaking of seats, let's go find them."

The place was busy, with lots of laughs and conversation. It was sprawling, with a second floor, and booths and round tables. The hostess led us to a quiet corner table and, after ordering drinks and meals, Felix sat back and asked, "How are you doing?"

"Lousy."

"Go ahead."

"My house burned down early this morning."

His brown eyes narrowed. "Not funny."

"I agree."

"Lewis . . . for real?"

"Just under two hours ago, I left Tyler Beach. The fire trucks were there, as well as a couple of cops and some people pretending to be my neighbors. Plus an officer from the State Fire Marshal's office, though it's pretty damn obvious the fire didn't start from somebody smoking in bed."

For what seemed to be a first for him, Felix was at a loss for words. Our wine and our meals arrived, and we took the opportunity to eat. Felix had some complicated pasta dish with tomato sauce, sautéed vegetables, and eggplant. I, on the other hand, had a fettuccine Alfredo dish with lobster meat and scallops, and we threw caution and ceremony to the wind and had a nice New Zealand Pinot Noir to go with everything. Along the way, I told Felix what I had been up to, including my trip to D.C. and back.

At one point, knife and fork in hand, he said, "Sorry about Annie Wynn. She seemed to be a grand woman."

"She is a grand woman," I said. "She's a strong, capable woman who is focused on getting her man elected president. She's not in some planning board campaign for a small town or city. Up there where she is, the air is pretty intoxicating. I can't fault her."

"You're a better man than me."

"Which I've told you many times," I said.

After we both paused to have another healthy swig of wine, I asked, "How's your Aunt Teresa?"

"Adjusting to her new condo."

"Her new what?"

"Condo. When I got her down to Florida, I did a quiet recon of her facility. Found out some muscular clean-cut men had been hanging around, asking questions about her and her favorite nephew. So I found her another place."

"Felix, I'm sorry to hear that."

He shook his head. "No worries. It's a step up from where she was, the kitchen is bigger, she has her own private Jacuzzi, and she tells me the pool boys are much more attractive than the ones at her previous place."

"But what's going to happen in the spring? When she wants to go back to the North End?"

His eyes hardened. "I fully expect that this mess will be settled long before spring."

I told him I didn't disagree with that, and when our dining finally slowed down, Felix said, "Tell you a story?"

"Sure. Cops and . . . well, people of your persuasion always have the best stories."

"Hah," he said, breaking off a chunk of bread. "I think I might have just been insulted. But knowing you . . . maybe not."

He chewed reflectively for a moment or two, then said: "Story begins in Providence. A number of years ago, when I was much younger, quicker, but still as handsome."

"Rhode Island?" I asked innocently.

"No, you knucklehead, Nebraska. Of course Rhode Island. Funny how Boston and New York make all the papers and bestseller lists about what passes for organized crime these days, but Rhode Island is the most mobbed-up state in the Union. Anyway, this was when the Patriarca family was on the ropes because the old man was in prison. So up on Federal Hill, you had two associated families who were trying to keep the peace. You had Nicky Giovanni and Tony Messina. Neither as bright as old man Patriarca, but they wanted to keep things on an even keel so business wasn't impacted."

"Fascinating," I said, spearing the last piece of lobster in my bowl.

"You kids are so impatient nowadays. So, one day Nicky Giovanni and Tony Messina are having coffee at some social club, and Nicky says, hey, Tony, you know, my house, the lawn and trees and bushes don't look so good, and my wife, Carla, she's busting my balls, you got any ideas? And Tony says, yeah, I got this Mick, his name is Callaghan, he'll do a good job for you, no problem."

"Ah, the Irish have arrived. Should get very interesting."

"Yeah, it does. So Callaghan goes over and maybe he's having a bad day, or maybe Nicky's wife Carla doesn't like the Irish, but Callaghan doesn't get paid for his work. Callaghan complains to Nicky, and maybe Nicky's having a bad day, and he tells Callaghan to piss off. So he goes to Tony, and Tony says, what, you're bothering me with this little crap? Go away."

I picked up the bottle of New Zealand Pinot Noir, finished off the bottle between our glasses. "Being as intimate as I am with the Irish, I guess this doesn't end well."

"Nope," Felix said. "In fact, one weekend when Nicky and his family were away, Callaghan went to the house, wanting restitution, so he stole this marble statue of the Virgin Mary, a statue that had come over from the old country and was nearly a hundred years old. So Nicky went apeshit, because he knew Callaghan had stolen it. So he went to Tony, wanting it back, and Tony said, hell, ain't my deal. You take care of it. And Nicky said, what the hell, you recommended the guy, and Tony said, doesn't mean he's my cousin, you idiot, and Nicky said, who the hell are you calling an idiot?"

"Sounds like Europe, about August 1914."

"Good comparison. Insults get worse, tempers rise up, and before you know it, you got a full-scale gang war breaking out. Guys in the streets getting shot, laundromats getting burned down, cars blowing up. Meanwhile, Callaghan, seeing what's going on and knowing that at some point blame's coming his way in the guise of two in the hat, tries to do the right thing and make it right. So late one night, he tries to sneak back into Nicky's yard and return the statue. But some nervous third cousin on guard duty sees somebody trying to climb over the fence with a sack slung over his back, and opens fire."

I took a healthy sip of the Pinot. "Not going to end well, is it."

"That's for sure. Poor Callaghan takes a round to his ass, falls off the fence, and drops the Virgin Mary on the sidewalk, whereupon it breaks into a zillion pieces. Seeing this as a sign from above, Callaghan gets his ass stitched up and takes the next Aer Lingus flight back to the home country. Eventually the gang war peters out, but my God, what a mess. Even though a peace was worked out, there are still old goombahs down there in Providence who are holding a grudge over that landscape guy and the broken statue."

I nodded. "End of story?"

"End of story."

"And the lesson, O wise one?"

"The lesson is, people and institutions can plan for a lot, but they often fail to plan for the unexpected. Like a grumpy landscaper. You're the unexpected piece in this little tale, Lewis. Curt Chesak and whoever's behind him, they expected to do what they wanted to do, and when things got a bit messy, the right word or the right phone call was made to tamp down the investigation. So in their world, Curt would be able to skate off to whatever next dark assignment waits for him. All is covered, all is contained, and whoever's paying the checks and pulling the strings, they get to remain unscathed and untouched. Then someone like you, a crazy Irishman who has this funny old-fashioned concept concerning loyalty, pops up."

I smiled. "Gee, that's the nicest thing anyone's said to me all day."

"You need to get out more."

"I am getting out," I protested. "Didn't you hear me? Just came back from a trip to our nation's capital."

"Point taken." He took a napkin, wiped at his fingers. "What now?"

"Keep on keeping on being the crazy Irishman. Why stop now? You know my original plan, Felix. I don't intend to give up."

"They burned down your house."

"Gee, thanks, I forgot all about that."

He drummed his fingers on the white tablecloth. "Okay, then. Anything else?"

From my coat I took out a small pad of paper and wrote a list for Felix. I passed it over to him. "I need what's here."

He read it and said, "Interesting. Looks like you intend to sail into harm's way."

"And then some."

He folded the list, made it disappear. "No problem. Can probably get it to you by later today."

"That'd be great."

"And where do we go from there?"

"Sorry, I thought I just heard you say the word 'we.'"

Felix said, "Lewis, please, you have vim, vigor, and a healthy sense of righteousness on your side. The guys you're going up against have just one thing on their side: bloody experience. I want to come along, even up the odds."

"No."

"Lewis. . . ."

The waiter came over, dropped off the bill. I picked it up and left enough cash to cover the tab and the tip. Still no credit card traces, thank you very much.

"Here's the deal," I said. "You've been with me on some very edgy outings in the past, for which I owe you so very much. But this one is different. This one is personal. And trust me, this isn't a comment on your skills and talents, but by being with me already on this little quest, you've been shot at, you've had to smuggle your aunt out of Boston, and you needed to find her new digs in Florida. I don't want them upping the ante on you, by either burning down Aunt Teresa's new condo or by putting a bomb in your Mercedes."

His eyes darkened and narrowed, and I suddenly felt sorry for all of those in the past who had crossed him. "Still don't like it."

"My apologies," I said. I took a large swig from my water glass, and I said, "And my apologies once again. I need to visit the head."

I slid my chair out and Felix said, "One of these days you'll tell me why you insist on calling the men's room the head."

"Old habit," I said. "One of my bosses back at the Pentagon was ex-Navy. So the walls were bulkheads, the floors were decks, and the bathrooms were the head. So I adopted his lingo."

"Bet you became Employee of the Year for that suck-up."

"Not even close," I said.

On the way back from my brief absence, there was a small crowd of diners waiting for their seats by the hostess station, and I took a moment to spare a glance outside at the parking lot. A steady rain was falling, and I saw a black GMC van slowly go by. It had a side window at the rear that was low to the ground, and which was blacked out.

I got back to the table, sat down, and said, "The bad guys have arrived."

Felix was sipping from a small white cappuccino cup. "Do go on."

"Just saw a surveillance van prowl the parking lot. Has one-way glass on the side that hides a specialized camera that scans license plates and runs background checks on the owners. Might be the State Police or Manchester Police, but I doubt it."

He took another sip. "Sit tight. I'll be right back."

Felix moved as fast and as silently as he always did, while I shifted my seat so I could see the entranceway and the far windows. I touched my Beretta and, oddly enough, felt fine. Around me were couples and groups of friends, dining, drinking, and laughing. No one seemed to notice the little drama occurring here in my corner of the universe.

Waited some more.

Felix strolled back, sat down with urgency. "There's another way out of here."

"I hope it's more than just the rear door out of the kitchen area. You have to give these guys credit."

"You have to give *me* credit," he said sharply. "There's a back set of stairs, leads down to an old access tunnel used when this place was one big happy mill complex. That's where you're going."

"And you?"

"I have my ways. Most important thing is to get you out of here, so let's get a move on."

I stood up with him and we strolled out past the hostess station, where the young lady gave Felix a wide smile. He led me to a function room, past an alcove that was used to store dishes and glassware. Felix opened a plain wooden door, flicked on a light. Old oak steps led down into the darkness.

Felix said, "The place is lit up now. Go down, take a left. At the third door on the right, go out, wait for me. I'll be along presently."

"How in God's name did you find this?"

"The nice hostess let me in on the secret."

"Really? In exchange for what?"

A slight smile. "A meal."

"Doesn't sound like much of a trade."

The smile grew wider. "The meal's breakfast. Now get going."

I got.

## CHAPTER NINETEEN

The stairway descended quite a way before it ended in a dirt cellar. To the right were wood pallets piled high with paper towels, napkins, and toilet paper. To the left was a brick archway. A series of overhead lightbulbs went off into the distance. I ducked my head and started walking. The dirt was well packed. It smelled of dirt and dampness and old things not disturbed in a long, long time. I moved the best I could. Other stairways went up to the left, no doubt to other parts of the old mill complex. I passed one door, bolted and locked. Another door, also bolted and locked.

Third door was the charm. It said FIRE ESCAPE on a sign up above, and there was a push bar to gain access. I pushed the door and stepped out on a narrow sidewalk. Rain was coming down. The door slammed behind me. I turned too late to get back inside. There was no door handle to get me back in. I pulled my coat tighter. I was at the other end of the brick building. The road was lined with parked cars. There were no entrances to other businesses over here. Just blank doors like the one I had just left.

The rain was coming down harder. I shivered, stamped my feet. All around me were the old mill buildings, full of memories and dust and old stories of immigrants speaking French, German, Italian, and Gaelic, working long hours, getting bodies bloodied and broken. It was getting dark with the thick rain clouds overhead.

Felix was nowhere about.

What now?

I pulled my coat around myself tighter. A wind came up, cutting through me. A car splashed by, headlights on against the heavy rain.

Where to go?

Felix had told me to wait.

So I waited.

I shifted my weight. The rain was a steady downpour. I thought about when this day was over, I could be home and turn up the heat and take a long shower, put on some fresh dry clothes, and then I stopped thinking.

I didn't have a home anymore.

It was now smoking timbers, wet books, charred clothes, and who knows what else.

I put my hands in my coat pockets.

My hair was soaked through.

A black van went up the road. I didn't pay any attention to it.

Pants were soaked through, too.

I looked up the road, which went up a slight incline.

The van had stopped at the top of the incline.

Then it made a three-point turn.

It was coming back.

Well, this was getting interesting.

The van came down the road, slowed, and stopped across from me. Engine idling, headlights on, windshield wipers flipping back and forth, back and forth.

The passenger's side door opened up. A man came out.

My right hand went up under my coat, slipped my Beretta out of my Bianchi leather shoulder holster. I brought my hand down and rested it behind my back.

No matter what was going to happen, I wasn't getting into that van.

The man had on black slacks, a long black coat, and a tweed cap on his large head. He looked both ways before crossing.

A careful man.

I switched the safety off the Beretta, pulled the hammer back. There was a round in the chamber. There was always a round in the chamber. I didn't want to waste time working the action.

The man sloshed his away across the street, stood before me. His hands were in his pockets. I decided then and there that if one of his hands came out of the pocket with a weapon in his hand, then I'd open fire.

I remembered my training. Aim for the lower trunk, keep on shooting, because the recoil would cause the pistol to buck, meaning subsequent shots would go right up the torso.

He stopped. Grinned. "Hey," he said.

"Hey yourself."

"Hell of a day."

"I've seen worse."

"You need any help?"

"Excuse me?"

"I said, you need any help? Shelter, place to stay, a warm meal?"

His right hand came out of his pocket and my pistol started coming up, until I saw he was holding a brochure. Clumsily, I brought my hand down, turned so he couldn't see what was in my hand.

"Not at the moment, but thanks," I said.

He held out the brochure and I cautiously took it with my left hand. "Catholic Charities," he said. "Just driving around in this awful weather, see if we can help people who are in need."

I nodded, folded the brochure in half. "I'm all right, honest. Thanks for stopping."

He touched the tip of his tweed cap. "Just looking to help."

"Glad to hear it."

He went back to the van. I stomped my feet, splashing up some water.

Hell of a day.

About fifteen minutes later, a light red Chevy pickup truck slowed down, and Felix was driving. He stopped in front of me and I stepped forward and got into the truck. The interior was warm and oh, so comfortable. I sat down and slammed the door.

Felix said, "You didn't think about waiting inside?"

"I like heavy weather." I rubbed at the console of the truck. "Not your usual style of driving."

"You complaining?"

"Observing."

We pulled out, got into the nearly empty streets of Manchester. I sat back. It felt good to be moving. Felix said, "Got what I could from what was available."

"Meaning what? You got supply dumps scattered around the state?"

"Around the northeast." Jazz music was playing from the radio.

"How did you do that?"

"Pretty simple."

"Nothing's ever simple when *you* get involved, Felix."

We came to a stoplight. He stopped, draped a big wrist and hand over the steering wheel, revealing a gold bracelet. "In my years of . . . self-employment, sometimes it worked to my advantage to arrange a cash discount in exchange for future services."

"Funny, you don't look like Don Corleone."

"Well, it's more than just favors. And I'd never do anything to humiliate or embarrass my former clients, or to put them in an uncomfortable spot. But due to . . . services provided, I have the ability to get transport, housing, meals, and other oddball items rather quickly. So be glad I've done so."

"Very glad. So, how did you get this pickup truck?"

"From an apple farmer in Bedford," he said. "He had an idiot son-in-law who kept on pressuring him to sell the joint, so another lifeless office park could be built on the property, make everybody a ton of money."

"Doesn't sound like something you'd do," I pointed out. "Get involved in a family squabble and all that."

"Yeah, but it was the son-in-law who had contacted me first. He had the oddest idea that I'd kill the old man for a sum of money. I told him that he was misinformed, and when he wouldn't take no for an answer, we had what diplomats call a frank and open exchange of views."

"I take it you prevailed."

"Don't ever doubt me," he said. "So I went to the old man and explained the situation, and in exchange for letting him know about his idiot son-in-law, and for allowing the poor boy to live, I had the use of the farm's spare pickup truck and free apple pies for the foreseeable future."

"And what about the idiot son-in-law?"

"Last I heard, he's still an idiot. And he's finally gotten rid of his crutches."

The light changed, we took a left, and it was good to be moving again.

Felix added: "By the way, now it's your pickup truck. As long as you need it. Just don't use it to haul around hay or manure or anything like that."

"That's what it's designed for, Felix."

"No, it's designed to give suburban men the illusion that they have deep roots to the land. Or something like that."

"Looks like you're reading *GQ* again," I said. "But another favor, if I may." I passed over a set of keys. "The Subaru I've been driving, it belongs to Kara Miles, Diane's partner. Can you get it delivered back to Tyler?"

He took the keys, tossed them into the air, caught them and put them in his coat pocket. "It'll be delivered with a full gas tank and a full car wash."

"Skip the car wash."

"Why?"

"I think the rust is the only thing holding it together."

About twenty minutes later, Felix dropped me off at a motel just off Interstate 93, called the Laurentian Peaks. "I'll be back in a couple of hours with your wish list," he said. "Then maybe you can take me out to an early dinner."

"Fair enough, since I'm using your cash advance."

Check-in was fairly straightforward, with a plump older woman with dyed black hair who spoke French to a man about her age, who sat in a corner, reading a newspaper with French headlines, half-watching a black-and-white television hanging from the white foam ceiling. From her directness and tone of voice, I imagined the guy was her husband. Or her long-suffering husband, if he ever got a word in edgewise to tell me.

Cash and my driver's license was good enough, and I got a real key with a triangular hunk of plastic and a white number 5 in the center.

"You need anyt'ing," she said, leaving the "h" out of the third word, "you jus' call up 'ere, eh?"

I nodded in thanks, went to my room, and dumped my clothes about halfway to the shower. I took my 9mm Beretta along and put it on the toilet seat, within easy reach, and after unwrapping two of those little soap bars, washed up and warmed up in equal measures.

I wrapped myself in a white towel and hung up my wet clothes in the bathroom. The room was small but clean, with a constant drone coming in from the nearby Interstate. Inside the nightstand were a Gideon Bible, and also one in French. On the far wall was a portrait of the famed Chateau Frontenac; next to that, a crucifix. I didn't have the number of the ACLU on speed dial on my cell phone, so I let it be. The television was a small color Sony, chained to a credenza; after a long, troubled nap, I watched a little news while waiting for Felix to show up.

Big mistake.

I caught the five o'clock news from the ABC affiliate in Manchester, and after a story about a shooting in the state capitol in Concord, the second story was about a suspicious fire in Tyler Beach. An earnest young man with blond hair, wearing a trenchcoat, and who looked like he had started shaving during the last Nielsen sweeps week, stood in front of the police yellow tape in the parking lot of the Lafayette House. Behind him was the smoldering wreckage of what used to be my home and garage. Because of the angle from the television camera, the garage was more in display than the house, which meant I got a terrific view of the tail end of my Ford Explorer, which had once been blue and was now charred black. It looked like the roof of the house had collapsed just over my bedroom. Beyond the bedroom, of course, was my office and my hundreds of books on the second floor, with plenty more on the first floor.

I had to stop watching, but I couldn't bring myself to move. A man and a woman, wearing blue windbreakers with STATE FIRE MARSHAL OFFICE stenciled on the back in yellow, and wearing light-blue latex gloves, seemed to be discussing something in my front yard, now cluttered with burned shingles and what looked to be a shattered window from the first floor.

Along with the images I saw, part of my overprocessed brain caught phrases, breathlessly spoken by the young member of the Fourth Estate.

". . . fire believed to be suspicious in origin. . . ."

". . . firefighters had difficulty fighting the blaze because of lack of nearby hydrants. . . ."

". . . historical structure, first used as a lifeboat station in the late 1800s, and then officers' quarters for the nearby Samson Point coast artillery unit. . . ."

". . . belonged to Lewis Cole, a reported magazine columnist. . . ."

". . . whereabouts unknown. . . ."

". . . reporting live from Tyler Beach, this is Abner Brewer."

I finally switched off the television.

"Get your facts straight, kid," I said to the blank screen. "I'm currently an unemployed magazine columnist."

A little while later, Felix rapped at the door, and after ensuring it was him and he was alone—by looking through the shade at the front window and a peephole in the door—I let him in, still clad in a towel, my Beretta behind my back.

"Based on what you're wearing and what you're carrying," he said, "it looks like you're either looking for love or looking for trouble."

"Or both," I said.

He was carrying two bags, one large and made of plastic, the other small and made of soft black material, looking like a duffel or equipment bag. He tossed the larger bag at me, which I missed catching and which fell to the floor.

"Now I know why you were always picked last for sports at the playground," he said.

I picked up the bag, peered inside. Pants and socks and shirts and a few other things. I looked up. "Pretty damn thoughtful."

"Only thoughtful if I got your size right," Felix said. "Besides, I don't want you coughing over dinner. It'd be damn impolite."

"I'll be right out," I said. "And lucky you, you'll be paying for dinner."

He managed a smile.

"I don't mind, so long as it doesn't make me late for breakfast."

It had finally stopped raining when we went out to dinner, which was just a short stroll down the block to a restaurant called Chez Vachon. Like my new place of residence, it was French-Canadian, and as we sat down I pointed that out to Felix. He smiled. "Sometimes you get the attention of knuckleheads who may be well armed but are lacking in the street smarts department. That's why I like to mix it up some, by not establishing a pattern of the kind of places I like to eat. Besides, they do a great pork meat pie. Give it a shot."

And I did just that, and surprised both Felix and myself by having an extra slice. It was spicy, hot, and very filling, and with a side salad and some wine, it fit the bill.

When we were at the coffee stage, I said, "Thanks for getting me out of Fratello's. How did you get out?"

"With no difficulty, which I found sort of insulting. They're after you, Lewis, not me. And that's not the way of the world."

"We all have our burdens."

"You seem to have your share of them. So where do you go from here?"

In my briefing back at the Italian restaurant, I had told Felix the details of my visit with the father of John Todd Thomas, the murdered Colby student, and where we were now. "So like I said before, I'm waiting to hear back from Lawrence Thomas. He's trying to track down the area where Curt Chesak is making his phone calls."

Felix said, "And then when you get a good location from this ex-spook, you plan to do what then? Go in as an avenging angel?"

"Go in avenging, that's for sure," I said. "But I'm no damn angel."

"Again, is it worth it?"

I stared at him, not quite believing the question. I said: "Less than an hour from here, one of the best friends I've ever had in my life is still in a coma. If that wasn't enough, the best home I've ever had, filled with memories and books and what few mementoes I have of my parents and my time in D.C., has been burned to the ground. If I didn't think it was worth it, Felix, I'd be back there, talking to the arson inspectors and my insurance company."

A slow nod. "I had to ask the question. I know from experience how . . . personal issues can cloud one's judgment."

"My judgment is as clear as a bell. And unlike Don Corleone and his crew, this definitely isn't business. It's strictly personal."

We sat quietly for a while, finishing our coffee, and he quietly said, "My original offer still stands."

"As does my original objection," I said. "This is going to be a one-man mission. Thanks for the logistics and the cash, but that's how it's got to be."

Felix nodded. "My turn for the bill."

"Wouldn't have it any other way."

# CHAPTER TWENTY

Back at the Laurentian Peaks Motel, there was just a moment of awkwardness when Felix and I stood there, just outside my room. He looked at me and I looked at him, and no words were exchanged, but there was the thought that this was it, the very last time we'd ever see each other. Not because of what had happened, but what was *going* to happen.

He shifted from one foot to another. His voice was soft. "Don't be a hero out there. Be careful."

"Be as careful as I can."

"You get into it, you feel like the odds aren't in your favor, get out. Don't be fancy, don't be pretty, just get out. If it means breaking things, running over things, or shooting whoever gets in your way, you fucking do it, Lewis. *Capisce*?"

I managed a slight smile. "Very *capisce*."

He moved quickly, suddenly, and he shockingly gave me a full embrace, slapping me on the back, murmuring "Good luck, all right?"

Felix stepped back, and he turned and strolled away.

I went into my motel room.

It took a long, long while before I fell asleep, and the sleep was light and restless, the hum of the Interstate traffic a constant background. More often than not, I was on my back, staring up at the ceiling, the sight of my burned-out home always in my mind.

And when sleep finally came, the sound of a ringing phone made me sit straight up, blankets and sheets around my waist.

The phone rang and rang, and I fumbled in the dark, switched on the light.

The phone was my loaner from Lawrence Thomas.

"Cole," I said, checking the clock. It was four A.M.

"Got it narrowed down," he said.

"Hold on, let me get pen and paper."

I swiveled around in my bed, found what I was looking for, and said, "Go."

"The second trace on that incoming call places him in a town called Osgood. Are you familiar with it?"

"No, but that'll change. Any address or location?"

"Unfortunately not, but I do have a search area, based on the cell tower the call went through."

"Go on."

"My . . . associates say that the call went through a cell tower on the top of a mountain called Flintlock Peak. From that cell tower, my associates say, plot a triangle from the tower, using a base point of magnetic north. From zero degrees to thirty-five degrees, you'll get a triangular-shaped search area, reaching to a lake called the Wachusett. That's your boundary."

"Could be a big area."

"I've already done a preliminary. It's a fairly rural town, and from Flintlock Peak to Osgood, from what I can tell, is farmland and forest. That narrows it down. There's not many businesses or residences in that triangle."

I yawned. "I'm on it."

"Are you leaving now?"

"No, I'm not."

"And why the hell not?" he nearly shouted.

"Because I've got work to do, supplies to retrieve, and breakfast to be eventually eaten," I snapped back. "Because I'm going in slow, but I'm going in right. This isn't going to be a Desert One fiasco, got it?"

He started talking again and I talked right over him. "That was early on in my career, when the hostage rescue mission to Iran failed. Lots of things made it fail, including too many fingers in the proverbial planning pie, and a commander in chief that insisted on being in the loop from start to finish. As of now, Lawrence, you're out of the loop."

"The hell you say."

"The hell I don't. You're in Virginia. I'm in New Hampshire. Based on those last two calls I received, Curt Chesak is on my turf, not yours. So I'm taking care of it. You got a problem with that, then go rely on somebody else. But I want this done too. And I'll do it right."

No words, just the sound of his breathing. I went on. "If I get another phone call from him, I'll let you know. Maybe that will help your folks narrow the search territory even more. But you've got to let me do this, Lawrence. I can't do it with you calling every hour or so, asking for updates. If all goes well, you'll get just one more phone call from me, telling you the job is finished."

He breathed some more. Coughed. I thought I heard a woman's voice in the background, no doubt asking why her husband was up at such a rotten hour. "All right," Lawrence said, voice shaking. "All right. I understand what you're saying. It makes sense. So go out there and do it, Lewis. But by God, do it."

"I will," I said, and that was that.

I managed to get some sleep, and in the morning I went back to Chez Vachon, where I consumed about a half-dozen crepes and half-dozen sausages, along with a couple of cups of coffee. I wasn't sure when or where my next meal would be; I wanted to make sure my tanks were topped off. Back in my motel room, I scratched furiously at my chin and under my neck, where an unfamiliar beard was growing. Time to take care of business.

I took a nice long shower, soaping up, and, with a couple of disposable razors in hand, did what I could do, shaving in the shower. A couple of times, the drain clogged up and I had to clean things up. When I had gotten dried and dressed, I opened the duffel bag that Felix had brought me, following my shopping list to the letter. I also checked my Beretta and my Bianchi holster, and then put it on, put my coat over it, and picked up the duffel bag and got going.

Outside it felt quite cold, and from the duffel bag I took out a Navy-style black watch cap, which I easily slipped over my head. I got in the truck and drove about twenty minutes to the Mall of New Hampshire, right near Route 101 and Interstate 93. I took my time wandering through the mall, admiring the Halloween decorations and displays, and then I ducked into an EMS store. EMS stands for Eastern Mountain Sports, and once upon a time they had three stores: one in North Conway, New Hampshire, the second in Boston, and a factory store at their headquarters facility in Peterborough. Now they had scores of small shops like this one in malls and shopping plazas, and some oldtimers still groused about how the whole feel and style of the place had changed over the years, probably with every change of ownership.

Me, I didn't care that much. I spent about thirty minutes in the store, getting what I needed, and in one corner of the store—past displays of crampons, ropes, and mountain-climbing gear for those brave folks who want to fight against the law of gravity—there was a wooden bureau with thin drawers. A few minutes later, I found what I was looking for: a U.S. Geological Survey map for the town of Osgood, with roads, rivers, streams, and mountain peaks listed, especially Flintlock Peak.

A woman came up to me. "Help you with something?"

I gently rolled the map in a tube so she couldn't see what I was examining. "I'm doing fine, thanks for asking."

She smiled. "Let me get a rubber band so that doesn't unwrap on you."

I kept my eye on her as she walked to the service counter and came back. Most of the employees in the store were just a few years over the state drinking age, and both the young men and young women sported tattoos, body piercings, and odd hair colors and styles. But this woman—whose nametag said PAMELA—was much older, nearly coming close to my demographic range. She had on hiking boots, socks, khaki shorts, and a black T-shirt depicting a Hubble Space Telescope shot of the Horsehead Nebula, with a caption stating "So much exploring, so little time." Her eyes were light blue and her hair was blond, with a few streaks of white along the side.

Pamela took the tube, snapped the elastic around it, and looked at my other items in a wire shopping basket. She smiled, revealing thin smile lines about her eyes and lips, which made her that much more attractive. "Going orienteering? Or hunting?"

Among my purchase pile was a compass, a small gas stove, a pair of 7 × 50 binoculars, a small knapsack, and some freeze-dried food packages, along with a couple of other things.

"A little of both."

She frowned, just a bit. "Really? Deer season's coming up. Is that what you're interested in?"

I shook my head. "No, no," I said. "I don't mind those who hunt, but it's just never been my thing."

"So what are you hunting for?"

I laughed. "Justice, what else?"

She laughed back at me. "C'mon, I'll take care of you up at the counter."

At the counter, Pamela rang up my purchases, asked me for my phone number and e-mail address, both of which I declined. She took that in good stride, put my goods in a plastic EMS bag, and then slid over a business card that had her full name: Pamela Howe.

"If you have . . . any questions about your gear," she said, her eyes bright.

I took the card, gave it a closer look. "If I do, you can count on it."

I walked out of the mall, the bag suddenly weighing heavy in my hand. Pamela's world was that of the outdoors and being in good shape and flirting with the occasional male shopper, with each day effortlessly sliding into another.

My world had been reduced to a simple one, where in a matter of days I was going to encounter Curt Chesak, and at the end of that day one of us would be dead.

More errands were run that day in Manchester. I got some more clothes at a JCPenney, found some more clothing at a hunting supply shop—where I had to slip the store owner an extra twenty dollars to get what I needed—and lunch was a quick stop at a Papa Gino's. I ate a small cheese pizza and drank a large Coke, and after washing up in the restroom, went to my borrowed pickup truck, out in the shopping plaza parking lot.

It was a fine fall day. I leaned against the warm truck fender, crossed my arms, and just let myself bake in the sun for a few minutes. Even though I was in a parking lot, there were fall leaves at my feet, gold and red and orange. They looked beautiful. Traffic was moving at a good pace over on the Interstate. I could be on the Interstate in less than five minutes, on the way up north, where the town of Osgood waited for me, along with Curt Chesak.

Or I could head south, and then east, try to pick up everything and just go on.

"Like hell," I said, and I got into my Chevy, and then got going to where I had to be.

Nearly two hours later, I was approaching Osgood. Nearly forty minutes earlier, I had taken an exit off Interstate 93 and followed a state road through two other towns before getting to Osgood. It was a type of New Hampshire town that looked great on calendars, Christmas cards, and presidential primary ads. It had a small downtown that consisted of a diner, a Citizens Bank branch, hardware store, town hall, a combination police station and fire station, as well as the usual and customary town common with its Civil War statue in the center.

I took my time going through the town, driving along a couple of side streets, before I kept on driving and left Osgood. To the left I could make out the far waters of Wachusett Lake, and off to the right were the low peaks, one of which was Flintlock Peak. I could make out a cell phone tower at the top, and the backs of my hands tingled, thinking about the voice of Curt Chesak going through the airwaves and bouncing right off that tower and coming to me.

I made my way to the lake, and there was a picnic area that was empty. It had two swing sets, some stone fire pits, and a half dozen picnic tables. I pulled into a finely packed gravel lot, rummaged through my belongings, and went out to the near table.

I unrolled my topo map and found four rocks to anchor the corners of the map. With my compass, I located the top of Flintlock Peak, and I put the compass adjacent to the peak, and then swung the compass around so the needle matched the true magnetic north indicated on the map.

There you go. Using the edge of a guidebook and a pencil, I drew a triangle that encompassed zero degrees and thirty-five degrees. The lines ended on the shores of Wachusett Lake. I stared down at the triangle I had just made, tapped my pencil in the middle. There were about a half dozen roads that were in the triangle. Somewhere Curt was hiding out there.

"Got you, you son-of-a-bitch," I whispered.

I started writing down the names of the roads. Spencer Lane. Tucker Road. Roscoe Street. Eric Street. Mount Vernon Street. Gibson Lane.

Then there was the crunch of tires on gravel, and I swiveled around.

A police cruiser was pulling in behind my borrowed Chevy truck.

I stood still, waited calmly, not making any moves. The cruiser was white and dark blue, with the markings of the Osgood Police Department on the side. A slim police officer came out, put on his uniform hat. He was about early thirties, which comforted me. A guy in his thirties has been on the job for a while, doesn't need to prove himself. A guy in his twenties would be full of himself, wanting to do something to show his chief and the police commission or whatever that he was an asset to the force.

Too much thinking. He approached. A slight smile. He had a prominent nose, bushy eyebrows, and black-rimmed eyeglasses.

"Good afternoon," he said. "Everything all right?"

"Absolutely," I said. "Just taking a break."

His nametag said TEMPLAR, and Officer Templar said, "A break from what, if you don't mind me asking."

So it began. The gentle questioning, leading down to a not-so-gentle conclusion. If it got to the point where he asked for the truck's registration, I'd be hard-pressed to explain how I was driving a truck registered to a farm in Bedford, belonging to a farmer whose name I didn't know. And then it could get really interesting.

"My work," I said. "I'm a magazine writer."

I took out my wallet, passed over my press identification card from the N.H. Department of Safety, along with my business card from *Shoreline*.

Officer Templar examined them both and said, "So you're a reporter, then?"

"A columnist, actually."

"And you write for *Shoreline*?"

Lots of questions. What was driving him?

"Used to," I said, putting a mournful tone in my voice. "I quit last week. My editor was a real bitch. Couldn't stand her. I'm trying to rustle up some freelance articles, make some contacts with other magazines."

"Here in Osgood?" He handed me back my business card and press identification.

"Sure. I'm working on an article about various discrepancies in households and income, even in small towns like Osgood, which I think represents the status of the nation as a whole. You know, the one percent versus the 99 percent. What I do is randomly select some households, maybe interview the owners, and get a nice cross-section of small-town life."

A slight smile from Officer Templar as he turned to walk back to his cruiser. "Sounds like a lot of work for a lot of nothing."

"That's what we writers do," I replied.

When he left, I changed my clothes in the shadow of my truck. I still didn't like the interrogation. In small towns like Osgood, it only took minutes for news of a stranger to zip through town.

Back in my borrowed truck, I drove back to the center of the town and went to the town hall. The parking lot was cracked asphalt, and I walked up the wide front steps of the town hall. The building was white; over the double doors, black letters announced OSGOOD TOWN HALL with the date 1858 underneath it. The doors were heavy, painted green. I walked in, the wooden floor creaking loudly as the door closed behind me. Before me was a bulletin board covered with notices for town meetings such as school board, planning board, and the selectmen. There were also notices for a ham & bean supper, a lost dog, two lost cats, and a flyer announcing a home cleaning service.

Up ahead was a waist-high counter, and a tall thin woman in her late fifties looked down at me as I approached. She wore round wire-rimmed glasses and had on a light yellow dress with tiny white flowers. I gave her my best inquiring smile, and she said, "Can I help you?"

"Gosh, I hope so," I said. "My name is Lewis Cole, and I'm working on a freelance magazine article."

I showed her my press ID, and she said, "My, I haven't met a real magazine writer before. The only writer I know is Sarah Gebo, she's a stringer for the *Union Leader*, lives over in Warren." She held out her hand. "Abby Watkins."

I gave it a quick shake. "Thanks, Abby."

"So, what are you looking for?"

Poor trusting Abby Watkins. At some time I would have to think of a way to apologize to her, but first I gave her the same story I had given Officer Templar: about getting information on a cross-section of the town of Osgood to write an article about economic differences and challenges, thereby using Osgood as an example of the economic challenges facing not only our region, but the country as a whole. She nodded at the apparent right places and I think the excitement value of being with a writer was rapidly approaching zero. Even with her eyeglasses, I could see her eyes beginning to glaze over.

"All right, I think I understand," she said. "What are you looking for then?"

"I was hoping to get some information on residences and businesses on these streets," I said, sliding over a sheet of paper.

She peered down at the list. "An interesting collection of roads. How did you get it?"

"Random, that's all."

Abby looked down, hesitated.

I said, "I always thought tax records like this were public information."

"Oh, they are," she said, head still lowered.

"Then maybe I should talk to the tax collector, or the assessor?"

That brought forth a laugh. "Sweetie, you don't know Osgood, do you?"

"True enough," I said. "But it seems like a nice town."

"Oh, it is, it is. But it's a poor town. Besides being the town clerk, I'm also the tax collector and the secretary to the selectmen, the planning board, and the zoning board of adjustment."

"Sounds busy."

"Oh, it keeps me jumping." She took the paper and said, "You're absolutely right: this is public information. Give me a few minutes, but just so you know. . . ." She paused.

"Yes?" I asked. "What's that?"

Abby seemed apologetic. "You're not a town resident. I'm afraid I'm going to have to charge you a dollar a page."

"Best deal I've heard today," I said. "No problem."

Within ten minutes I got photocopies of what's called the tax cards for each property listing, paid the Town of Osgood twenty-one dollars in cash, with a receipt for expenses for my nonexistent magazine article. In the parking lot next to my pickup truck was the Osgood police cruiser with Officer Templar sitting inside. He gave me a cheerful wave and I returned the favor. I got in the truck, drove down a block to Osgood Finest Pizza. Before going in, I popped open the glove compartment and memorized the truck's owner: Bedford Pleasant Farms. I wasn't going to give Officer Templar an opportunity to trap me with an inopportune question.

Osgood Finest Pizza, like most pizza places in New Hampshire, was owned and operated by Greek-Americans. Not sure why, but the food was always good. A chubby young lady with a thick black ponytail and a cheerful smile in a white uniform with red apron took my order, and within ten minutes I was sitting in a booth by myself eating a hot steak-and-cheese sub, with a nice cold Coke. Feeling a bit concerned about my current diet, I had decided to splurge, so I also had some low-fat baked potato chips.

The sandwich was hot, the steak well cut and tasty, and the Coke did its usual fine job of quenching my thirst. Unfortunately, my diet experiment didn't end well, since the low-fat chips tasted like pressed cardboard sprinkled with salt.

A few minutes later, I was in my borrowed truck again. I started up and drove east, and I came upon a low-slung motel called Peak's Paradise. I pulled into the parking lot. Waited. Looked around the lot and the building.

No.

Officer Templar seemed pretty interested in my activities. I didn't want to be stationary in one place, to pen myself in one location to have to answer a lot more questions. Instead I backed up and drove down one narrow road, and then another. I found a hunting trail or path and backed the truck in, moving slowly and easily, a few branches scraping the side.

I sat and took stock of the tax cards I had received. There were twenty-one names, twenty-one addresses. Where to start? I started culling by going through the list, being brutal in eliminating properties that I couldn't see Curt Chesak staying in. Each property card, besides listing the owner, address, and value of the property, also gave a description of the building: everything from number of bathrooms and bedrooms to a photograph. So residences that consisted of mobile home trailers, double-wide trailers, or distressed properties that had the cliché front yard of bathtubs, old cars on blocks, and truck tires were discarded.

Not fair, but I wasn't looking to be fair.

After that first pass, I ended up with eleven possibilities. I checked my watch. About three hours before dusk came my way. Plenty of time to do a recon and see what I could learn. I started up the truck and started out on my quest.

All of the roads were built the same. A single-lane paved country road, with no sidewalk, no center yellow line, not much of anything except asphalt and drainage ditches on each side. Just like the roads back in Lee, where I'd had that wonderful encounter with Mister Marvel, philosophy expert. As I took my time going up and down the various roads, I made it a point to slow some as I went by the properties. There were a couple of working farms, with wide pastures, barns, with cows, sheep, and horses, and a couple of access lanes blocked by metal gates. Most of the other homes were single-family residences, up close to the road. There were kids at play, tossing balls around, riding bicycles or horses. It was a fine fall day. Halloween decorations were out on porches and at mailboxes, from skeletons to ghosts to witches to bundles of corn stalks.

And on the mailboxes were names from O'Halloran to Finch to Dupuis.

Nothing that said Chesak.

Nothing shouting out that Curt Chesak resided here.

Nothing.

Driveways and homes and everything so innocent and up-front. Hard to believe that a killer was out there somewhere, and as the hours slipped away, my frustration started to build. Maybe he wasn't out here. Maybe he'd just happened to be in the area when he had made those phone calls.

Maybe.

The last house had the name Smith. In other circumstances, I would have found it hilarious. It was a nice-looking two-story home, on a slight rise, and in the front yard mom and dad and two young girls bounced around with a soccer ball while a white German Shepherd barked along and played with them.

No evil there.

I turned around and left.

## CHAPTER TWENTY-ONE

Back to the little lane where I'd hidden out before. The Peak's Paradise motel once again beckoned to me, with the siren song of a hot shower, soft bed, and free HBO, but I manned up and decided to continue on my own. After the truck was backed in, I lit up a small gas lantern that I had purchased from EMS earlier today and, with flashlight in hand, I strolled down to the country road. I turned around and was pleased to see no light escaping out to the road.

Back to the truck, I unrolled a mattress pad and sleeping bag. I sure hoped it wasn't going to rain tonight. Huddling in the cab wasn't my idea of fine sleeping.

With sleeping arrangements set, I started up a gas stove and, working carefully and following directions, I heated up a freeze-dried meal of beef stew. If I hadn't eaten in a week, it probably would have tasted pretty good. I washed up, went into the woods to do my business, and then took the tax cards and crawled into my sleeping bag. With a headlamp perilously balanced on my forehead, I examined each one and looked again, to see what I was missing. The numbers were all there, and they weren't adding up.

They weren't adding up.

I was getting sleepy.

In a little bag near my head, I took out my cell phone. Dialed the number for Kara Miles. It rang and rang.

No answer. Didn't even go to voicemail.

Hung up. Put the phone back in the bag.

It was getting colder. I put my hands in the sleeping bag, stared up at the sky. Looked for stars. Didn't see a single one. Thought a lot about Diane, over there in Exonia. Wondered if she dreamed in her coma. And if so, what did she dream about? Her long years at the Tyler Police Department? The bad guys and girls she had put away? Me? Kara Miles and the other loved ones in her life? Or did she dream, over and over again, of those last few minutes of the violence, when Curt Chesak and the others were coming at her, pipes and lumber in their hands, rising up, knowing that it was too late to reach for her weapon, the blows falling and falling. . . .

The rain started about an hour later.

I was just about a foot longer than the truck cabin's width, which meant a long night of being curled up on my side, legs knocking around, and I dozed here and there, and when the light finally started streaming into the windshield and directly into my face, I got up, stretched, and walked around the truck. I was cold, stiff, sore, and my unanswered phone call to Kara Miles was on my mind.

No more.

No more phone calls to Kara. What was done was done. I was going to do my job. That's it. No more dialing and re-dialing that memorized phone number. . . .

Numbers.

The numbers didn't add up.

The rain had stopped a while ago. Dead leaves from oak and maple trees were all around me. I shuffled around, packed up my stuff, and went back into the truck. Started up the engine, let the heat roll over my legs as I unfolded the topographical map of Osgood I had gotten at EMS. I let my cold fingers trace the lines of the roads and streets in that magic triangle where Curt's cell phone had been located.

On the topo map, little squares marked each residence along the roads. I spent a good amount of time in the morning, matching the little squares with the roads. I did it once, twice, three times.

Tucker Road.

There was a little square, a distance away from the road, that wasn't listed on the tax cards.

On the north side of this little square was a property listed for Swinson. On the south side was a property listed for Keller.

But nobody was listed for the mystery square on Tucker Road.

Nobody.

But the topo map didn't lie.

Something was there.

I put the map aside, put the truck in drive, and left my little refuge.

On the outskirts of Osgood I stopped at an Irving gas station, one of the many outposts of the Canadian oil company archipelago. Fueled up the truck, got a coffee and a pretty good cinnamon Danish. I drove out to the far end of the parking lot, had my breakfast, thought things through.

My own past dribbled through my mind. Code words. For some reason, code words were bouncing around. In my little corner of the DoD universe, missions were never called missions. They were called pizza deliveries. We might have had pre-op planning sessions that took months, that involved air and naval assets, that inserted extraordinarily dangerous, highly trained and dedicated service members (Navy, Army, Air Force, Marines, or—yes—Coast Guard, take your pick) that resulted in death, destruction, and general mayhem.

But they were called pizza deliveries. For a joke, I guess, but also to insulate us poor civilians in the rear from what was actually going on in the front line.

My turn, though, to go into the front line.

Pizza delivery.

I went back to Osgood Finest Pizza and ordered a large cheese pizza. I got back into my truck, drove off to Tucker Road. The Swinson place was a gorgeous new home that, if it were a bit bigger and on a lot a bit smaller, would be called a McMansion. Brickwork and shrubbery and finely trimmed lawn, nice paved curved driveway. The number on the mailbox said 10. I went past the nice home and stopped for a quick moment. A scraggly dirt road with a metal gate blocking the entrance. The gate was rusted, leaning to one side, weeds growing at the base. It looked pretty old and beaten up.

Except for a metal post, with a keypad that controlled the lock.

I kept on driving.

The Keller home was an old Cape Cod that sometime in the past had had a porch constructed on the front. The driveway was dirt. In the rear part of the yard, part of it was fenced off and chickens moved around. The number on the mailbox said 14. I pulled up in front of the house, deftly stepped out and went up to the porch with the pizza in my hands. The floorboards creaked loudly as I stepped to the door and knocked on it hard and firm.

The door swung open and a white-bearded man peered at me. He had on patched blue jeans, work boots, and a green cardigan sweater. His eyes were a twinkling blue, and he said, "Sorry, bud, didn't order that."

"Yes, sir, I know you didn't," I answered with a sheepish tone. "Thing is, I'm supposed to deliver this to 12 Tucker Road. But I can't find 12 Tucker Road."

The guy opened the door wider. "Sorry, bud, there ain't no 12 Tucker Road. There's me and then there's the Swinsons, next butt-ugly house over, which is number 10. But no number 12."

"Damn," I said, moving the pizza box from one hand to another. "I thought for sure that dirt road and gate over there was number 12."

"Well-l-l," he said, drawing out the last letter. "It should be, but there's some sort of non-profit or conservation easement over there, don't get taxed. Plus you take that dirt road up about a half-mile, you'll find a christly big hunting lodge, belongs to some outfit from away."

*Found you again*, I thought, *found you again.*

"Funny to have a hunting cabin up there, it being conservation land."

He shrugged. "People from away. Go figure. Got money to piss away, they do. Sometimes they don't even bother driving up the road. They take a helicopter in and out. But sometimes you can hear 'em shooting away. I don't mind, but Mister Swinson, the asshole, 'scuse my French, he's originally from New York and don't like the sound. But it's their land, right? They can do what they want."

"Good for them," I said, holding up the pizza box. "But it still means someone's pulling a prank, and I'm gonna get hit for this."

The guy eyed me, and I said, "Look, you want this? Free? No charge? Otherwise it's just gonna go to waste."

"What kind is it?"

"Plain cheese."

"Hah, I'll take it," he said, holding his hands out for it. "Wish it was pepperoni, but we all can't get what we want, am I right?"

"Right as you can be," I said, handing the pizza over to him.

I took my time that afternoon, prepping for my second pizza delivery of the day. I repacked and rearranged my sleeping bag, food, stove, and extra clothing, along with my weapons and a few other items. I drove along Tucker Road again until I found another overgrown wide trail that led somewhere deep into the dark woods. I carefully backed the truck up the lane until I couldn't see the road anymore. I switched off the engine. Thought some. It had been a relatively short drive from Manchester to here, but in a lot of ways it was the longest trip I had ever taken. On the seat beside me were my personal cell phone and the special cell phone I had gotten from Lawrence Thomas. I picked them both up and put them in the side pockets of my knapsack.

I juggled the truck keys for a moment, and then lowered the visor, put the keys there, and put the visor back up. On the back of a takeout menu from Osgood Finest Pizza, I scribbled a note:

*Please contact Felix Tinios of North Tyler to ensure the return of this truck. Thank you.*

Underneath the note I scribbled Felix's phone number, and I slid the menu into the visor.

I got out of the truck and shouldered my knapsack, which felt pretty damn heavy. I patted the side of the truck, said, "Thanks," and walked away.

Most people who get lost in the woods think their cell phone is a magic mystery tool that will lead them in and out with no difficulty—and if there *is* difficulty, well, that's why there are cops and Fish & Game officers. Obviously they're just sitting around, eagerly anticipating yet another phone call from a lost hiker. Yet a topo map and a compass will always mean you will never, ever get lost. From what my first and only pizza customer of the day had told me, the hunting camp was at the end of that dirt lane, both lane and little rectangle marked on the map.

Using the compass, I determined how many degrees I had to set to make a fairly straight line to a ridge that overlooked the hunting camp. From where I was, all I did was to sight in the compass to a landmark ahead of me, like a boulder or wide pine tree or a stand of birches. Once I got to that point, I found another landmark. Repeat as necessary.

Which I did, until I got to the ridgeline and saw the hunting camp beneath me.

Some camp.

I took out a pair of binoculars, scoped the place out. It was a house, a pretty good-sized home that wouldn't look out of place along the pricier parts of North Tyler and Wallis. Wooden and two-story, it looked like it had been here for quite a while. The shingles appeared to be cedar, and the yard was a few acres and mowed. At the rear of the house was a concrete landing pad, with an enormous H painted in the center. A post with an orange windsock was some distance away from the concrete. There were two satellite dishes on the roof, along with a set of very tall antennas. Bushes were scattered around the yard.

At the front of the house, I could just make out a dark green Hummer, the civilian version of the famed Humvee.

Only the best for Curt Chesak and his friends.

But how many friends?

It was tempting to stroll down and start the job, but that was stupid. No need to rush.

I slipped off the ridgeline and worked my way down to the rear of the yard.

Dusk was falling by the time I got to where I wanted to be. Like most areas of the state, there are ghost stone walls that travel through wooded areas that had once been farmland. Hard to believe, but there was a time when more than ninety percent of my state was clear-cut for farms. Now, just a hundred or so years later, the ratio has reversed: most of the state is now forested, having reclaimed the farms, the descendants of the original owners now living in Ohio or Indiana or any other place where the land was cheaper and richer.

What worked for me was that the edge of the home's landscape butted right up against a stone wall, which gave me great cover to watch things. With my knapsack and most of my weapons left behind, I crawled up to the stone wall and waited. I was now wearing the favorite outfit of snipers and Scottish game men, called the ghillie. It's a suit one wears that has leaves, twigs, and branches placed all over, so when you stop, if you do it well, you blend in with the scenery. Years and years ago, some old-timers with leathery skin and sun-squint wrinkles around their eyes had told me what it took for good surveillance and tracking, which was three things: patience, patience, and patience.

Which meant it took me over a half hour to slowly crawl along the forest floor until I reached the stone wall. And another fifteen minutes or so to take out my binoculars and position myself just right.

By then darkness had fallen and, one by one, lights were lit inside the home.

I settled in for a long wait.

Through the night, I saw shapes and shadows move beyond the windows. It was impossible to determine how many men were in there. Once, a light went on in an upstairs bathroom, and I saw a muscular young guy with a short blond haircut take a shower. If I'd been someplace else and *was* somebody else, that might have proven interesting, but he wasn't Curt Chesak, whom I desperately wanted to see.

Eventually from one of the larger windows to the rear, I spotted the light blue glow that mean a television was in play.

I waited.

It grew darker.

Waited some more.

Out in the woods I could hear creatures scurrying through the fallen leaves. Once an owl hooted loud and long just a few yards away from me, almost causing me to jump up like I had been stung by wasps.

Lights went on, lights went off.

I slowly moved my binoculars around, keeping my view on the house.

One by one, slowly and gradually, all the lights went off.

I kept still, watching. My eyes adjusted more to the darkness.

There were little glows of light coming from the house, from those little bits of electronic gear and machines that are always on, all the time, illuminating just a touch to let their human masters know they're up and awake.

But it looked like everyone in that house was asleep.

I waited another hour, and then spent another half-hour crawling back so enough distance was put between me and the stone wall.

Thus ended the first day.

# CHAPTER TWENTY-TWO

My camp wasn't really a camp, just a hollow in the woods where I felt comfortable taking some shelter. I used a headlamp with a slight beam to put a ground cloth down, then a thin mattress pad, and then my sleeping bag, still damp from the previous night's adventure. I put everything within easy reach and then settled down for dinner. I opened up a freeze-dried packet of chicken and rice, but I didn't dare light a fire or a stove. Maybe the guys in that alleged hunting camp were kicking back and taking it easy, and maybe they were on hyper-alert, with night-vision gear and thermal imaging devices. So I poured in the correct amount of water and ate it cold. If I hadn't eaten in two weeks, it probably would have tasted pretty good. Dessert was two Hershey's chocolate bars. I cleaned up and undressed and scooted into the sleeping bag, and I shivered until the down bag eventually warmed me up.

In the darkness I reached out with my right hand, touched a sheet of plastic. Underneath the plastic were a flashlight and my 9mm Beretta. I was all set. I settled in and looked up through the tree branches, saw a couple of stars, and fell asleep.

I awoke with the daylight, at about 7:15 A.M. I got out of my bag, stretched, made a temporary latrine about fifty feet away, and went back to my little campsite. Breakfast was water and a couple of granola bars. I brushed my teeth, then got my gear wrapped up and hidden at the base of a tree trunk that had lots of gaps and holes. Dressed and geared up once again, I went back to the stone wall and settled in again.

Some voices from the house. Television, radio, or real guys?

Couldn't tell.

The sun was shining right into the upstairs bathroom window, so I couldn't tell if anyone was showering or not. Not that I was curious in that sort of way, but if I saw a bearded guy showering, at least I would know the firm count of men in the house was at least two.

The morning dragged on. Ants walked over my hand. At some point a fat woodchuck waddled right by me, about ten feet away. I should have felt tired, bored, or weary, but no, I was doing okay. Watching that house and waiting to see if Curt Chesak was really there or not was like having a giant dry-cell battery nearby, feeding me energy. I felt like General U. S. Grant, feeling feisty and like I could wait here all fall and winter if I had to.

On my back I had a Camelbak hydration pack for water, and I sipped during the morning and kept myself hydrated.

Then it got very interesting, very quickly, when two men with shotguns appeared.

They came from my left, moving slowly, about twenty feet apart. I saw them out of the corner of my eye, and if it was possible to freeze even more, that's what I did. I saw their weapons first, pump-action shotguns, held out, barrels moving left and right as the two men scanned the area in front of them.

I tried not even to blink.

They came closer. They were wearing blaze orange vests, hats, and camouflage pants. Hunting licenses dangled from safety pins on their vests. Both men were heavyset and bearded.

Hunters.

Shotguns.

I don't hunt, but I have no problem with those who do. My only problem was that they were following the stone wall, and in about sixty seconds or so the closest one was going to get one hell of a surprise when he stepped on my back.

Damn.

I held my breath.

They got closer.

I could smell wood smoke coming from them.

A voice. "Hey, Darryl?"

"Yeah?"

"Take a break?"

"Sure, why the hell not."

They stopped and lowered their shotguns. Both checked to make sure the safeties were on—thanks, guys!—and leaned the shotguns up against two adjacent oak trees. They both sat down on the stone wall, stretched out their legs in the leaves.

"George, where the hell is this meadow you've been saying?"

"Another twenty minutes, thirty tops. We just follow this stone wall, get past this place, and we'll be there 'fore you know it."

"That's what you said a half hour ago. Only a half hour left to go."

"Yeah, well, I don't think the pheasant will mind, so lighten the hell up, Darryl, okay?"

A few more murmurs of voices, a plastic water bottle passed between them, two cigarettes lit up. They both used lighters and took deep drags from their cigarettes. They talked low for a while—I caught bits and pieces of conversation about mortgage payments, the upcoming presidential election, and wives—and then the one called Darryl raised his voice some and said, "So, how's it going with you and Marcia?"

No answer.

Darryl said, "C'mon, George, if you can't tell your brother, who can you tell?"

"Shit," George said. "It's like this, I know she's going through becoming a teenager and all that, but it's driving me freaking crazy. The other night, I came home from work and she wanted to talk to me about green energy and how I was contributing to the destruction of the planet 'cause I was workin' at the mill. You know, all I wanted to do was to kick back and have a beer, watch some ESPN, but Margaret tells me I need to pay more attention to her, with all the hormones kickin' in and shit. So I tried to be polite and say, well, green energy sounds cool and stuff, but that's down the road, and right now we got bills to pay, and the mill's the best place around here for a guy like me to get work."

The other man said, "Sounds reasonable."

A heavy sigh. "Christ, at her age, I don't think Marcia knows how to spell 'reasonable.' So she said if I was right sure the planet was important, I'd make sacrifices now to help save energy and stuff, prevent climate change and global warming, and I said okay, if you want to start saving energy, let's get rid of the TV in your room, your hair dryer, and your damn cell phone, you can start tonight if that's so important to you, and then she started getting teary-eyed and said I was making fun of her, and I was part of something called the patriarchal oligarchy, and it wasn't fair that her class should be called on to sacrifice first, and then she stormed upstairs and wouldn't come down for dinner, and Margaret got all pissed at me for getting Marcia all wound up, and crap, all I wanted was a beer and some ESPN."

Another heavy sigh. "What the hell is an oligarchy anyway?"

Another brief wait, and his brother said, "Christ, I'm sorry I asked."

When their break was over, they stripped their cigarette butts to make sure there were no leftover embers to start a fire—again, good job, guys!—and then one went to retrieve his shotgun, and the other said, "Hold on, gotta take care of business here."

He traipsed over a few yards, stopped about two feet away from my shoulder, and in a very few seconds something liquid started splashing against my back. I closed my eyes, gritted my teeth. The little shower seemed to go on for a long time, and there was a grunt of relief. "Man, that second cup of coffee was killing me," George said. "Thought for sure my damn bladder was going to explode."

"Good for you," Darryl said.

*Yeah*, I thought. *Good for you. Now get the hell out.*

Darryl retrieved his shotgun, and he and his brother started talking and walking.

On George's first step, a bolt of pain hammered my left ankle.

"Shit!"

George took a tumble into the leaves and I bit my lower lip to keep from crying out. The damn guy had just stepped on my ankle and fallen.

Darryl said, "You okay?"

"Shit, yes, but damn it, what the hell did I trip on?"

I bit my lower lip even harder. Trembled. I didn't dare move my head. I just bit and held my breath and waited.

"I don't know," Darryl said. "Could be a rock or a limb underneath all those leaves."

"Cripes, I guess so. Hey, give me a hand up, will you?"

"Okay."

Some more words were exchanged and then their voices drifted off.

I relaxed some, let out a breath of air. My lower lip ached, as did my left ankle.

And I stunk like a urinal.

Lunch was two more Granola bars, two more Hershey bars, and some lukewarm water from my Camelbak. My lip eventually improved, but my ankle ached like the proverbial son-of-a-bitch. Later in the day, I heard the hollow *boom-boom* of shotguns being fired, and I hoped the two brothers were having a better day than I was.

Meanwhile, all was quiet at the house, which still hadn't told me whether or not it was Curt Chesak's rural fortress of solitude.

So I waited. And smelled. And ached.

In the afternoon it got warm and despite my adventures of the morning, I started feeling sleepy as the fall sun beat down on me and my little hiding place, and the heavy weight of my ghillie suit on me. I yawned a couple of times, and then I dozed off for a few seconds, and then jerked up when I realized I was drifting off. I tried spraying my face with my Camelbak water, but it was too warm to jolt me awake. I stretched and bent and bit my lip again, and I felt like I was losing the battle, that nothing was going to prevent me from falling asleep.

Until I heard the sound of an approaching engine.

It grew louder and louder, and the way the engine was thrumming, I knew exactly what was coming my way.

A helicopter.

I slightly turned my head and I saw a shadow flash overhead. It went over the house and then came back, a standard four-passenger dark blue

Bell helicopter. Old memories came to me of helicopters, none of them particularly pleasant. The helicopter slowly came down, and I had to admire the pilot's skill as he placed his machine square in the middle of the H painted onto the concrete.

Then the rear door to the house opened up, and a smiling Curt Chesak strolled out.

My hands quivered some as I watched him come out. I had no trouble recognizing him, since I'd had a personal interview with him just a couple of weeks before. He was carrying a black overnight bag and was with another guy who seemed older, and who was speaking loudly to Curt as the two of them approached the helicopter.

My Beretta was in my right hand, the binoculars in my left.

Damn, not a good shot, not a good shot at all.

I should have brought a rifle. Even one without a telescopic sight and with only open iron sights, it would have been an easy shot to nail him in the chest with no difficulty at all.

But all I had was the Beretta and a couple of other things that wouldn't do.

Damn, damn, I thought. Why didn't you bring a rifle? Why not?

And it sickened me to acknowledge, but a dark and angry part of me knew why I only had a pistol: because I wanted Curt to get a good look at me and know exactly why he was about to be killed. A rifle shot from fifty yards away wouldn't do that. Oh, the ultimate goal would be achieved, but I wouldn't be as satisfied.

The two men got closer to the helicopter, ducked low to avoid the spinning blades.

Damn, damn, damn.

Because of my pride and vanity, my one chance to get the son-of-a-bitch was fading away, for within seconds he'd be at the now-open door to the helicopter's cabin, and he'd be gone.

Damn.

And how would I feel, and what could I say to Lawrence Thomas when that happened? That Curt had gotten clean away because of my arrogance?

For the first time in a while, I felt I had lost it all.

The two men got to the helicopter. Chesak tossed in the overnight bag, shook the hand of the older man, who then climbed into the cabin.

Chesak stepped back. Closed the door. Waved.

Moved back, head still low.

The engine noise increased, the helicopter lifted up and back, and then it was gone.

By then, Curt was back inside the house.

I let my breath out. Didn't even realize I'd been holding my breath.

I lowered my Beretta, took a swig of water. That had been too damn close.

So, what now? Chase after Chesak right now, surprise him as he's settling back in?

Yeah, right.

There was Curt, and the guy I had spotted the night before taking a shower.

Didn't mean there were only two of them in there.

Oh, I was sure there weren't thirty or anything, but that didn't mean I was about to embark on a suicide mission.

Not yet, anyway.

So I settled in, waited some more.

The afternoon dragged on. At one point I slowly moved away and used a convenient tree to urinate against, almost laughing at the thought that at least I wasn't pissing against some guy pretending to be a tree trunk. I ate another granola bar, took a couple of Ibuprofen for my aching ankle, and slowly crawled back to my hiding place and let the afternoon drag away. A couple of times I heard something rustling in the leaves about me, but I never did see anything, which wasn't surprising. A squirrel at play in the woods can sound like a coyote trotting up to you if you let your mind get away from you, and I was desperately trying not to let that happen.

The house was quiet again.

What could they be doing in there? Playing cribbage? Working the controls on some sort of video game? Surfing the Web for snuff videos? Discussing tips and techniques on how to kill people?

I yawned a couple more times. It was getting cooler. I was running plans and options through my head, wondering how much longer I could stay out here. I had food and water for a few days, and reasonable sleeping accommodations, and enough firepower to hopefully get the job done when the time came, but what I was missing was vital: good intelligence.

What I did know was important enough, but I still didn't know how many were in there, if they were walking around armed, and what the interior of the house looked like. I could burst in right now, filled with fury and the confidence that I was doing God's work in settling justice, but that wouldn't be worth anything if I ended up in a laundry room on the first floor, a bullet through my forehead.

I stretched out my legs.

The sun was starting to set. Lights came on inside the house.

The rear door opened up.

Someone stepped out.

Chesak?

I focused my binoculars. The man stepped out into the yard, stopped, stretched his arms like he was taking a break.

With the binoculars, I could easily make out his face.

It wasn't Curt Chesak.

It was Heywood Knowlton, history professor at Boston University.

# CHAPTER TWENTY-THREE

I kept my view on him. He walked slowly and randomly, his head bent down like he was in serious thought mode. He had on a light-tan jacket but no hat, and I imagined his bald head was quite cold. His moustacheless beard seemed more scraggly than before.

He stepped closer. I quietly moved to the left. There were a couple of low evergreen trees between the two of us.

I didn't hesitate.

I went over the stone wall, got into a crouch. I ran across the finely mowed rear yard, just as Knowlton had turned—head down, still apparently deep in thought—and I got him from the rear. Even though I'd been on the debate team in high school, I plowed into him like an angry NFL linebacker paying for two alimonies. I stayed on top of him as he fell, making sure I had a hand on the back of his neck, to push his face into the grass.

He let out an "oomph!" but that's all I was going to allow. I dug the muzzle end of my Beretta into his right ear, and into his left I said, "Not a damn sound. Not a peep. You call for help, they'll be coming out to help a corpse. Got it? Nod your head."

He nodded his head.

"Put your arms out where I can see them," I said.

The professor stretched out his arms.

"We're going for a walk in the woods. Move with me. You say a word, you resist, you try to run away, trust me, Professor Knowlton, you'll be a dead man."

He got up, legs trembling, and he let me propel him back across the lawn, over the stone wall, and into the woods. I grabbed my little bag as we went past, and I was very pleased that he had carefully listened to every word I had said.

Almost restored my faith in higher education.

Near my campsite I tied his arms together at the elbows, an uncomfortable position and one that was almost impossible to wiggle out of. I sat him down against a pine trunk and got a small flashlight, and I stood across from him, stripped off my ghillie suit. It felt good to be free. I sat down on a small rock, flashlight and pistol in hand.

"Well, professor, didn't philosopher John Dewey say the most effective way of learning was to have a great teacher sitting on the end of a log, with an eager student on the other?" I motioned with my Beretta. "Plenty of logs out there in the forest, but I think we'll make do."

He seemed to catch his breath, find his voice. "You . . . you . . . I know you. Shit. Yes. Cole. Right? The magazine writer who came into my office a few days ago."

"A gold star for the teacher. Hey, gold stars. Was that another idea from John Dewey?"

"Dewey was overrated."

"Maybe so, but he lived to be in his nineties and probably died in his own bed. If you want to do the same, start talking to me."

"Go to hell. I don't have anything to say to you."

I went over, slapped him twice—hard—across his face. I stood over him. "Whatever ivory tower you live in, professor, is a long, long way from here. So let's start with the basics. How many are in the house now?"

He coughed, cleared his throat. "Three."

I slapped him again. "How many?"

"Three."

Another hard slap that pushed him to the ground. "Jesus! Stop that, all right? There's only three in the house."

Breathing hard, I sat back on my rock. "Curt Chesak and who else?"

"Two minders."

"Their names."

"One is Corey. The other is Brad."

"Which one is the blonde?"

"Corey. Jesus, Cole, what the hell is this all about?"

"I'm after Curt Chesak. Remember? He nearly killed a friend of mine."

Knowlton spat out some saliva. "A friend? You're doing this for a friend?"

"Yep." I lifted my Beretta so he could take a good look at it in the dying light. "What are the three of them doing right now?"

"Cole . . . you don't know who you're messing with."

"And neither do they. I don't have much time. Answer my questions, fully and quickly, or I'm going to hurt your knees. It won't kill you, but you'll be in pain and walk with canes for the rest of your life."

His breathing quickened. "A friend . . . not even a family member . . . a friend. . . ."

"You should try it sometime. Now. The rear door you came out of. Is it locked?"

"No."

"You sure?"

"Christ, yes, I'm sure!"

"The three in the house. What are they doing at this minute?"

"Corey's in the kitchen. Getting dinner ready. Brad's in the living room next to the kitchen, playing Halo or some damn thing. There's an office upstairs. Last I knew, Curt was there, checking e-mail or porn, I don't know."

We spent another minute or two, discussing the layout of the house, and then I stood up. Time was slipping away like ice melting in my fingers. "Here's how it's going to be. You stay put for at least the next half hour. Do anything else, and I'll hurt you. Either now or later. After the half hour is gone, do what you want."

"How the hell am I supposed to know when thirty minutes have passed?"

"You're an educated man, figure it out," I said. Then I looked down at him and said, "What happened to you? And why did your house get burned down?"

He shivered. "I had screwed up. After the demonstration at the power plant, I was supposed to drop out of sight, so the cops and you and anybody else couldn't question me, couldn't keep Curt's name in the papers. But I didn't want to leave campus . . . and they punished me. Now, I'm stuck with them until things cool down."

"Then what? Go back to being a tenured revolutionary?"

"Going back to school, being a resource and advocate for true change." His voice grew defiant. "And don't bother asking me who Curt works for or who pays him! You won't get that out of me!"

I holstered my Beretta. "News flash, professor. I don't care."

I was now at the stone wall, ghillie suit still off, equipment bag in hand. I quickly got to work. I was sure the three over there were expecting the not-so-good professor to return for dinner at any moment. I had on plain black sneakers, green fatigues, black wool watch cap on my head, light amber shooting glasses, light black leather gloves. I had adjusted my leather Bianchi holster so my 9mm was across my chest for easy access. On my left arm I had put four lengths of sticky gray duct tape. At my belt was another weapon, and an open net bag for a few other items.

I suppose I should have said a prayer or a word or something, but I had no time.

I went over the stone wall and started running to the house.

In a matter of seconds, I was at the rear door.

It opened up easily enough.

There was an entryway and pantry, and I went through there quickly. No time for sneaking or stealth. The men in the house were expecting someone coming back, a snotty professor full of himself and his thoughts.

Into a wide kitchen. Warm and the smell of beef being sautéed. Pots and pans hanging from ceiling beams. Open door to the left. Big island counter in the center. Man at the right, stirring something in a Calphalon pot over a huge gas stove. Not looking over. Pistol on his hip. Jeans, sweatshirt, short blond hair. He said, "Jesus effin' Christ, Heywood, what took you so long?"

A matter of steps. He was big, he was smart, and he moved whip-fast when he realized that I wasn't Knowlton.

But it was too late for him. When I got into the kitchen, my right hand went into the open net bag, came out with a black instrument the size of a large TV remote, an Acadiana stun gun, gotten the other day from Felix. I clicked it on and by the time Corey swung to the right and was reaching for his pistol, I shoved the stun gun into his ribs and pulled the trigger.

He grunted, arched his back, and fell to the tiled floor. On the ground, I nailed him again. Another spasm, and fortune favored me, because he rolled to his side. Back into my cloth bag, out with two plastic Flex-Cufs. I slipped one over his arms, drew it tight, did the same for his ankles. I tore off one of the duct tape strips, slapped it over his face. I looked to the left, through the opening. Noted windows, ornate door leading outside, assorted couches and chairs, and loud sounds of things being blown up.

"Hey, Corey!" a voice said. "You drop something in there?"

I grabbed his bound ankles, dragged him across the tile floor, made sure he was hidden behind the center island. I moved around and yelled out, "Yo! Brad! C'mere!"

On the other side of the island, I stood up, waited by the open door. Brad came through; he was wide and big, legs like tree trunks, wearing jeans and a tight red T-shirt. He moved faster than Corey when he realized something was wrong in the kitchen, and even without spotting me, he spun and flashed out with a long arm and heavy fist. He caught me on the side of the head, knocking me into the wall, but I managed to stun him on his arm. He swore and fell back, rubbing his arm, shaking it, and I pushed myself off the wall and went at him. He swung again and I ducked down, slipped and fell on my knees.

My knees hurt like hell.

I gasped from the pain.

But I slammed my right arm up, stun gun still held firmly, and caught him in his flat belly.

He cried out, sank to his knees. I got up, woozy and light-headed. I jolted him in his ribs, his hands and arms drawn up, and he collapsed. He tried to struggle as I Flex-Cuffed and gagged him, but in a couple of minutes he was on the floor, near his companion.

I went to the stove, turned the flames off. I was sweating and breathing hard, and my knees and head ached, but there was no turning back.

I was committed.

I put the stun gun away.

The 9mm Beretta was now in my hand.

I went hunting.

The living room was clear. Bookcases, bar, some old landscape paintings, fireplace, and large screen television, showing some imaginative alien landscape, frozen in motion, sound still blaring. On the other side of the room was a wide staircase, leading upstairs. I took a series of deep breaths, went to the staircase, and stayed to the left, moving as fast and as quietly as I could.

I went upstairs at a light trot, keeping to the left side of the stairs. My Beretta was held out in the approved two-handed combat stance. Top of the stairs.

I moved left, to the office that Knowlton had mentioned.

Wide wooden desk. Computer and monitor. More bookcases. Long draperies.

It was empty.

Damn.

Whirled around, sped down the hallway, past one open bedroom, bathroom, and—

To the right. Closed door. Sound of movement inside. I leaned over, twisted the doorknob, kicked the door open.

Curt Chesak, standing by a bed. Hair wet. Fresh out of a shower. Fully dressed, bulky black turtleneck sweater, khaki pants.

Pistol and waist holster on the bed in front of him.

"Hey," I said.

He laughed. "The avenging angel has arrived. Creaky knees and all."

"Knees are hanging in there. You know who I am, don't you."

"Christ, yes."

"And you know why I'm here."

"Oh, spare me. You don't have the balls."

"You killed a college student, nearly killed my best friend, and have raised all sorts of hate and discontent. That's all I need."

He shrugged, grinning. "What can I say? Born to be bad, I guess. You know, Lewis—"

"Shut up."

It all happened so very, very fast. He was good. He leaped to the bed and I saw it all in my mind's eye: Curt grabbing the pistol, rolling to the floor, moving up, weapon in hand, spraying all twelve rounds in my direction.

Gunfire broke out, loud and ear-shattering.

Curt looked very surprised.

I shot him once, twice, and then three times in the chest. He fell back against the near white plaster wall, eyes stunned.

Some, I suppose, would have felt a sense of triumph, or closing the circle, or getting the job done. But I didn't have the luxury to wait around and figure everything out. I didn't wait.

I reached down, picked up my three empty and warm cartridge casings, and got the hell out of there.

I was halfway down the stairs when something loud and hard hammered my right leg, and I tumbled down to the first floor.

It felt like my right leg had been torn off at the thigh, rotated, and pushed back against my hip. The pain made me gasp. I ended up in a tumble on the floor. I moaned long and loud. The smell of burnt gunpowder was strong. I crawled, turned, and sat myself up without screaming. A pretty damn good accomplishment.

Up on the top of the stairs, Curt Chesak looked down at me, eyes ablaze, weaving back and forth, a pistol in his hand.

He tore at the front of his black turtleneck, revealing a Kevlar vest wrapped about his torso.

"Son of a whore. . . ." he gasped. "You think I've gotten . . . this far . . . without . . . precautions. . . ."

He fired again. I closed my eyes, flinched.

He had missed.

I started moving back, using my hands, scooting on my butt. My right leg felt as hot as molten lead and about as useful. I couldn't find my Beretta. He took one step, and another.

"Broke a shitload of ribs . . . you did. . . ." he gasped again. "But . . . I'll still walk . . . out of here . . . alive. . . ."

The living room. Moved toward the living room. Front door. Looked as big as a barn door, but I had to get outside. Had to.

He stumbled on the stairs, caught himself with his free hand on the banister. He let out a groan and fired at me again.

This round blasted through a window.

I came upon a coffee table. Wedged myself up using both of my arms and my good leg. I tried to forget my right leg. Tried to forget the roaring pain. The grayness of what I was seeing. I got up on my left leg, started hopping, dragging, gritting my teeth. Looked back. Saw a stream of shockingly bright red blood behind me. Wondered foolishly how so much blood got there in such a quick time.

"Cole!"

A couch in front of me.

I rolled over the back of the couch as another shot ripped out, striking my left foot. I screamed again as my right leg hit the back of the couch, then the cushions, and then the floor.

Music was still playing from the television. I was on the floor. The front door seemed even bigger but looked to be a mile away. I was in front of a fireplace. I dragged myself over to the front of the fireplace.

I heard a whimpered squeal from behind me, and then the same noise again, deeper.

My chest was pounding, I was panting, and everything about me grayed in and out.

Up at the fireplace, I grabbed a poker, flipped around. I didn't faint from the pain.

A quick and good moment.

Curt Chesak staggered around the couch I had just flipped over. My blood was smeared on the couch and its cushions.

He stood still, weaving. "All this . . . this . . . for a kid you didn't even know . . . and a dyke who's a vegetable? For real? Christ. . . ."

I held the poker out. He laughed. "Last stand . . . of a good man . . . hmm? You got hit in the thigh, Cole . . . I could stand here . . . and just watch you . . . bleed out. . . ."

My hand wavered. It seemed like the poker was getting heavier with each slippery second passing by.

He grinned. It was one damn scary look. Shadows seemed to move.

Curt raised his pistol. "So . . . close . . . your eyes . . . if you please. . . ."

I spat at him. "To hell with you."

His grin grew wider.

The pistol was now level with his eyes.

He stared down at me.

Stared.

Gasped.

Sighed.

His arm fell to his side, his pistol clattering to the floor.

From one moment to the next, his face turned the color of an old T-shirt.

Then he collapsed.

Revealing a short dark-skinned man standing behind him, wearing a black jumpsuit.

Suraj Gurung. The Royal Gurkha Rifleman who worked now as a driver for Lawrence Todd Thomas, late of the CIA.

In his left hand he held the wicked sharp curved knife called a kukri, which was dripping blood.

## CHAPTER TWENTY-FOUR

He put the knife in a scabbard at his side, came to me quickly, knelt down. "Are there any others in the house, Mister Cole?"

"Just the two in the kitchen."

A quick nod. "We have already met."

"How . . . he had a Kevlar vest on. How did you get him?"

"I saw his shape from the rear. I severed his spine, just below the vest. Quite simple, it was."

He had a small knapsack on his back, which he shrugged off. "You are bleeding profusely, Mister Cole."

"Getting shot tends to do that."

From the knapsack he took out a medical kit, some bandages and compresses. He had a small pair of scissors, which he used to quickly split open my pants leg. He expertly went to work, tied off something on my thigh, and said, "I have arrived here in time, luckily, is this true?"

"Quite true," I said. "How in hell did you find me?"

His smile was wide and white. "Mister Lawrence, he is a very wise man, is he not?"

I remembered the super-duper spy cell phone he had given me back in Virginia. A phone that no doubted carried a tracking device.

"A very wise man. How long have you been following me?"

His hands worked quite fast on my leg. "Long enough. I was in the woods with you, watching you watching the house. I even saw those two huntsmen make water upon your back. You did very well, not moving."

"Didn't have a choice."

"Do any of us?"

He sat back, as if to admire his job. "Excuse me for a bit, I have something to do. Please close your eyes and relax. I will be back most presently."

I sat up against the fireplace, took his advice, gritted my teeth. I think I passed out, because it seemed like Suraj was back within seconds, kneeling in front of me. "I have a quandary," he said, his voice concerned.

"Tell me what it is," I said.

"Mister Lawrence, he told me that I was to follow you, to make sure the job was done, to bring back proof and to ensure you are not harmed. But, alas, you are harmed. And I am concerned to move you. If I do so, the bleeding will no doubt resume and put you in deadly peril. But if I were to call for medical assistance and stay with you, then I cannot complete my task. So it seems—"

I interrupted him. "Get out, then. Get out and when you're far enough away, make the call."

He nodded. "Is that fair to you?"

"Very fair. But will you do me a favor?"

"But of course. I will be honored."

I pointed to the other side of the house. "In the woods back there, you'll probably find a man with a beard, arms tied up, wandering through the woods. If you find him, set him free. Don't harm him. Just free him."

A pleasant nod. "It will be done." He went back to his kit. "I have morphine."

"Will it put me to sleep?"

"Most likely."

"Then I'll tough it out. I have a task to complete as well."

Such a wide smile. "I cannot imagine what."

"Then don't worry. And get moving."

He gently touched my shoulder, said, "Go with God, Mister Cole," and then he stepped back. He picked up a heavy green trash bag, bulging at the bottom.

And the shadows moved, and he was gone.

I waited and waited, caught my breath, and I pushed myself up. Grimaced. The pain seemed to roar right up my right leg to my gut and chest and to the back of my head. I went through the living room, to a door that led—I hoped—to the garage. It opened up easily enough. I took another deep breath. I fumbled with my right hand, found a light switch.

Lit up the place.

I looked around.

There.

A gas can, next to a riding lawnmower.

I hopped over, gritting my teeth even more, grabbed the gas can and managed to do so without falling over. Back into the living room. To the drapes by the other side of the room. I tugged and tugged and they came free. They fell to the floor, and to my surprise and delight, I found my Beretta. The both of us had gone through a lot, and I hated the thought of losing it. I picked it up, tried twice to put it back in my holster, missed each time.

Time. Running out of time.

I slipped the pistol into my waistband. Picked up the gas can again. Kicked the drapes against the wall. I opened up the gas can, tipped it over with my foot. The stench of gasoline came quickly to my nostrils as the gasoline burbled out over the carpet and to the drapes.

I tore off my gloves, put them in the pile as well, along with the remaining tape on my arm, the stun gun, and my equipment bag.

Back to the fireplace, picked up a box of matches. Sweat was running down my back. I took my handkerchief out, opened the door. And stepped outside into the blessedly cool and free air.

I turned and started lighting off the matches. One, two, three. Each time I lit the match I tossed it into the living room

They all sputtered out.

Sirens were sounding off in the distance.

Another match flared, flew to the living room, where it fell at the right place. Flames rolled and roared up, and I took the box of matches and tossed it into the now-roaring flames.

I slowly and carefully backed away, and the last thing I saw was the body of Curt Chesak, on the floor, arms at its side.

With no head.

Outside, I walked as far as I could from the house. There was a large boulder to the right of the driveway, and I sat down. I took my Beretta out of my waistband and dropped it to the grass. I tried my very best not to move my right leg. From one of my pockets, I took out a small flashlight, lit up the surroundings. My Beretta was there. I aimed the flashlight at my left foot, which was tingling. I moved my foot about. Nothing seemed to hurt, nothing seemed to be bleeding. I twisted my foot about, saw the heel of my torn sneaker. Lucky shot for me, not so lucky shot for Curt Chesak.

Over at the house, the interior was a bubbling orange, and then a near window shattered, and there was a *whoosh* and roar as oxygen rushed in to feed the fire. The flames bulged out and up and spread up the near walls. Something morose seemed to settle around my spirit, thinking once again of my poor house back in Tyler Beach, seeing once again the flames dancing around the place that had been my home for years.

I suppose I should have also felt something profound at that moment. Of justice being served. Of a debt being paid. Of Diane Woods, in a coma miles away, who'd never have to fear this man ever again.

Instead, my right leg was hurting so much that I gasped every few minutes. I was cold. My hands were shaking. And I had a desperate need to urinate.

Nothing profound, but damn true.

Sirens were louder.

I looked down the driveway. Red and blue lights led up the far trees, and I saw headlights approach. I held my arms out, and waited.

As chance would have it, Officer Templar was the first on the scene. He came up to me, flashlight in hand, and I said "I'm unarmed, but I'm shot. Right leg. I also have a pistol on the ground in front of me. It's on safe."

"I'll be damned . . . Cole, the writer?"

"The same."

"What the hell's going on here?"

"Wish I could say."

Two fire engines came up the driveway, and I felt better seeing an ambulance from the Osgood Volunteer Ambulance Squad bring up the rear.

Part of the house's roof collapsed in a shower of flame, smoke, and sparks.

Less than a half hour later, I was in an emergency room bay at the famed Dartmouth-Hitchcock Medical Center in Lebanon, New Hampshire. Surgeons and nurses fussed and worked over my wounded leg.

By then I had drugs going into my system and the ache of my right leg seemed to lift right up, like a lake mist, and then I was told I was going to surgery, and that seemed very fine to me.

I woke up here and there, sipping some water and beef broth from very helpful and beautiful nurses who took good care of me, and I was once led around my hospital room to do something important, like pee in a bottle, and when I finally woke up for real, one arm had an IV tube running into it and my other arm was handcuffed to my bed.

Interesting combination.

I peered down at my right leg. Heavily bandaged and suspended in air.

Lay back down in bed. Tried to relax, and by damn, I did fall asleep.

Again I woke up, and a young nurse in scrubs with fine blond hair bustled around, checking my vitals, checking my bandages, and she gave me a bed bath and apologized in advance for assaulting whatever was left of my dignity, and, remembering the scores of times I had been in the hospital before, I just smiled and let her do her work.

A tall surgeon with big hands and small, laughing eyes came in and gave me a thorough medical debrief of my gunshot wound, explained the surgery, and said in a hopeful tone that major arteries and tendons had been missed, and while the leg would ache like the proverbial son-of-a-bitch on occasion in the future, I should have a relatively clean recovery.

He shut his clipboard and glanced down at my handcuffed wrist. "Medically speaking, you're going to be in fine shape, Mister Cole. As to legally speaking . . . I'm afraid I can't help you there."

"Not a problem. I appreciate what you and everyone else have done."

He looked back at the door. "There's someone here to see you from the State Police. I've been asked to let him in if I think you're ready to be questioned. But if you'd like to take another day or two off. . . ."

I shook my head. "Go ahead, let him in. I don't mind."

The doctor nodded. "Very well. I'll see you again later tonight."

He left and a minute later, Detective Pete Renzi came in, not looking particularly happy as he closed the door behind him.

Renzi scraped a chair over, sat down. He looked very much like a man trying to keep things under control. I kept my face as bland as possible, looking right back at him.

Then he lost it.

"You stupid damn fool! You didn't goddamn listen to me, did you! Went out bumbling on your own, got a bullet in your leg, probably damn near got killed after I had warned you . . . and what happened in Osgood is not only the lead goddamn story in every newspaper and television station in New England, it's even made the friggin' *New York Times* and all the major networks!"

He paused, face red, breathing hard. I moved some, the handcuff rattling on my bed railing.

"Gee, dear," I said. "We never talk anymore."

I didn't think Renzi was the kind of guy to slap a handcuffed patient, but he sure looked tempted. "Let me tell you what we got going on in Osgood, okay?"

"Sure. I'm not going anywhere."

And I rattled the handcuff once more for emphasis.

He leaned forward. "You want to know why? I've got you, with a bullet in your leg. You were found about fifty feet away from a remote luxury home that was burning to the ground when police and fire units got there. State fire marshal's office quickly determined the cause of the fire was arson. And when we poked through the ruins, we found three bodies. All male. All missing their heads. Care to say anything about that, Lewis?"

"Not at the moment."

"I didn't think so. Plus there's the fact that your own house burned down a few days ago, also by arson. Hell of a coincidence, don't you think?"

I rattled the handcuff again. "They happen, don't they."

"In my line of work, we hate coincidences."

"Sorry to hear that."

"We'll see just how sorry you can be, Lewis."

I moved some in my hospital bed, thrilled I could move without a bolt of pain searing its way up my leg like lightning.

"Go ahead."

"Here's the deal. Not open to negotiation."

"Gee, I love it already," I said.

"Look, you've managed to skate through a number of things over the years because of your relationship with Detective Woods. That's understandable. But she's still in a coma, and she's not in a position to help you. Nobody can help you."

"Except for you, right?"

"Right now I'm your best friend, Lewis. So the deal is, tell me what the hell you were doing up there, who those people are, and what the hell happened. Tell me and I'll be on your side. I'll do what I can to protect you, and I'll do what I can with the Attorney General's office."

I rattled the handcuff again.

"Am I under arrest?"

"Depends on what you say."

"Then I can't say anything else, Detective."

He sighed, stood up, and officially put me under arrest, using the standard Miranda warning.

"What charges, then?" I asked.

"Arson, for one. Three homicides, for another, if we're lucky."

"Won't stick."

He gave me a sly smile. "Sorry, Lewis. You're not in Wentworth County any more. Here, you've put Grafton County in a bad spot, you were found next to the destruction of one of the oldest and finest homes in Osgood, and three burned bodies without heads tends to get people's attention. Not particularly something that a judge will let you out on bail for. I got a strong feeling they're going to go hardcore on your ass."

"I suppose I'll just have to do my best," I said. "Is this when I get my sole phone call?"

He took out his cell phone, switched it on, and passed it over to me. "I'll be right back."

I dialed a number from memory, back when a special woman resided in Boston, and left a detailed message with the young man who answered. Then after I said good-bye, Detective Renzi came back into my room, held out his hand.

"You got your call," he said. "Let's have the phone."

"How about another phone call?"

He took the phone away. "State says you get one, and you just got it. And in case you think about breaking free and shuffling away, there's going to be a state trooper sitting outside your room."

"Didn't expect anything else."

"Glad to hear it."

Later that night, the same nurse as before with the colorful scrubs and the fine blond hair came in to help me with dinner. Her name was Lynn. My meal was sliced turkey with gravy, stuffing, and mashed potatoes, and she helped me cut up my food so I could eat it with one hand. When I was done, she came back and helped me clean up and looked at my empty plate.

"Looks like you have one heck of an appetite."

"If you knew what I had been eating the past couple of days, you wouldn't be surprised."

"Really?"

"Helpful hint," I said. "Gourmet freeze-dried food isn't."

She laughed and said, "You know, you don't look like a dangerous criminal."

"Really, I'm not," I said. "I'm quite gentle."

"So what are you being charged with?" Lynn asked, picking up my dinner tray.

"Trespassing with evil intent, I think."

That got me a cheerful laugh, and I said: "Ask a favor?"

"As long as it's not a handcuff key or a file."

"My room phone is dead. I'm sure the State Police had something to do with it. Could you call somebody for me?"

She shifted the tray, seemed reluctant. "Just a friend," I added. "She's in a coma in Exonia Hospital, and I just wanted to check on her condition."

She bit her lower lip, said, "Give me a sec."

Lynn went out and came back with a pen and notepad. I gave her Kara Miles's name and phone number, and she left. Five minutes later, she came back and said: "Your friend Kara says it was good to hear from you, she hopes you get out soon, and nothing's changed with Diane."

I nodded. "Thanks. I appreciate it."

Another smile. "Glad to help a prisoner of society."

After she left, I settled into my bed, winced just a bit, and checked my television. The listings for the evening included "It's the Great Pumpkin, Charlie Brown," and I saw that as a good sign.

# CHAPTER TWENTY-FIVE

The next morning at about 11 A.M., my little hospital room was fairly crowded. In addition to myself, there was Detective Pete Renzi; a fierce-looking young woman in a dark gray power suit, who was an assistant attorney general for the State of New Hampshire; a tall balding man with black robes, who was District Court Judge Jaden Bobbett; and Raymond Drake, an attorney from Boston, who was my representation. Drake was wearing a well-cut suit that was probably worth more than my entire wardrobe—or what was left of it—and he was definitely the most unpopular man in the room.

For one thing, he was a lawyer—insert your own lawyer joke here—and for his second strike, he was a defense attorney, and for his third strike, he was from the dreaded People's Republic of Massachusetts. Even though he had been admitted to the New Hampshire Bar, he was still considered an outsider by Renzi, Judge Bobbett, and the assistant attorney general.

Still, he was *my* outsider. Some years ago, while practicing in Boston, he had come up against someone who was a business associate of Felix Tinios, and a disagreement arose. Drake was used to settling disputes in well-lit courtrooms with rows of benches and comfortable chairs, but his opponent was more inclined to see things in black and white. Long story short, Drake found himself on the proverbial one-way trip out to Boston Harbor, wrapped in chains in the back of a cabin cruiser, when Felix had intervened and saved him.

Ever since then, he's been in Felix's debt, and has always helped for free when the time came.

Like now.

The assistant AG, with a severely cut blond hairstyle and wearing black-rimmed glasses, got right to it. "Your Honor, in this matter, the people are seeking a remand for Mister Cole. He is linked to an arson that destroyed a home worth nearly a million dollars that was of great historical importance to the town of Osgood, and we believe he will soon be linked to the matter of three male homicide victims who were later found in the debris."

Drake smiled. His skin was always permanently tanned, and he wore gold rings and jewelry on both wrists. His gray hair was finely cut and trimmed, and his blue eyes seemed bright with the thought of going to battle on my behalf.

"Your Honor, if I may, I've gone over the preliminary paperwork, and it seems that traces of gasoline were found on Mister Cole's pants cuff and one of his sneakers," he said in a calm voice that sounded like it belonged on NPR. "The state fire marshal's office has also determined that an 'accelerant' was used to start the fire in question in Osgood. Now, the way I see it, the only connection between Mister Cole and the fire is that in both cases, hydrocarbons are involved. But I don't see any evidence that the gasoline found on Mister Cole's pants is the same type of accelerant used in the fire. He could have gotten gasoline on himself in filling up his vehicle. Or trimming hedgework. Or cutting down a tree."

The assistant AG instantly responded. "We'd also like to point out, Your Honor, that a few days ago, Mister Cole's home in Tyler Beach was destroyed by arson. It's reasonable to infer that the house in Osgood was burned down in some sort of act of revenge."

Drake didn't let that one slide. "Your Honor, the Osgood residence that burned down is owned, as far as we can determine, by a real estate trust company based in Los Gatos, California. To think Mister Cole burned down a house in Osgood due to a grudge against someone thousands of miles away is a stretch. My learned friend from the attorney general's office looks quite presentable today; one could infer that she was chauffeured here in a limousine, but I think we would all agree that's a fairly poor assumption. Again, where is the evidence?"

The attorney general was a spunky sort and didn't give up easily. "Your Honor, once the fire was extinguished, arson investigators and the State Police located three male bodies in the debris. Initial medical examination determined that they had died prior to the fire being set. Two of them appeared to have been bound, and all had their heads severed."

Judge Bobbett blinked a couple of times, got Detective Renzi's attention. "Do you have any more information to add to that, Detective Renzi?"

"I do not, Your Honor."

"I see."

Drake spoke up. "If I may . . . Your Honor, it's said that all three men were missing their heads. Have their heads been located?"

Renzi shook his head in disgust. "Not at the present time."

Drake smiled, gestured toward me. "As you can tell, Your Honor, my client has been grievously wounded with a bullet to his right leg. Is the State truly saying that my client managed to overcome three men, sever their heads, and set the house on fire, all with a bullet wound to his leg?"

The judge looked to Renzi and the assistant attorney general. She said: "The investigation is continuing, Your Honor, and the State is confident that more evidence connecting Mister Cole to these crimes will be found shortly. That's why we're asking for no bail. It's obvious that Mister Cole is a threat to the community."

Judge Bobbett said, "Well, Mister Drake, you've heard what the State has to say. What amount would you be seeking for bail for your client?"

He held out his tanned hands. "Your Honor, we recognize the severity of the crime, but Mister Cole has resided for some time in Tyler Beach, has connections to the area, and with that bullet wound is definitely not a flight risk. We think one hundred thousand dollars, cash or surety, would be quite equitable. We would also agree to Mister Cole surrendering his passport and wearing a monitor bracelet."

"Is he employed?" the judge asked.

Drake paused, and I knew the judge had struck home with the question. "Mister Cole has been a long-time columnist for the Boston-based magazine called *Shoreline*. He has left their employ and is now a freelance writer."

Judge Bobbett looked at me. "Is that true, Mister Cole?"

"Yes, sir."

"Have you sold many articles since leaving your job?"

"Not a one, sir."

"And Mister Cole, do you have a permanent residence?"

"Not at the moment, sir. As the assistant attorney general so capably pointed out, it burned down a few days ago."

"I see . . . Mister Drake, we certainly have a situation here, don't we."

"That we do, Your Honor."

"It might be good for all concerned for your client to give the State Police a full and truthful account of what happened that night in Osgood."

Drake hesitated. "It might be good for all concerned, Your Honor, but I must look out for the best interests of my client. Which is why I'm advising him not to say a word."

A brief nod. "Which is your right. Well." Judge Bobbett looked down at his papers and said: "This is how it's going to be, I'm afraid. Mister Drake, you have done an admirable job in representing your client's interests, but at the end of the day, we have a home destroyed, three dead men with their heads missing, and your client. Who, by chance, was in the vicinity of said home, with accelerant evidence on his clothes and a bullet wound to his leg. Mister Cole could do the right thing and tell investigators what happened. He's decided not to. His right. But I'm going to agree with the State's request. No bail."

That was that. Detective Renzi looked happy, the assistant attorney general looked happy, and the judge looked somber. Duty done.

Some paperwork was exchanged and examined, and the judge said: "Mister Cole, once your doctor says you can be moved, you're going to be transferred to the Grafton County Jail's medical wing. From there, we will be in contact with your attorney for an upcoming date for a probable-cause hearing."

"I understand, sir."

The judge gathered up his papers, put them into a soft leather briefcase. "If I can say something unofficially, I've looked at your background. Over the years, you've been in police custody on a number of occasions, but you've never been prosecuted. I'd say that today, your luck has run out. Despite what your attorney has advised you, do consider cooperating with investigators."

"I'll certainly keep that in mind," I said.

Judge Bobbett said, "I doubt it, but I had to say it."

Then the full complement of legal and police authorities of the State of New Hampshire left, and Renzi closed my hospital door behind him.

Drake moved his chair closer to my bed. "Sorry, Lewis. Did my best. That sucked."

"Oh, don't be so hard on yourself," I said. "At least you get to go home tonight."

"Yeah, but it's a hell of a drive. Interstate 89 has got to be the most boring road in all of New England."

"Agreed. So what now?"

"You tell me."

"Thought it was the other way around."

He laughed. "Sure. In normal cases. But this ain't normal, Lewis. So I'm going to do my very best to get you out, and if I can't do that, I'll do my very, very best to get a not-guilty verdict if and when this goes to trial."

I slowly nodded. "Can't ask for more than that."

He began putting his own papers away. "Anything else you'd like to tell me about what's going on?"

I looked out the window at the near peaks of the White Mountains. So very fine, so very far away. "Over the years, I'm sure you've seen those action-adventure movies, right? The ones with high-powered conspiracies, dark shadows, bad guys. Usually there are lots of gunfights, explosions, and fires. Action, action, action. But if you look closely at those movies, there are always some innocents in the background who get hurt, get killed, get run over. They're forgotten within seconds. The big guys, the protagonists, they go on their way."

Drake just looked at me. I continued: "This time, the ones who got hurt, they have friends who don't forget."

He said: "From what I've been told by Felix, your friend was a cop. Part of her normal duties."

I shook my head. "Nothing about this was normal."

He closed his briefcase. "I see. Felix sends his best wishes, you know. He'd be here, but he's in the middle of . . . something."

"Understood."

He got up. "I'll see what I can do to make your stay at the county jail comfortable, Lewis. I'm afraid neither the food nor the nursing help will be as attractive."

"I'll get over it."

Drake moved his chair back to where it belonged. "I hear every now and then from Annie Wynn. She's doing well for Senator Hale. She's going places."

"I know. I saw her a few days ago in D.C."

Drake patted my foot on the way out. "Way I hear it, she's going places without you."

"True enough."

"A pity."

"You'd think."

Then I was left alone.

Lynn, the nurse from before, came by to help me with dinner, which was a pork chop, rice, and salad. She again cut up the food so I could eat with one hand, and she examined my handcuffed hand and tsk-tsked and put some lotion around my wrist.

"Looks like you're going to be leaving us in a bit," she said. "Off to the fine lodgings of the county."

"Any chance you'd be coming along?"

"Hah," she said, rubbing my wrist some more. Her fingers were firm and strong. "No chance, I'm afraid." Lynn stopped and wiped her fingers dry with a piece of tissue paper. "We don't get official word, just rumors, but it seems the State thinks you've done some bad things. True?"

I pondered that for a moment and then said, "According to the laws of New Hampshire, I guess I did."

"You don't seem too worried."

"It was the right thing to do."

She smiled, took away my dinner dishes. "I sure hope you're right."

"Me too."

Later that night I had to use the bedpan, and Lynn did her work quickly and professionally, and she offered me a sponge bath, which went just as quickly and professionally. As she helped me get back into my hospital slacks and shirt—being quite careful around my bandaged thigh—Lynn said: "Some interesting scars you got there, Lewis. I'd guess this isn't the first time you've been in a hospital."

"You'd be right."

"What happened to you, then, if you don't mind me asking?"

Lots of random thoughts came up for air in me mind, all revolving around that day in Nevada years ago, when I'd been the lone survivor of a training accident, when my DoD section had unintentionally crossed into a classified testing range and had been sprayed with something that, officially, the DoD wasn't even supposed to have. Everyone in my section had died except me; but as a lasting gift, I had been plagued with non-cancerous tumors over the years that would suddenly appear and have to be cut out.

Eventually it would no doubt kill me.

But not tonight.

"I got them in the service of my country," I said.

She got up, bent down, kissed my forehead. "God bless you, then. Sleep well tonight, and . . . I do wish I could be there for you at the county jail."

My eyes were open. My hospital room was dark, save for a few lights associated with monitoring equipment. To the right was the window, overlooking the distant mountains. There were no lights up on the peaks. Below was a parking lot for the hospital. Nothing was moving. In front of me was a television, off, hanging from a stand set in the ceiling. Empty chairs and a table on wheels flanked my bed.

My heart was thumping. Mouth dry. I felt like I couldn't move.

The door to my room was slowly opening, casting a pillar of light across the tile floor.

I knew what was going on.

They were coming for me.

I tried to scramble with my right hand, to get the call button.

I couldn't move.

A form came into view. Male. Dressed in black. Something strange was on his head. He moved his head. I recognized it right away. Night-vision goggles.

I tried to call out.

My mouth so very, very dry.

He came closer, moving with no sound, moving like dark fog.

No call button.

I thought of rolling off the bed.

Couldn't move.

Mouth dry.

Heart thumping, racing, almost choking me with its speed. I was now panting.

The man stopped next to me. A hand moved. Light from somewhere glinted off something metallic in his hand.

A blade.

Knew exactly what was going to happen next, knew all it would take would be a quick snap of the blade to my throat, and it would be over in seconds.

The blade descended.

I shouted.

Chest seized.

My eyes opened again.

I rolled to the side, shaking, my handcuffed wrist clanking along. One hell of a bad dream.

One hell of a bad dream.

There was a cup of water with a flexible straw. I grabbed it with my free hand and drank and drank until the cup slurped, empty.

I fell back against the bed. My heart was still thumping along, and my bedclothes were soaked through.

One *hell* of a bad dream.

I wiped my face and stretched out, wincing as a shot of pain burst out from my thigh. I eased my breathing, rested my head against the pillow.

A memory floated up to me, of my time back at the Puzzle Palace, when my section was responding to the news of an embassy attack in the Mideast, back when they weren't such a common occurrence. We were trying to make sense of the information that was flowing in, and one of my fellow section members had shaken his head and said, "Pizza deliveries . . . sometimes they can go both ways."

My breathing slowed down, my racing heart began to ease.

Pizza deliveries can go both ways.

# CHAPTER TWENTY-SIX

Two days later was moving day. I didn't have much in the way of personal belongings—most were now in the custody of the New Hampshire State Police—but I did get a little plastic bag with a toothbrush, floss, and toothpaste. Two polite deputies from the Grafton County Sheriff's Department came into my room, one pushing an empty wheelchair. Paperwork was signed and exchanged, and the older of the two deputies—who had a florid handlebar moustache and a nearly bald head—tried to be gracious and polite with the whole process. His partner was tall and young, with close-cropped black hair, and eyed me suspiciously, like he wished I would make a sudden break for it so he could put a round in my good leg.

The older man, Deputy Lindsay, moved the chair close to my bed. "Mister Cole, this is what we're going to be doing today. We're in charge of transporting prisoners to the county jail. There's a bed in the medical facility that's waiting for you, though I'm sure the help won't be as attractive as what you're used to."

"I'm sure," I said.

The other man, Deputy Bronski, glowered at me, holding a manila envelope. Both men wore tan slacks and brown uniform shirts with brown neckties. Wide leather utility belts held their usual equipment of pistols, handcuffs, and pepper spray, along with radios that had microphones clipped to their shoulder epaulets.

Deputy Lindsay went over to the left side of the bed, and he quickly undid my handcuff. I wanted to prove how strong and noble I was by not rubbing the wrist, but I couldn't help myself: I rubbed and rubbed the wrist, feeling like I was scratching at an itch that had been tormenting me for nearly a week.

Lindsay pocketed the cuffs and asked, "You need help getting into the wheelchair?"

"If you hold the chair steady, I should be able to make it."

By now, my leg was no longer in some sort of suspension system. I tossed off my blankets and sheets and, gritting my teeth, managed to rotate around and put both feet on the floor. Lindsay held the chair fast and, after a few deep breaths, I got out of bed and into the chair.

It felt good to be out of the bed.

That nice feeling lasted about ten seconds.

"Sorry, Mister Cole," Lindsay said. "Rules are rules. Put your wrists together."

Wrists together, the handcuffs went back on with a metallic snap. He took a white cotton blanket and put it around my lap and down my legs. "If you'd like, put your hands underneath the blanket so no one can see them."

I shook my head, rested my cuffed wrists on the blanket. "It was a fair pinch. I've got nothing to hide."

Deputy Bronski led our little procession out into the hallway, and Deputy Lindsay pushed my chair along. The lights seemed very bright and everything seemed so clean, and I didn't want to think much about what my lodgings were going to be like later that day. Passing the nurses' station, I got a few sympathetic smiles from the Dartmouth-Hitchcock pros, and that felt fine. We got an elevator to ourselves, and I twisted my head back to Lindsay.

"Excuse my ignorance, but where the hell is the county jail?"

"North Haverhill," he said. "We take Interstate 91 and get off on one of the state roads. Just over a half hour."

"Sounds quite scenic."

Bronski spoke up, voice low. "No worries, you won't see shit."

We got out in a main lobby area. Patients and family members swarmed around the elevator banks, but as our trio went out to the glass doors leading to the outside, it was like we were made of garlic and the people were vampires. They all backed away and turned their eyes, save for one little boy, wearing a Batman sweatshirt, who stared at me with wide, wide eyes.

If I had just persuaded him not to follow a life of crime, I guess this little public display was well worth it.

Bronski slapped a square button that opened up a set of doors, wide enough for the wheelchair to go through. Outside, the cold air snapped at me like a blast of A/C, and I took a deep breath, enjoying the taste and smell of outdoor air. Off to the right, parked right up to the curb, was a brown-and-tan GMC van with a gold sheriff's department shield, and a long line of lettering announcing GRAFTON COUNTY SHERIFF'S DEPARTMENT. Lindsay wheeled me to the pavement and off to the rear of the van. More family members were strolling up to the main entrance and, seeing me and the van, they all walked around in a wide circle.

"Look how popular you are," Bronski said.

"And they don't even know me yet," I said.

Lindsay laughed. He parked my wheelchair and opened up the rear of the van. I was impressed. There was an elevator system in the rear made for wheelchairs. Lindsay toggled a couple of switches, and a platform unfolded and lowered itself to the ground. I was wheeled in, the chair's wheels were locked, and in a couple of minutes everything was squared away. Bronski was up forward in the cab, with a mesh screen separating him from his dangerous prisoner.

The rear of the van was spare, metal and utilitarian. Benches lined both sides, and metal rings were set into the floor and the sides. I was set in the middle, wheels locked, and Lindsay took some heavy-duty bungee cords and secured the chair even more.

He leaned over, rapped the rear of the mesh. "Ski, we're good to go."

Bronski grunted, spoke something into his microphone to Grafton County Dispatch, started up the engine, and we were off.

In just a few minutes, we were on Interstate 91, heading northeast. Bronski had been wrong. I was seeing shit, although only through the rear windows with mesh wiring embedded in the glass. The landscape was wooded low hills and mountains in the distance. There wasn't much left in the way of foliage. My wrist ached where the handcuff was cutting into the skin and bone. Deputy Lindsay leaned forward, wrists on his thighs, thick hands clasped together.

"You feeling okay?"

"Not bad."

"Leg hurting?"

"Enough to know I got shot."

"Jesus, that's what I heard," Lindsay said. "Who the hell shot you?"

I smiled at him. "A nine-millimeter pistol."

"Hah," he said. "I mean, who? Who shot you?"

I smiled wider. "A mysterious gunman." He stayed quiet. I added: "Nice try, Deputy. Don't worry about it."

He grinned. "Hey, I gotta try. Never know what might happen."

"I'm sure," I said. "For all you know, somebody might confess to the Lindbergh baby kidnapping. Or Jimmy Hoffa."

"Guy can dream, right?" he asked.

A few minutes passed. I said: "Excuse me for saying this, Deputy, but you don't look like a cop. You've been a sheriff's deputy long?"

"About five years."

"What did you do before then?"

"Firefighter. City of Nashua. Got my twenty in, got the wife and kids, and headed north. Nice piece of land, raise some chickens, pigs, and beef. Figured if and when things collapse, we'll make it through. In the meantime, I get out of the house, meet some interesting people, and add to my pension."

"Sounds great."

"Better than a lot of other people are doing here, that's for sure."

A few more minutes. I cleared my throat. "Deputy Lindsay, could I ask a favor?"

"Hmm?"

I raised my hands up. "I know it's against the rules and all, but could you take off the cuffs? Please? My right wrist is really aching."

"Christ, no."

"C'mon," I said, moving my hands over my bandaged leg. "You think I'm going anywhere with this bum leg? Do I look like I can overpower you? Please. Besides, your buddy up there driving looks like he'd like to pump a round in the back of my head, just for the hell of it."

He looked up at the mesh screen, looked back at me. I quieted my voice. "Take the cuffs off, treat me just like a patient, and I'll put my hands under the blanket. Keep my mouth shut. Your partner won't know. We pull into the jail, put them back on, and that's it."

Lindsay seemed to be thinking over something, and then he came to me, worked quickly, and undid the cuffs. I put my hands under the blankets, rubbed both wrists this time, and said, "Thanks."

"Don't know what you're talking about," Lindsay said.

About two minutes later was when it happened.

Bronski took an exit that put us on Route 25, and the road was narrow and curvy, with farms and pastureland and a few mobile homes out there in the distance. Old stone walls and barbed-wire fences, and herds of sheep and cows at work. I looked out at the passing rural landscape, wondering what my view would be like once I got to the county jail. I also thought about what Attorney Drake was doing on my behalf at this very moment, and spared some thoughts for Diane and Kara and Felix.

And here I was, alone in a sheriff's van, heading to jail.

I was thinking so much that I almost missed the vehicle that was now behind us.

It was a black Chevrolet Suburban, with tinted windows and no license plate up forward, which meant it wasn't local, since New Hampshire requires vehicles to have license plates both fore and aft.

It had pulled out from a dirt driveway, sped up, and was now closing in behind us.

"Deputy Lindsay."

"Yeah?"

"Check what's coming up on our tail. The Suburban."

He leaned over, looked to the rear. "So?"

"Deputy, in about one minute, we're going to get ambushed. Better call for some backup."

He flipped back to me, the friendly look entirely gone. His eyes were glaring at me, face flushed, as his hand went down to his holstered pistol. "You bastard, you set us up! That's why you wanted your handcuffs off!"

"If I was setting you up, I wouldn't warn you. You don't have much time. Deputy, get to it, call backup!"

His eyes didn't leave me as he evaluated my words, and he said, "Move, and you'll be the first one hit."

"Take a number," I said. "Those guys are after *me*."

Lindsay took his pistol out and, with his other hand, toggled the radio microphone on his shirt epaulet. "Dispatch, dispatch, this is Grafton Mobile One."

Static crackled back at him.

His voice louder, "Dispatch, dispatch, this is Grafton Mobile One."

More static.

"I think they're jamming you," I said.

"Shit."

He tried his cell phone, said "shit" again, and tossed it on the floor.

The Suburban sped up, getting closer. Lindsay pushed by me, rapped on the mesh wire separating us from the cab. "Ski! We got trouble! My radio's not working, and we got bad guys on our asses!"

Ski said something back; Lindsay said: "Then haul ass! See if we can make the jail in time!"

The van lurched as Ski sped up, and Lindsay came back, checked his pistol, took me in with a look, and asked, "Who's after you? Same guy who shot you?"

"His friends."

"They're pretty pissed off."

I said: "Whatever happens, don't get involved. Keep your head down and—"

"The hell with that," he said with determination. "You're our responsibility."

The Suburban came almost to the rear bumper, and then a hell of a thing happened. The van's engine cut out and the Suburban passed us and Lindsay said, "The hell just happened?"

"They've just killed your engine."

"How the hell did they do that?"

"I'm sure it's top secret somewhere."

The Suburban sideswiped the van, up forward Ski shouted, and the van skidded and went off the road, into a drainage ditch. Lindsay scrambled to keep his balance but he fell, as my county wheelchair and I fell on top of him.

# CHAPTER TWENTY-SEVEN

I screamed as my bandaged leg hit something, and there was a god-awful banging and tearing noise as the van came to a rest on its side. I was sitting on the tilted floor, and Lindsay was crumpled up in the corner, bleeding from his head, part of the lift mechanism pinning his legs down. I shuffled over to him, checked his pulse in the neck. Steady and strong. I only had seconds to do something. His pistol was in his lap. I grabbed it, wasted a second or two to find a spare magazine, couldn't find one. There were shouts and a loud *bang* coming from outside.

I went back to the rear, popped open the door, and it flopped open. I lowered myself to the drainage ditch, dressed only in pajama bottoms and top, with thin hospital slippers on my feet. My feet were instantly soaked.

I peered around the edge of the van. The Suburban was parked just a few yards away, engine running. Driver was still inside, ready to speed away when the job was done. One man was approaching the still form of Deputy Bronski on the road. Another was flanking him, giving him cover. Made quick professional sense. Taking care of the closest armed opponent. Both had on jet-black fatigues, boots, web belts, black Navy watch caps, with earpieces and microphones set before their mouths. Each had a stubby automatic weapon in his hands, looking like a variant of the popular Swedish-made H&K 95.

I was spotted by the far man and he said something sharp and quick, and I think I surprised all of us when I fired first, sending off at least four shots as they quickly flopped to the ground and rolled to one side, weapons rising up.

By then I was trying to make my way through the woods.

"Trying" was certainly the word of the day. I had to drag my bandaged leg behind me, the slippers were about as useful as wet cardboard, and after a couple of yards I was shivering from the thin clothing I was wearing.

I glanced back several times as I moved as fast as I could, going up a tree-covered rise, not thinking much of anything except to make some distance. Making distance meant time, and time meant the increasing chance that somebody would be coming by this rural road and would think enough of seeing a county sheriff's van on its side to make a phone call.

Illusions? Had none. These were two very professional, cool, and capable men on my trail.

I paused, panting. Thought I saw some shadows moving down below, about fifty feet away. Two more shots from my borrowed Glock 10mm. Which meant about six rounds left.

Hell of a last stand.

I kept moving, tripped, and fell. Yelled out. Rolled over, sat up, looked at my leg.

The bandage on my right leg was seeping blood through my thin cotton pants.

"Day just keeps on getting better," I whispered.

I got up, my slippers now black with dirt and debris, as well as my pants legs below my knees. Shivering hard now. Watching through the woods, boulders, and brush. Feeling at that very moment what a deer felt like in these woods every November.

More shadows moved down there.

Damn, they were good.

I kept moving, panting, crying out every now and then as a sharp rock or stick poked into my feet.

More distance made, but I was slowing down. To the right, an old cellar hole appeared, from some farm that had tried to make it here a century ago and had failed. I had a brief thought of going into the hole, burrowing in, and hiding, but those guys back there probably had thermal detection devices with them. Trying to hide in a hole like that would just make their job easy.

Above all, I didn't want to make it easy for them.

I kept moving.

The hill got steeper and steeper. It felt like ice picks were being jabbed into my lungs. A shot from behind me.

I whirled, saw one of the gunmen slipping behind a birch tree. I brought up the pistol and pulled the trigger.

Nothing happened.

Nothing happened.

I moved another foot or two, tripped once more, swirled and fell flat on my ass, my bottom now soaked through. I grimaced and stretched my legs out. I was sitting against a thick old pine tree.

I pulled the trigger again.

Nothing.

It was jammed.

I clawed at the action.

Jammed.

A spent 10mm cartridge was jamming the works.

I looked up.

The two gunmen were moving quickly and silently up the slope of the hill, not too far away.

Looked around on the ground for a stick or a length of wood or an abandoned screwdriver to pry out the empty cartridge.

Nothing.

Tried with my finger, broke a fingernail.

Raised my head.

The two men were so close that I could see that the one on the left had black bushy eyebrows, and the one on the right had thin fine blond eyebrows. Both had their weapons up to their shoulders, aiming right down at me. I even saw that the guy on the right had a shotgun-type weapon slung over a shoulder, which I thought was overkill.

Hah.

I threw the jammed pistol at the near gunman. Here we go, I thought. The circle was about to be closed. Was almost killed by my government some years ago in Nevada, and now the job would be finished in a minute or two, in my home state, by my government or somebody else out there associated with them.

They came closer.

I cleared my throat. "If you're hoping for some begging, you're wasting your time."

The gunman on the left brought a gloved hand up to the microphone in front of his lips, murmured something, paused, and then nodded his head, like he had just been told something. He held up his right hand, palm up, and turned, ensuring that his partner saw the motion.

He came closer, knelt down on one knee in front of me.

"How you doing?" he asked, his voice deep Southern and relaxed.

"Had better days."

"No, you haven't," he said.

"I think I'll be the judge of that."

He grinned, revealing white teeth that could put him on a *GQ* magazine cover. "Nah, you're wrong, Mister Cole. 'Bout ninety seconds ago, we just got orders to cancel the op. So you're good to go."

I took a breath. The cold air tasted pretty fine. "You wouldn't be lying, would you?"

He shook his head. "Nossir, wouldn't do that." He eyed me and said: "Can see you're bleeding like a son-of-a-bitch. Wish I could stick around and help ya, but we gotta get movin'."

"Like you helped the two deputies?"

"Ah, they'll be copacetic, just you wait and see. Guy in the van's got a dinged head, other guy's out with a nap."

"Looked pretty permanent to me."

"Nossir," he said emphatically. "Ivan over there nailed 'em with a vortex gun. Drops 'em for about a minute or two, long enough to secure 'em."

"What the hell is a vortex gun?" I asked, again looking at the stubby shotgun-like weapon on the second gunman's back. Ivan spotted me doing it and said something loud and piercing in what seemed to be Russian. The man in front of me turned his head, spoke Russian crisply right back at him. A long time ago I could have puzzled out what they were saying, but those days were long gone.

"Sorry, classified," he said, standing up. "And Ivan's getting hot to trot. Made his bones back in Chechnya, can't stand to be sittin' still in one place. Don't you worry, once we're clear, I'll call the cops, tell 'em where to pick you up."

I suppose I should have kept my mouth shut, but I couldn't help myself. "Just like that? You want to help me out, and five minutes ago you wanted to take my head off?"

He grinned again. "That's the job. Just following orders."

"Stuff like that would keep me up at night."

He slung his automatic rifle over his shoulder. "Maybe so, but you know what? I love it. I do what I have to do because of who I am, and I let somebody else worry about right or wrong, east or west, left or right, Muslim or Christian. All above my pay grade, and that's fine with me."

He touched his forehead with his forefinger. "Keep cool, bud. Looking forward to never seeing you again."

Then he turned, said something in Russian again to the gunman called Ivan, and in a matter of seconds they were ghost shadows among the trees.

# CHAPTER TWENTY-EIGHT

A week and a presidential election later, I was standing outside the main entrance to the Grafton County House of Corrections, leaning on a metal cane, wearing donated clothing from the county. It was a cold, crisp day, and I was supposedly a free man. Buildings behind me were surrounded with coils and coils of concertina wire. A black Chevrolet Impala came up to the parking lot and stopped, and Detective Pete Renzi stepped out of the car and walked over to me.

When he stopped, he dug out a pack of Marlboro cigarettes and lit one up, took a deep drag.

"So you're smoking again."

"Damn observant," he said, taking another deep drag. "The past couple of weeks would drive anybody to smoke, thanks to you."

"Sorry about that."

"Not here to get your apology."

I leaned some more on my cane, felt the sharp wind cut through me. I kept quiet. He dropped the cigarette, ground it out with the heel of his shoe.

"Don't you feel bad, nearly getting two sheriff's deputies killed?"

"They weren't killed," I said. "Banged up a bit, but they weren't killed."

"And you can't say anything about the Suburban that drove you guys off the road, or the two gunmen?"

"I've made at least two statements to the county attorney and the state's attorney general. Don't feel like saying anything more about that. Go check the interview transcripts if you're still curious."

I had a strong feeling he didn't like what I'd just said, but I didn't care that much. I was feeling the cold and I just wanted to leave.

Renzi said, suddenly, "I've been with the state for quite a few years, and I'll be damned if I've ever seen anything like what happened. All the evidence associated with you and this case—your clothes, your shoes, even your damn socks—disappear from a locked facility at the state's crime lab. Gone. Which meant a shitstorm came my way and swept up some poor crime techs, barely making enough salary to support a family."

"Guess you know I had nothing to do with it, being the guest of the county and all that."

"Oh, I don't know about that, Lewis. For a while, I was sure your pal Felix Tinios had something to do with it, but he had the typical ironclad alibi for the night the theft occurred. The bastard even had the same kind of alibi the night the Osgood house burned down. And here you are, free to go. No evidence, no probable-cause hearing, no trial. Congratulations."

"Somehow I'm not feeling the sincerity, Detective."

He took out the pack of cigarettes, looked at it, and then put it back into his coat. "Seems like a long time ago, I warned you off the matter of Curt Chesak. It's obvious you went ahead and did what you wanted to do. Are you still on the job?"

"I've got more important things going on at the moment," I said, raising up my cane a few inches.

"I'll take that as a 'no.' So let me ask you this. There were three male bodies found in the house after it burned down. Safe to say Curt Chesak was one of them?"

"You being a detective and all, I thought you might already know that."

"Hah," Renzi said, his voice flat. "Problem is, no fingerprints. Any recovered DNA hasn't been matched with anything in any DNA database we've been able to access. Plus there's the matter of the heads."

"Find them yet?"

"No," he said. "And no heads means no skulls, no teeth, and no dental records. Unless something turns up shortly, this is going to be one honking big cold case. And I don't like cold cases, especially when I'm looking at the guy responsible for putting this case in the freezer."

I shifted my weight on my right leg, pleased that the pain was throbbing at an acceptable level. "Heard any news about Diane Woods?"

"Couple of days ago, heard nothing had changed. Still in a coma."

"Thanks for the information," I said. "Wasn't able to make any calls while I was inside."

"You're welcome."

Dead leaves skittered across the asphalt. Thought for a moment or three. "Tell you this, Detective. If I may, your job is about making sure justice prevails. Trust me when I say this: justice has prevailed."

"Who made you judge and jury?"

"Me," I said. "Saw that a real judge and jury wasn't ever going to decide this, and I wasn't going to allow that to stand. A decision that I will think about forever, and a decision that I'm glad I made. And if I may, trust me on this, it's over, it's done, and the matter is closed."

"Only if I say so."

I nodded. "Agreed. Only if you say so."

We stood there in the cold wind on a fall day, and Renzi said: "Ah, Christ, enough of this. You know what? It kills me to say this, but I think you did a good job. I'll always deny saying this, but yeah, I'm glad to see that justice prevailed for Diane Woods. It just pisses me off mightily that you did it, that I couldn't, and that you're going to get away with it."

"Not without a few bumps in the road."

"Yeah. What's the deal with your leg?"

"Still attached to my hip, but it's going to hurt for a long time to come."

"And your house?"

"Last I saw, it was still burning. Not sure what's going to be left when I get back to Tyler Beach."

"Hell of a thing."

"Yeah."

Another few moments passed, and he said, "Well, I'm heading back to Concord, see if there's anything new about the crime lab break-in. But I'm not holding my breath."

"Seems like a wise choice."

"Give you a ride?"

I spotted a vehicle coming up the paved access road. "No, I'm all set."

"Good. Hope you have better days."

"You too."

As Detective Renzi drove off, a black stretch limousine pulled in, bearing Massachusetts license plates. It made a circuit of the parking lot, like it was trying to show the inmates inside what was waiting for them if they got out, kept their noses clean, and, most important of all, if they made the right friends.

The limousine pulled in front of me, the rear door opened up, and Felix Tinios came out, breath misting some in the cold air. He had on a charcoal gray cloth coat that went down to his knees, red turtleneck shirt, gray slacks, and black shoes. His face was tanned and his black hair was set and perfect, and he came up to me, slid an arm through mine.

"Come along, my friend," he said. "It's time for you to go home."

"Not much of a home left." I started walking, using the cane, leaning on Felix.

"True enough. Should have thought better before opening my mouth. Hey, I heard there was a fire up here, more than a week ago. Where you were found sitting outside on the front lawn. Hell of a coincidence, eh?"

We reached the open door of the car. "They started it," I said.

"And you sure as hell finished it."

"I sure as hell did."

The interior of the limousine was warm and comfortable, with a very attractive young woman sitting on the other side. A built-in round table was between us and her, and there were plates and covered containers and little cans of Sterno flickering along. The woman looked to be in her mid-twenties, with olive skin, dark brown eyes, and long black hair braided to one side. She had on a short black skirt, black stockings, high-heeled shoes, and a tight yellow ribbed blouse that was quite low-cut.

I settled in as well as I could, stretching out my bum leg. Felix sat next to me, closed the door, and motioned to the woman. "Lewis, I'd like to introduce you to Angela Rossini, an alleged second cousin of mine from the Old Country."

I leaned over, extended my hand. She smiled wider, took my hand in hers, and said, "*Buongiorno, Lewis.*"

"Nice to meet you too," I said.

She released my hand and spoke to Felix. "*Mi dispiace, Felix, lui è bello ma ha davvero gli odori!*"

"So, what did she just say?" I asked.

Felix patted my good leg. "She thinks you're cute and that you could use a bath."

"Tell her thanks for the first part, and apologies for the second. Sponge baths from male attendants tend to just hit the highlights."

The limousine purred its way out of the jail's parking lot, and in a few minutes we were covering the same ground I had passed more than a week ago.

I didn't give it a second glance.

"And who's driving? Angela's brother?"

"No, a former associate . . . and let's just leave it at that."

"Fine."

When we got onto the Interstate, Angela went to work, removing covers and preparing dishes. In a few minutes I had a white linen napkin on my lap, with a large square plate that had beef tenderloin, some sort of crispy potato side dish, and a salad. Glasses of Chianti were also poured, and I ate the best meal I had consumed in a long time as we moved south and then east.

When I was finished, I asked Felix, "So, who's Angela? For real?"

"For real, she is a second cousin. According to her paperwork and birth certificate, at least."

"What's she doing here? Besides serving lunch."

"She's an astrophysicist from some college in Rome. Couldn't find a job, like most of her generation. I got her over here a few days ago, thought she'd be a good companion for you on the ride back. Talk about stars, planets, galaxies. Help pass the time."

"You know I don't speak Italian."

He wiped his lips and hands with his napkin. "Shit, Lewis, do you see 'stupid' tattooed on my forehead? She claimed she spoke English when she e-mailed me a few weeks back."

"Along with a photo?" I asked innocently.

"Never mind that. So here she is . . . well, what you see is what you get. I told her I didn't like being lied to like that, and she said if I had to, I should punish her."

She started collecting our dishes, smiling all the time. I tried hard not to stare at her long legs and her smooth cleavage.

I failed.

"So, are you going to punish her, or what?"

Felix sighed. "I'm struggling with that. She is a second cousin, after all."

"Maybe she lied about that too."

He smiled. "Hell, didn't think of that. Thanks, bud."

After a few more pleasant smiles, I leaned back in the comfortable seat and asked, "Do you know anything about Diane Woods?"

"Not a thing. How about you?"

"A couple of weeks ago, talked to her partner Kara Miles. Nothing had really changed. Still in a coma. Since then, I didn't have access to a phone."

Felix dug into a side pocket, handed over his cell phone. "Go for it."

I dialed and after four rings, it went straight to voicemail.

Did it two more times.

I handed the phone back. "I'll try later."

"Sure," he said. "So, where do you want to go?"

"Exonia Hospital."

"Okay."

Felix helped Angela with some more of the dishes, the two of them speaking to each other in Italian, and once he said something that seemed to anger her, for her face turned red and her voice went up a notch or two. But I checked her eyes, which were saying something else entirely.

When Felix was through, I asked, "Aren't you going to tell your associate?"

"Tell him what?"

"Tell him where I want to go."

Felix laughed. "Didn't have to. I told him from the start that's where we'd end up."

"Good call."

He folded his arms. "Detective Renzi meet up with you?"

"Just before you showed up. I understand he spent some quality time with you as well. Thanks for backing me up."

"The truth is always a good defense."

"Who told you that?"

"Oh, I get around."

With the wonderful meal, wine, and companions, accompanied by the gentle drone of the limousine, I put my head back and quickly fell asleep. Like every other time in the past several days, I saw the same thing before I drifted away: Curt Chesak in his bedroom, me shooting him three times. Meaning to shoot him dead. To kill him. To end his life.

The rational part of my mind had no problem with that. He had done me harm, had done Diane harm, and had killed a college student whose only sin had been working for his father.

That was the rational part.

But deep in my heart and in the marrow of my bones, no matter what I had said to Detective Renzi, there was doubt, there was anguish.

Ultimately, I had not killed Curt Chesak, but the intent was in my actions.

I slept on the drive south, but not particularly well.

When the limousine slowed down as it made an exit onto Route 101, about another half hour before we reached Exonia, I woke up and stretched. Angela handed me two warm and moist towels, which I used to wipe my hands and face. When I was done, she poured small cups of very strong coffee for Felix and myself.

As we sat there, Felix asked, "Did Attorney Drake meet your needs?"

"Met and then some."

"He has a message for you. Hold on."

Felix took out an envelope, which he passed over. It was cream-colored, made of heavy stock, and had HALE FOR PRESIDENT in the upper left-hand corner, accompanied by a familiar address. And speaking of familiarity, my name was handwritten with blue ink in the center.

Quite familiar.

Felix and Angela pretended not to look at me. I examined the envelope one more time, reached over, and toggled a switch that lowered the window. I tore the envelope in half, in quarters, and then slipped the scraps out the crack of the window, whereupon the passing windstream snatched them away.

I raised the window back up, and we were all quiet until we reached the Exonia Hospital.

I got out of the limousine and looked back in and asked, "You feel like coming in for a visit?"

Felix laughed. "I admire Detective Woods, I respect Detective Woods, but I don't particularly have fond feelings for her. You go ahead. I'll stay here with Angela. We'll be here as long as it takes."

"Thanks, and do me a favor. No limo rocking when I come back."

He reached over, started closing the door. "With this suspension system, you won't see a damn thing."

I walked slowly into the main entrance of Exonia Hospital to the near elevator banks, and then I got off at a familiar floor where the ICU was located. I was pretty much ignored as I went past the nurses' station, didn't see Kara or a police officer keeping watch outside Diane's room.

I walked faster.

The door was open.

I walked in.

The room was empty.

I stood there, not moving, my first thoughts being that perhaps she had been taken out for an X-ray or MRI or some other procedure, but no, the room was clean, there were no balloons, cards, or flowers on the window counter, and the bed was neat and well made.

A male nurse came by, and I said, "Excuse me, do you have a moment?"

"Sure," he said, stopping. He held a clipboard in his hand and wore multi-colored scrubs and white shoes.

"Could . . . could you tell me where Detective Woods is? The woman who was here?"

"Oh," he said. "She's gone. I'm sorry. Didn't you know?"

## CHAPTER TWENTY-NINE

There was a roaring in my ears and my legs quivered. Gone. Just like that. While I was being kept in prison. Gone. All that fighting and shooting and tears and pain and lies . . . and for what?

She was gone. The nurse started to walk away and I managed to move my tongue. It seemed suddenly thick in the back of my throat. "Wait," I said, hating how weak my voice sounded. "Wait just a second."

He came back to me. "Yes?"

"Can . . . can you tell me any more? About which funeral home she was taken to? For services?"

He looked at me blankly, and then gave me an embarrassed smile. "Sir, sorry, I should have been more clear. When I said she was gone, I meant she's been discharged. She's been transferred up to the Porter Rehab and Extended Care Center. You know where that is?"

The thought of asking directions never came to me. My first thought was of taking my cane and wrapping it around his young, empty head.

"I'll find out."

The Porter Rehab and Extended Care Center was in an office park adjacent to the Porter Hospital, about a half-hour north of Exonia. It was two stories and made of brick, and I limped in with no problem, taking an elevator to the second floor. Felix and Angela and Felix's associate stayed back in the limousine, which took up three parking spaces. As before, Felix begged off going in with me, saying he was going to try to teach Angela some English phrases while I was away.

I eyed him as I got out of the limo. "Need some tips on what to say about heavenly bodies?"

I got a knowing smile from him as the door closed behind me.

On the second floor of the rehab center, the hallways were wide and had waist-high wooden railings for the benefit of its patients. I passed a large room which had exercise equipment and a mock-up of a dining room and kitchen, where patients were at work trying to recover from a host of injuries.

Diane Woods was in Room 209, and there was a Tyler police officer named Milan, whom I knew, sitting outside. He was leafing through *USA Today* and just nodded at me as I passed by. I quietly walked in, seeing Kara Miles curled up on a settee, fast asleep. I paused and took in Diane.

She was on her back, head propped up on a pillow. There was a feeding tube going into her nose, taped in place. The bruises and marks on her face had improved, meaning she was looking at least somewhat like the Diane I knew. Monitoring devices were hooked up to her wrists and hands. I stepped in closer. Her eyes were closed, and her mouth was sagging open, and her lips were cracked and dry.

She was breathing on her own, but it was a labored, rasping noise.

The windows overlooked a field, and in the distance, Air Force aircraft were landing and taking off from the nearby McIntosh Air Force Base, over in Lewington. Kara kept on sleeping. On the sill by the windows, get-well cards were crowded in a long row.

I came in even closer. It was Diane, no doubt about it, but the spark, the light, the life I knew, wasn't there.

Maybe it was gone, maybe it was hidden, but it wasn't there.

I kissed her forehead and slowly walked out.

"Where to now?" Felix asked when I got back into the limousine.

"Tyler Beach."

"You sure?"

"No doubt."

About forty minutes later, we were on Route 1-A, hugging the New Hampshire coastline, the winds coming up, the surf breaking harshly against the rocks. The fine homes of Wallis and North Tyler were lit up with golden lamps, and then we came upon a number of motels and restaurants, and then a long stretch of rocks and boulders the size of small cars. Up ahead was the Lafayette House, and the limousine made a left turn into its parking lot.

It stopped before the dirt driveway leading down to my home. I got out and Felix joined me. Without asking, he took my arm, helped me down the rough dirt road. With each step, my insides felt heavier and heavier. I didn't say anything, just kept on looking, observing, evaluating, until I reached the front of my home, with its small, scraggly lawn.

The smell of burnt and wet wood was still strong. To the right was a jumble of broken beams, shingles, and burnt planks that used to be a small outbuilding that served as a garage. From inside the destroyed garage, my Ford Explorer was a charred mess, resting on burnt and melted tires. Close by was my two-story house, which was now mostly one-story. Most of the roof to the right had collapsed where my office and bedroom had been. The area had been covered with a blue tarp that rattled as the wind came up. The whole area was still surrounded by yellow crime-scene tape, which flapped and twisted from the sea breeze. The waves crashed in behind my house. Chunks of burnt wood and shingles were piled up in front and to the side of my house.

My legs were shaking. I just looked and looked.

Felix still held on to my arm. He said: "Did I ever tell you the story of my Uncle Vincent? He had a place outside of the North End. One day the place blew up because of a natural gas leak, but he was one suspicious bastard and started a one-man gang war."

"No, you've never told me that story."

"You want to hear it?"

"No, I don't."

I broke away from his grasp, went to a point in the yard where there was a chunk of concrete and bricks back from when this place had been a lifeboat station during the late 1800s. I clumsily knelt down, wincing from the pain in my thigh, reached under the brick, and took out a small lockbox, which I opened. I took out a key, limped past Felix, ducked under the crime-scene tape, and unlocked the door. I had to bump my hip twice against the door to open it up. There was no power, of course, so I couldn't switch on any lights that might be working, but what I saw stunned me.

Save for chunks of plaster and pieces of burnt lumber that I could make out, the place was empty. No furniture. No rugs. No books, no bookshelves.

Had I been robbed?

"Lewis?" said Felix.

I turned. "You," I said. "What did you do?"

He shrugged. "What do you think? I'm an expert at salvaging things, picking up stuff that fell off a truck. When the smoke had cleared, I hired a crew, got in and took everything out that was still in reasonable shape. Books, rugs, some furniture. It's all spread out in a large storage facility over on Route One in North Tyler. A guy I know is doing his best trying to get the smoke out of your stuff. Sorry, your computer was a loss. Along with a hell of a lot of books."

"That's okay," I said, still not believing what I had seen. "I always do backups of my computers. Books can eventually be replaced."

Felix came to me, also ducking under the tape. "So there you go. Did what I could."

I reached over, grasped his shoulder. "More than I could have imagined."

Back at the parking lot, Felix said, "Welcome to crash at my pad, long as you want."

"No, that's all right," I said. "I'll stay at the Lafayette to start, until my bank account gets drained."

"What are you going to do tomorrow?"

"I'll figure it out then," I said.

For the next few days, I got into a routine of sorts. I would sleep soundly but without waking particularly refreshed, go downstairs to have an overpriced and over-caloried breakfast in the Lafayette House's dining room, and then putter around in the morning on a variety of errands and cleanup. On the first day, I rented a Honda Pilot that had great legroom, so I was able to drive around even with my injured leg, which meant I could visit Diane every day. Kara was so happy to see me that at first she burst into tears.

"I can't help it," she said, as we stood next to Diane's quiet form. "She's breathing on her own, and sometimes her eyes open up, but she really isn't responding. And if I don't put more hours in at work, I'm going to get fired. So maybe you could sit with her some, so I can catch up on work. And . . . Jesus, Lewis, what happened to you?"

"Bee sting," I said. "Bad reaction."

"Lewis. . . ."

"Let's just leave it like that for now. Look, what can I do?"

She wiped at her eyes. "Just sit with her, okay? Like you said, even in the deepest of comas, patients can hear what's going on. So talk to her, or read to her."

"I'll run out of things to say in a while," I said. "What kind of books does she like?"

"Classic mystery books. Like Agatha Christie. I always teased her about that, that she was bringing her work home with her when she cracked open one of those books. But she said she just enjoyed the plots and the detectives, except for that Belgian one."

"Hercule Poirot."

"Yeah," Kara said. "Diane called him 'that insufferable Belgian twit.' So don't pick up any of those."

"I won't."

Before I left, I kissed Diane again on the forehead, and said, "Kara, by the way, you won't need that Tyler cop sitting outside anymore."

Her face looked puzzled. "What happened?"

"Time passed, that's what."

"Does that have something to do with your leg?"

I slowly walked toward the door. "Everything. Something. Nothing. Diane's safe, that's all that counts."

So on the second day, I spent some time with Diane, just reading from *Ten Little Indians*, and about the second hour, I was startled when her head rolled to me and her eyes opened up. I dropped the book and stood over her, and her eyes rolled around, unfocused, and then she closed them.

I picked up the book and having lost my place, started reading again from the previous chapter.

I knew it didn't make any difference, but I wished it had.

The day after that, I went to the Tyler Museum, a tiny wooden building set off a large oval lawn that was the Tyler Town Common, the place where its militia drilled back in the sixteen and seventeen hundreds, and what was now a nice park. The building is only open a few hours a week, and I was lucky in getting to one of those special hours when I arrived.

Larry Cannon, a retired shipworker from the Porter Naval Shipyard up the coast and the museum's sole curator and volunteer, met me in the main room, which had a series of glass display cases that showed interesting bits and artifacts from Tyler and its beach from the early years right up to the time when Tyler was named an Official Bicentennial Community back in 1976.

Larry was in his late sixties, and even though he didn't have to, he dressed up each time he was at the museum, with a dress shirt, bow tie, and gray slacks. He had a gray moustache and beard and wore reading glasses perched at the end of his nose. Besides running the museum, his other work consisted of traveling hither and yon, taking spectacular photographs of lighthouses.

He shook my hand as I got past the doors and said, "Damn, so sorry to hear about your house. I hear it was arson? True?"

"Unfortunately, very true."

"Damn. Any idea who might have caused it?"

"A literary critic who doesn't like my columns, I guess. The investigation is still continuing, according to the State Fire Marshal's office."

Larry folded his large leathery hands and leaned on a glass counter that held old coins and bills from the Revolutionary War period. "It was a hell of a shame, not only about your home, but about the history before it was converted into a house."

"Which is why I'm here, Larry," I said. "A couple of years back, we had a chat at the Tyler Town Days. You said that somewhere in the archives, you had some original blueprints and plans for my home, covering at least fifty years. I was hoping I could see them at some point."

"You plan on rebuilding?"

"You know it," I said.

Larry rubbed at his bristly beard. "I know we've got the plans. It'll take some digging, but I can get them for you. But I got something else that might interest you. My brother-in-law Gavin, he's in the home contractor business and specializes in old homes, old barns, stuff like that."

"Go on."

"Thing is, I know he keeps lumber he don't use, and he's got a christly big barn in Tyler Falls that's full of planks and timbers that are up to a hundred years old. Some even older. It'll be pricier than hell, but if you were wanting to do your remodeling job right, I could hook you up with him."

I smiled. "That's fantastic."

Larry shook his head. "Again, I'll warn you. It'll be a right pricey job, to do it right."

I headed for the door. "Pricey is fine. I want to do it right, and then some."

On the third day after my return home, pricey was no longer fine.

Adrian Zimmerman was an eager young man with fine black slacks, long leather coat and leather briefcase, and a small digital camera that he used to take photos of my house and what was left of my Ford Explorer. His hair was light blond and he shook his head a lot while walking around the rubble, and he looked like he had bought his first razor blade a month ago. He was a claims agent for the insurance company that covered both my home and car, and when he was done, we went back up to his Buick, where he breathed on his hands and rubbed them together.

"Mister Cole, it's obvious you've suffered a tremendous loss, but I'm afraid we can't do anything for you at the present time."

I kept a pleasant smile on my face that didn't match my words. "And why the hell not?"

"It's out of my hands, really, and the local office. Your case has been bumped up to regional. You see, preliminary investigation here is that your home fire began as an arson. Then, from police and news media reports, we also know that you were a suspect in a similar arson, just a few days later, up in Osgood."

"All those charges were dropped."

His smile was still wide and sincere. "Perhaps they were, but it still raises a number of questions, so regional plans to take its time answering before proceeding on any claim."

"That's not fair, and you know it," I said. "I've been a customer for years, never once late for a payment, not once ever filing a claim."

"Fair has nothing to do with it, I'm afraid. In these troubled times, Mister Cole, with your connection to two arsons, there will have to be a very thorough investigation before my company will assume liability and issue a payment."

"Look, I just want to get things going here. Don't you understand?"

"Of course I understand, Mister Cole, but look, even if a settlement is reached in another several months or so, my recommendation is that the residence be razed and a new structure be built in its place."

"It's been here for more than a hundred years!"

He shrugged. "A hundred or a thousand, it's still nearly burned to the ground."

There were a few more words exchanged, with him getting calmer and cooler as I got angrier and hotter, but after a while I just gave up and he drove off, still smiling and in a good mood, in his company car, which I no doubt had had a hand in buying for him.

Another day, this time with drinks at the Lafayette House bar with Felix in attendance. We both had Sam Adams beers and overpriced appetizers, and after munching through scallops wrapped in bacon and some jumbo shrimp, he said, "Confession time. Let it out."

"All right," I said. "For the first time in my adult life, I didn't vote in the presidential election. Couldn't get an absentee ballot at the Grafton County Jail."

"Not much of a confession. What do you think of the results?"

"The American people have spoken. Who am I to disagree?"

"Even with one bum leg, you're dancing pretty good. So. Confession time. Let it out."

I got another Sam Adams, another round of jumbo shrimp, and I let it all out. From the time I left Manchester in Felix's borrowed pickup truck, to my surveillances in Osgood, to the encounter with the pheasant hunters, my later encounter with Professor Knowlton, and my raid of the house, the shootings, my wounding, the arrival of the Gurkha soldier, and the subsequent fire.

Felix said nothing, but grunted at some high points—or low points, depending on one's point of view—and then he seemed quite impressed with what had happened to my aborted transfer from the Dartmouth-Hitchcock Hospital to the Grafton County Jail.

When I was through and took another long swallow of beer, he asked, "Feel better now?"

"Just a bit."

A manicured thumbnail of his worked the edge of the Sam Adams label. "From the two hitmen receiving orders not to bag you and tag you, and the fact that all the evidence connecting you to the fire in Osgood has disappeared, it seems to me that I sense the cool clammy hand of the federal government at work."

"Or at least a dedicated retiree."

"True enough. I guess the Gurkha's arrival with three heads impressed him enough that he went out of his way to help you."

I lifted my nearly empty bottle of beer. "Here's to federal retirees."

Felix clinked my bottle's neck with his own. "Why not?"

After he took a swallow and put the bottle down, he said, "Speaking of retirees, what are you up to now?"

I kept my mouth shut for a minute or so and then leaned over the table. "Don't rightly know. I'm at the proverbial loose ends. I have no job. My savings are being drained on a daily basis with my room here and my car rental. Plus I've also dropped a hefty deposit on some nineteenth-century lumber that I'm going to use to rebuild the house, and my contractor is pushing me to start work right away, before the first snows come."

I took a moment to fold a spare white napkin that was on the table. "But if I do that without the insurance company's approval, they'll be so pissed they might turn down my claim."

"Go on."

"What? There's no more on."

"The hell there isn't. I've known you for quite some time, my friend. I know you've been down some dark trails before, but this is the first time you came up to a man, face to face, and shot him three times. Three times in the chest. You weren't meaning to wound him, or scare him. You meant to kill him."

"I didn't succeed. Most I did was break a few ribs and maybe his sternum before he encountered a man who brought a knife to a gunfight."

"A very big knife, I know, but no matter who put him into the ground, at that very moment, you were a killer of men. And that's bothering you, that's troubling you, no matter how many wisecracks you make or how many beers you drink."

"When did you become such a sensitive soul?"

"I'm not, as a number of law enforcement officials will attest. But I know what it's like to be you, at that moment. Me, I had the upbringing, the experiences, the training. But what got me through, the very first time and since then, was the thought that I was doing right. I was making some sort of rough justice, outside of the cops and courts, but that whoever encountered me deserved what happened."

I slowly nodded. Felix said, "What you did, can you honestly say that it was the right thing to do? That justice was done for Diane and that CIA retiree's son?"

"I can," I said, thinking some more. "I can . . . but sometimes I think it was all futile. Diane is still in a coma, Lawrence Thomas and his wife are still mourning their son, and in my goal to seek justice, I lost my house, my savings, my job, and nearly my life."

"But justice was done."

"Yes."

"And you know it, and I know it, and Lawrence Thomas knows it, and I'm sure Kara Miles suspects it. So take what you can, Lewis. You're here with me, enjoying a cold beer, fine food, and even finer conversation. Those particular bad guys have been put away. And tomorrow, you'll plug along, and day after day, it will get better. Promise."

"But no guarantee for Diane."

"None, sorry to say. But none of us have guarantees. A rogue tidal wave could come up here and snatch us away, or that Renzi detective might decide to come in here and arrest us both. You just do what you can."

His words were making sense, and would probably make better sense tomorrow, but I wanted to change the subject, so I did. "What's new with your second cousin, Angela? She fitting in?"

"Hah," Felix said, finishing off his Sam Adams. "Oh, yes, I sense some family blood in her, because she is, in fact, not an astrophysicist. Poor dear appears to be confused about the difference between astronomy and astrology. But I'm sure she'll fit in somewhere."

"So she lied to you, but she got here to the States, probably on a green card you helpfully arranged. Mission accomplished for the young lady."

"Nicely put."

"Plus she got to meet you," I said. "What an extra benefit."

"Some days we all win."

# CHAPTER THIRTY

The next day started off with me feeling like a winner, but ended quite differently indeed.

I came down to the lobby, trying to decide if I was going to have breakfast in the Lafayette House's fine dining room, or go get something a bit more basic at one of the local diners that are scattered along Route 1 and Route 1-A. I was tired of eating fine breakfasts that not only clogged my arteries, but also made me feel heavy and bloated for the rest of the day. Besides missing everything else about my burned-down home, I also missed just grabbing meals from there and cooking for myself.

I was thinking through what to do when the decision was made for me: Lawrence Thomas was waiting for me at the entrance to the dining room.

I went over, still using my cane, leg still aching, and he smiled and nodded at me.

"So good to see you," he said. "Buy you breakfast?"

"A deal," I said, and the helpful hostess gave us a corner spot that had a great view of the ocean, the Lafayette House's parking lot, and a bit of blue that marked the tarpaulin that was still nailed and secured to the collapsed roof of my house.

We made some chit-chat about the weather, about travel, and after our respective meals were ordered, he said, "A few words of appreciation before we eat."

"The appreciation is all mine," I said. "If it wasn't for you sending Suraj to tail me, I'd be a dead man."

An appreciative nod. "You bear no ill will, then, for my having you followed?"

"Absolutely not. It worked out . . . he seems quite the soldier."

Cups of coffee arrived and, as he was working his spoon in the mug, he said: "Not to mince words, but he's a killer. A sweet, loyal, and capable man, but a killer nonetheless."

"He said he owed you his life in Afghanistan. What happened?"

Lawrence gently *tap-tapped* the side of the spoon against his mug. His voice became reflective. "We were at a remote forward operating base, near the Pakistani border. Conducting cross-border surveillance. One night we were attacked. Surveillance can go both ways, you know. The night was long and bloody. I was at the wire, too, an M-4 in my hands, doing what I could. Suraj and his squad were incredible. One outpost . . . they ran out of rounds and one of the Gurkhas was swinging at the Taliban with a machine gun tripod. In the morning, it was a mess, but we had held on. Suraj had taken a round to the belly. He was triaged to be left behind. When a medevac flew in, I insisted they take him along. Some would say I insisted too much."

"How much was too much?"

He took a genteel sip from his coffee cup. "I put my Colt pistol against the helicopter crew chief's head and told him that either Suraj was going, or his brains were going to be splattered across the near bulkhead. He saw the error of his ways and found a way to take him."

"I can see why he has such loyalty to you," I said. "If I may . . . how did he get . . . the heads to you?"

Lawrence looked shocked. "They didn't come to me . . . I mean, please, what do you think, I'm a barbarian?"

I couldn't think of an answer, and Lawrence went on. "They went to a trusted colleague of mine at the Agency, in charge of a forensics division. Through dental records, photographs, and DNA analysis, we were able to identify the three individuals."

I could see our waitress approaching. "You used that information later, didn't you? To cancel the op against me."

He smiled. "Very good analysis," Lawrence said. "That's exactly what I did. You know the phrase 'walking back the cat'? That's what I did, once I got Curt Chesak's real name and the names of the two other men. Walked back the cat until I got to their overseers. I contacted them, told them to cease and desist any activities against you and your friends, or else their activities would be made public."

The waitress was very close. "Thank you," I said. "I owe you one. I owe you a lot."

She stopped by, and the dishes were being put on the table. He said, "Would you like to know who they were?"

"No," I said. "I wouldn't."

He had a cheese-and-eggwhite omelet, while I made do with buttermilk pancakes, sausage links, and real maple syrup, which was dispensed in little jars because the real stuff is so much more expensive than the cane-sugar syrup made to look brown that is dispensed at most restaurants.

When breakfast was done and the dishes were cleared away, Lawrence said: "One more piece of business to settle, if I may."

"Go right ahead."

He took out a cell phone—and it looked standard, not like the 007 phone he had given me before—and he dialed a number, paused, and said, "It's time" and hung up.

Lawrence picked up his cup of coffee, and I was about to do the same, but my hand froze.

Coming across the floor of the restaurant, with a disturbed look on her face, was my former boss, Denise Pichette-Volk of *Shoreline* magazine.

Lawrence stood up, wiped his hands on his napkin, extended his hand. "Denise, so nice to finally make your acquaintance. Do sit down."

She looked about the same as when I had last seen her, at the magazine's offices in Boston, though her black hair had been trimmed some. She had on dark slacks, a black sweater, a tan cloth overcoat, and some multi-colored scarf that looked like it had been made by human hands over many, many hours.

I looked at her, she looked at me, and she said, "Can we make this quick, please?"

Lawrence sat down. "Certainly. Care for some coffee, juice, something to nibble on?"

"No." Her voice was flat.

"Straight to business, then?"

"That's what I said."

I cleared my throat. "Gee, nice to see you, too, Denise. How's things?"

Her face darkened, but she didn't say a word. Lawrence said: "Some time ago, Anthony Seamus Holbrook was running that shop, wasn't he? A retired admiral."

"That's right," I said. "He's out on medical leave, which is why . . . Denise came aboard."

She leaned back in her chair, stuffed both manicured hands in her pockets. Lawrence said, "Oh, yes. The official story."

This was getting interesting. "What the hell do you mean by that?"

"I mean that I know Admiral Holbrook. Our paths have crossed a few times in the past years, and a few months ago he was called back to active duty. All secret, of course, but in his years in the service, he managed to make some . . . contacts with officers and elected officials who are now in positions of power in a variety of governments. These officials tend to value old men, with their knowledge and experience, and that's what the good admiral has been doing. In his place, Denise came aboard. But let me say that, in spite of her no-doubt good intentions, she exceeded her authority in the matter of you, Lewis. And once Admiral Holbrook found this out, he was not happy."

I couldn't help myself. I was grinning. "Let me guess. I'm getting my job back as a columnist."

Then I stopped grinning when I heard what Lawrence said next. "Not exactly," he said. "You're going to have Denise's job."

This time it was Denise's turn to smile, as small as it was, and I turned to Lawrence and said: "You're kidding."

"No, I'm not. I talked this through with Admiral Holbrook, over a phone connection that sounded like it was active when Mister Bell was tromping the streets of Boston. We both agreed that you had been treated poorly, and that compensation should be arranged. Instead of giving you back your columnist job, we believed it would suit both you and the magazine for you to become its editor."

"I don't want the job."

"Hear me out, Lewis. You won't be by yourself. Denise has agreed to stay on as a consultant and help you."

She was still smiling, and I was hoping to erase that expression. "Excuse me again, but I find it hard to be in the same *state* as her, never mind sharing an office or work responsibility."

"You proved by what you did for me that you have an extraordinary range of talents and drive. Don't sell yourself short."

"I'm not selling anything," I said sharply. "You are, and you're doing a lousy job." He started to talk again, and I interrupted him. "Wait a sec. You said the Admiral has been called back into service. Have *you*?"

His face was expressionless. I said, "When I first started at *Shoreline*, the Admiral told me that the magazine was sometimes used as a resource or cover to help out certain agencies. That's still true, isn't it? Damn you, you're trying to call me back into service, aren't you?"

Denise spoke up. "This Boy Scout chatter is really getting me excited, but if you don't mind, I'd rather leave."

She got out of her chair, waved bye-bye with her right hand like an eight-year-old girl, and said, "Good luck, Lewis. Welcome aboard. I hope you choke on it."

When Denise had left, I said, "Hear me once, and that's it. I'm not going to be an editor. I'm not working in Boston. I'm not coming back. I like my life just as it is, and nothing you say will change that."

Lawrence smiled gently. "And what life is that? Daily visits to a comatose patient? No job? I know your monetary status right down to the penny, Lewis. Your burned-out house is across the street, open to the elements. What are you going to do when the winter storms start up in a week or two? And I know you don't have the funds to get it repaired."

I resisted an urge to look out the window.

I also resisted an urge to sock him one.

He said, "Appeals to your patriotism might not work. You've been around way too long for that. But an appeal to your realistic nature should. The job would pay well. You can keep your house here for weekend visits. Maybe set up an apartment in Boston. Widen your circle of friends."

My voice was bitter without even trying. "I'd hate every goddamn second of it."

Now it was his turn to get up from his chair. "Spend some time working on your résumé, Lewis. See what that might get you. Try to figure out if working at McDonald's or as a supermarket bagger will help you get what you need."

"I want to talk to the Admiral."

"Sorry, no can do. He's in a place where he can't be reached."

"Why in hell are you doing this?"

A slight, apologetic shrug. "You said it yourself, just a few minutes ago. You owe me one. I'm taking you at your word. And this one is it. There's going to be a staff meeting at the magazine tomorrow in Boston at eleven. Dress the part . . . and don't be late."

# CHAPTER THIRTY-ONE

The next twelve hours or so moved like I was in amber, slow and out of focus. When morning came back the next day, I had a light breakfast—at last—of coffee and toast in the Lafayette House dining room. As I slowly ate, this time I took a place by the window where I could see the flapping blue tarp that marked a safe harbor of mine that was now broken, never to be fully repaired, a fatal harbor to trap unwary mariners.

Back up in my room, I got dressed in a new light-gray suit, the first one I had owned in many years. I had a problem getting the pants over my bandage, so I cut if off with a pair of grooming scissors and tossed it in the trash. I wondered what the maid would think later of what I had done.

Before getting dressed, I looked at the sutured wound in the mirror, gently touched it, admired the bruising and scabs. I saw the other scars on my body, ones that had come to me because I had come up against a system that would never, ever take no for an answer.

Once dressed, with a necktie that seemed to choke me, I looked in the mirror.

Could not recognize the person looking back.

I slowly walked downstairs and out into the cold air of the parking lot, to my rented Honda Pilot. Started it up, backed out of the lot, and then on to Route 1-A.

I managed to avoid looking at the place that had once been my home.

I checked the time.

Plenty of time.

I drove off to the interchange that got me onto Interstate 95. If I took a right, I'd be heading to Boston.

If I took a left, I'd be heading to Porter.

Another time check.

Why not?

I turned left.

At Room 209 of the Porter Rehab and Extended Care Center, I had the place to myself, save for its star patient. Her hair had been washed and trimmed since I had last been here, and her hands were still on top of the covers, still motionless. Her breathing was still raspy, her eyes still closed.

I pulled up a chair and sat down. I had forgotten to bring an Agatha Christie novel, but so what. So I just held her hand and sat and waited, and tried to think of something noble to say, and came up empty.

I looked up at the clock. I was going to be late.

So what. They'd have to get used to me and my management style.

I sat for long moments more, just hearing her breathing, the occasional *bleep-whir* of the medical devices hooked up to her, and the sound of people outside her quiet room, moving about and laughing and talking and living.

I gave her hand a squeeze, got up, and kissed her forehead.

"Later, Diane," I said, and turned to walk out.

I was halfway to the door when she started coughing, coughing and hacking.

I went back to her, found a tissue, wiped at her lips and her chin. The coughing and wheezing went on, and I was about to ring the call button, when it suddenly stopped.

There was a deep breath, her back arched.

I took her hand.

My eyes had a hard time focusing.

Then her head turned.

Her eyes opened.

Her eyes opened.

I squeezed her hand.

She blinked.

Blinked.

I didn't dare move, breathe, or do anything.

Her tongue came out, ran across her dry lips, and it moved again. I leaned in to her, staring at her eyes.

A whisper.

A whisper, getting louder.

"Lewis?"

It seemed like a bright light was shining into my face. I took my other hand and covered my eyes for a moment. Then I squeezed her hand again.

"Right here, Diane," I said. "Right here."

"Oh," she said.

She closed her eyes and I was about to yell out about the unfairness of it all, that she would slip away now, and her eyes opened and her face creased up just a bit, just the tiniest bit, like she was trying to smile.

"Lewis," she whispered. "So happy to see you. I'm so tired. Promise me you won't leave."

I squeezed her hand even harder, ignored whatever time it was, or whatever time it was going to be.

"I promise."

# ACKNOWLEDGEMENTS

The author wishes to express his sincere thanks and gratitude to Otto Penzler, who first gave Lewis Cole a home twenty years ago and is still looking out for him; Claiborne Hancock, Phil Gaskill, and everyone else at Pegasus Books; my agent, Nat Sobel; my wife and first reader, Mona Pinette; Alex Trebek, who knows why; loyal reader and correspondent Alfred E. Betts, Royal Navy (ret.); Frank and Lori Balantic, fellow lake dwellers; and to the friends and fans of Lewis Cole—especially Denise Lamontagne—who so eagerly awaited this book. I promise I won't be as tardy next time.